Praise for
STILL WATER

"Complex characters with gut-wrenching backstories propel this twisty mystery towards its shocking conclusion. **I was engrossed!**"

Robyn Harding, bestselling author of *The Party*

"**Utterly compelling and intriguing**, *Still Water* is a **very clever whodunit**. . . . My husband thought I was ignoring him while I was reading this book. I wasn't. I just forgot he existed because I was so engrossed."

Liz Nugent, bestselling author of *Unraveling Oliver*

"The tension in this book is sharp enough to cut. . . . **If you liked *Still Mine*, you'll love *Still Water*.**"

Tyrell Johnson, bestselling author of *The Wolves of Winter*

"As **swift, intense, and vengeful** as the river it describes, this book is a **must-read**."

Roz Nay, bestselling author of *Our Little Secret*

"Instantly captivating, **mysterious, and relevant**—Amy Stuart has done it again!"

Marissa Stapley, author of *Things to Do When It's Raining*

Praise for
STILL MINE

National Bestseller

"An **impressive debut**, rooted in character rather than trope, in fundamental understanding rather than rote puzzle-solving."

The Globe and Mail

"A **gripping page-turner**. . . . Add to that, Stuart has an ability to tap into the dark psychology behind addiction and abuse, and to bring these complex struggles to life in a way that stays with you for days."

Toronto Star

"Stuart has created a likeable heroine, complete with some pretty serious flaws. Between Clare and the other characters of Blackmore, the story is both **haunting** and **compelling**."

Vancouver Sun

"Stuart is a sensitive writer who has given Clare a painful past and just enough backbone to bear it."

The New York Times

"Delivers all the **nail-biting** moments of a fast-paced thriller. . . . You'll find yourself turning the pages faster and faster."

Elisabeth de Mariaffi, author of
The Devil You Know

"An **intricately woven** thriller. . . . A **vivid** and haunting debut."

Holly LeCraw, author of *The Swimming Pool*

"A **haunting** treasure of a book that burrowed its way into my psyche as I read it. . . . Not since *The Silent Wife* have I been rendered so power-lessly riveted by a psychological thriller. I can't wait to read what Stuart writes next."

Marissa Stapley, author of
Things to Do When It's Raining

"A **tense** and **absorbing** read. . . . Stuart paints a vivid picture of the stark mountain town, Blackmore, and the cast of shadowy characters who inhabit it."

Lucy Clarke, author of *The Blue*

ALSO BY AMY STUART

Still Mine

STILL WATER

A NOVEL

AMY STUART

PUBLISHED BY SIMON & SCHUSTER

New York London Toronto Sydney New Delhi

SIMON &
SCHUSTER
CANADA

Simon & Schuster Canada
A Division of Simon & Schuster, Inc.
166 King Street East, Suite 300
Toronto, Ontario M5A 1J3

This Simon & Schuster Canada edition May 2018

SIMON & SCHUSTER CANADA and colophon are trademarks of Simon & Schuster, Inc.

For information about special discounts for bulk purchases, please contact Simon & Schuster Special Sales at 1-800-268-3216 or CustomerService@simonandschuster.ca.

Silhouette bridge design by Tony Hanyk, tonyhanyk.com.
River image © Shutterstock

Book design by Ellen R. Sasahara

Manufactured in the United States of America

1 3 5 7 9 10 8 6 4 2

Library and Archives Canada Cataloguing in Publication
Stuart, Amy, 1975–, author
Still water / Amy Stuart.
Issued in print and electronic formats.
ISBN 978-1-4767-9045-9 (softcover). —
ISBN 978-1-4767-9047-3 (ebook)
I. Title. PS8637.T8525S87 2018   C813'.6   C2017-906712-5
                                                 C2017-907236-6

ISBN 978-1-4767-9045-9
ISBN 978-1-4767-9047-3 (ebook)

For my parents,
Dick and Marilyn Flynn;
with infinite love and thanks

SUNDAY

Clare jolts upright, her hand at her mouth to stifle a scream.

This room is blue with moonlight. Clare is on a single bed, its rusted joints creaking beneath her as she adjusts to sitting. She blinks. Bare walls, high ceiling, cobwebs wound tight in the corners. There is an open window, a hot wind lifting the corner of her bedsheet. The door is closed. Another single bed is pressed to the far wall, a woman lying facedown, asleep, as still as a corpse.

A voice in Clare's head. *Do you know about this place?*

The woman in the bed lets out a long whine. Clare studies her in the low light. She looks to be in her midthirties, her face gently lined but tense even in sleep. She rolls onto her back, one arm flapped over the side of the bed. There is a zigzag of scars on her forearm and palm. Defensive scars, Clare knows. The kind that come from fending someone off. They spoke only briefly after Clare arrived last night, shook hands, maneuvered around each other in the small space. *Raylene*, she'd said. Her name is Raylene.

The painted hardwood floor is warm under Clare's feet. She stands and tiptoes to the window. This room is on the second story, a porch roof extending below her. Two hundred feet ahead, a river churns. A willow tree is perched so close to the water that its thick roots curl over the edge of the bank. A wooden cross has been nailed askew to its trunk. Clare twists her hair into a bun, then crouches to catch the breeze on her neck.

Do you know about this place?

Yes, Clare thinks, eyes on the wooden cross. I know about this place.

This morning, there was the ocean. Two days ago, Malcolm Boon in the doorway of Clare's room, a folder in hand.

I have a new case, he'd said. *A woman and her child have disappeared.*

How many days since she and Malcolm absconded from the hospital in Blackmore before the police could question them? How many days and nights did Clare spend in that motel room, drifting in and out of fitful sleep as she healed from the gunshot wound? She can muster only flashes. Bandages peeled back, the angry pink of her shoulder. A meal eaten on an unmade bed. A dusty glass of water Malcolm gave her to wash down the pills. The tide in and out on a beach. Malcolm there, Malcolm gone. And then, Malcolm arriving with the folder, offering her a new assignment.

I think you'd be good for this case, he'd said. *It's a place called High River. A place for women like you.*

Something had roused Clare then. Her second case. A chance to right the wrongs of her first effort, to prove she might actually be good at this work. For twenty-four hours she'd pored over the folder: Sally Proulx and her two-year-old son, William, swept away days ago by the same river Clare watches out this window now. She'd papered the wall of her motel room with the timeline and backstory, photos and police reports. Photos of Sally in her previous life, before she and William arrived in High River. As Clare worked, a strange energy bolted through her. She couldn't sleep. She wouldn't talk to Malcolm. She cut back on the pills, holding her breath against the waves of pain and nausea. This time, she would be prepared. She would invent a version of herself that fit in at High River. Go under-cover. Learn from her mistakes. It only occurs to her now that Malcolm probably chose this case because he knew it would hit too close to home for Clare to refuse it.

With a gasp, Raylene sits up in bed, eyes wide. "No!" she says. "No."

Her eyes search the room until she spots Clare crouched at the open window.

"It's okay," Clare says.

Raylene's eyes are unfocused, afraid.

"You were dreaming," Clare whispers. "Go back to sleep."

As if never awake, Raylene slides down the bed until her head lands softly on her pillow.

Rain. Clare extends her hand through the open window to catch the first drops on her palm. She can never remember her own dreams. It used to suit Clare to forget, to abandon the details of her life before this one, those many months on the run before she met Malcolm Boon. Before Malcolm hired her to do this strange work of searching for lost or missing women, before her first case in Blackmore. Before the bullet wound and the blur of days spent recovering at that seaside motel. As they drove to High River yesterday, southward to this thick heat, Malcolm kept such quiet that when he spoke, his voice startled Clare.

Remember, he said. *We got lucky on the Blackmore case.*

We got lucky, Clare repeated, hand resting on the shotgun wound just inches from her heart. *Lucky.*

What I mean, Malcolm said, *is that missing women don't always turn up alive.*

Forget luck, Clare wanted to say. Instead she looked out her window in silence, any change in the landscape masked by the gas stations and fast-food joints on repeat at every interchange. Mile after mile she mulled the details of the High River case. The little boy and his mother. Fixating on the details of the case distracted Clare from the pain in her shoulder, from the panic, the need for one more pill to take the edge off. She committed everything in that file to memory, every detail of Sally Proulx's story absorbed, Clare an actor learning her part. This time, she will play Sally's friend, a more direct route into the story than she took last time. But now that she's here in High River, Clare feels uncertain she's made the right choice in agreeing to take on this case. She stares at the white cross, at the swaying tentacles of the willow tree. Her chest hurts. Her shoulder hurts. It feels hard to breathe in this heat. She thinks of the letter from her husband that she carries in her bag.

I can't forget you, my Clare. You're still mine.

Eighteen, Clare thinks. Eighteen days since she left Blackmore with Malcolm, driving west to the ocean and that motel, the letter from Jason in her back pocket. Two hundred and twenty-five days since she left Jason, sprinting through the snowy back fields to the car she'd hidden under a sheet. A long-planned escape from a vicious husband. A life left behind months ago. But no matter how much time passes, she can't seem to stop counting the days.

Do you know about this place?

It was Raylene who'd asked her this question as they lay in the dark last night, hours after Clare first arrived. Clare had feigned sleep instead of answering. Yesterday she'd felt certain she was equipped for this. She'd felt certain she'd learned all she could about High River, that this time her cover would be rock solid. Clare glances over her shoulder to Raylene, curled into fetal position, a pained look on her face as she sleeps. Clare looks back at the river, then presses the window all the way closed, her hands shaking with pain or withdrawal or panic, she can never tell which anymore.

It doesn't matter if I'm ready, Clare thinks. I'm here.

It is morning and Clare sits at the kitchen table, a breakfast spread in front of her. There is music playing in another room, a song too folksy and quiet for Clare to discern the words. Helen Haines washes her hands at the sink, wooden cabinet doors askew on their hinges behind her. What does Clare know of Helen? That she wears old jeans and a plaid shirt untucked. That she must be a decade older than Clare, forty-something, her dark hair streaked with gray and wrapped in a tight bun. That she owns this grand house and the eighty acres it sits on. That she invites women seeking refuge to stay here with her, women on the run. Women like Sally Proulx. Women like Clare.

This time yesterday Clare stood on a patch of grass at a gas station hundreds of miles from here, watching from a distance as Malcolm filled the tank, cell phone warm to her ear, counting the rings on the other end of the line.

My name is Clare O'Brien, she said when Helen Haines finally answered. I am a friend of Sally Proulx's.

Well-rehearsed lies, only her first name true. There had been a long silence before Helen cleared her throat and asked what Clare wanted.

I need a safe place to stay, Clare said. And I know Sally is missing. I want to help.

Hours later Clare stood at the gate to this strange house with her duffel bag at her feet, swatting at the flies that swooped in the stillness. Across the road from the gate a field of young corn stood ablaze in the pink light. Farmland and trees stretched in every direction. Thick with heat. Too reminiscent of home. When Clare emerged through the bend of trees arching over the long driveway, the first thing she noticed was the river. The willow tree. This house. And standing before it all on her front steps, hands in the pockets of her faded jeans, its matriarch, Helen.

"How did you sleep?" Helen asks, still hunched over the sink.

"Not terribly well," Clare says. "I had a nightmare."

"The heat can do that." Helen wipes her hands on a dish towel and sits across from Clare. "And you traveled pretty far."

"I did."

The story Clare told Helen had her traveling from the east and not the north. Helen will know nothing of Clare's actual trip with Malcolm, the turn inland from the ocean, southward on busy highways, the sun high and blaring through the windshield, a full day of driving until he'd deposited her at a nearby gas station and she'd called the taxi to take her the rest of the way. Helen will know nothing of the curt and fumbling goodbye Malcolm offered as he unloaded her bag from his truck, a strained nod in her direction before driving away, the parking lot gravel too wet from rain to kick up under his wheels.

"I have to say," Helen says. "I was surprised to get your call yesterday."

"I debated coming at all," Clare says.

"Sally never spoke of you."

"No," Clare says. "I don't imagine she would have."

Clare pauses, mirroring Helen's frown.

"We don't advertise this place."

"I know you don't."

"And yet you knew about it."

"Because Sally told me," Clare says.

"And now we've been in the news." Helen looks to her feet, anxious. "You didn't say much last night."

"I was overwhelmed," Clare says, a half-truth. "Arriving here. That cross nailed to the willow tree. It threw me."

"I hate that cross," Helen says. "Markus put it up."

"Markus?"

"My brother. He lives across the river. It's a memorial to our parents. But now . . ." Helen trails off.

"Well," Clare says. "I appreciate you giving me the chance to rest."

"Sally didn't talk about home," Helen says. "Where she came from. Some women do. Some tell you everything. Some don't. She mentioned her mom. A sister, once, I think. She and William seemed pretty alone in the world."

Clare lifts a salt shaker from the table and clutches it hard in her fist. She thinks of the details on Sally's family from the file, a mother dead and a sister across the country quoted in a story about Sally's disappearance as saying they'd long been estranged. No father. Few friends. Sally Proulx and her son, alone. It's hard to pinpoint how it happens, how the isolation sets in for women when a marriage turns bad.

"Did you see Raylene this morning?" Helen asks.

"She wasn't in the room when I woke up."

"She often goes for walks before the heat settles in."

"Is it just you and Raylene in the house?" Clare asks.

"And you," Helen says. "And Ginny. My daughter. I really only have room for two or three women. Less when Ginny is home for the summer."

"I haven't met her."

"She's a late riser. And she'll glare you down like a bear. Just ignore her."

Ginny, Clare thinks. Virginia. The only photo from the case file had been culled from social media, a hazy profile shot of a young woman in a bikini top and flowing skirt, arms bent loosely overhead, the river swirling fast behind her. Helen stands again and returns to the sink. The room is large and square, a long harvest table at its center. A back door leads to a stretch of untended field and then a distant grove of trees. So much like home, Clare thinks again.

"There are two detectives working Sally's case," Helen says. "I know they'll want to meet you."

"I'm happy to talk to them," Clare says, smiling to ward off the surge of dread at the prospect.

Helen stares at Clare, rapping her ringless fingers against the table, her nails cut square. There is a simple beauty to Helen, skin golden from summer sun and eyes a deep brown, but she does nothing to play it up. Clare thinks of her own mother, yanking the brush through her hair and dabbing on lipstick before so much as opening the door to receive the mail. You have standards or you don't, she'd say to Clare as they roamed the cosmetics aisle of the drugstore. There is no middle ground.

"I don't know much about what happened to Sally," Clare says. "Maybe you can fill me in."

"Other way around," Helen says. "I need you to fill *me* in."

"On what?"

"Sally should not have told you about this place. I'm having trouble getting past the fact that she did."

"She sent me one e-mail. One e-mail. Telling me where she was. A week later I see on the news—"

"Telling you where she was. You see?" Helen rubs at her forehead. "Who knows who else she told?"

"No one, I'm sure. Sally—"

"She wasn't supposed to do that. It's the only rule. The only rule I have. I invite women here. They don't just decide to come. They don't invite each other."

"I understand," Clare says. "I'm sorry."

"What if she told her husband? Or someone else?"

"I doubt she would have done that," Clare says. "She knew who to trust."

"No she didn't," Helen says.

In the file the only pictures of High River were from the initial missing persons report, the details of this refuge laid out in the plain language of police-speak. For years Helen Haines had housed women who needed a safe place to land, sometimes for months or years at a time. It might have been a refuge a week ago, Clare wants to say to Helen, but now it's a crime scene.

"Eat," Helen says.

Clare picks a muffin from the basket and rips it in two, grateful for the reprieve. The first bite is so moist it dissolves on her tongue. She wants to cry at its sweetness. With a swoosh the back door swings open and Raylene steps into the kitchen. In the daylight Clare can glean the details, Raylene's black hair wavy down her back, her skin and eyes a dark brown.

"See anyone?" Helen asks.

"No," Raylene says. "Not since yesterday. I think they've called the search off." Raylene plops into the chair next to Clare. "Sorry. I don't remember your name."

"Clare is a friend of Sally's," Helen says.

"What?" Raylene shifts her entire body to face Clare. "Why didn't you tell me that upstairs? Last night?"

"We only spoke for a minute," Clare says.

The smell of coffee has overtaken the room. Helen pours a cup for each of them, laying out the cream and sugar at the center of the table. Raylene drops a heaping spoon of sugar into hers and stirs so that her spoon clanks against her mug, eyes never leaving Clare.

"She never mentioned any friend named Clare to me," Raylene says. "And Sally told me everything."

A mosquito lands at the center of the table. Clare lowers her fist to squash it. "I hate when people say that," she says.

"Excuse me?" Raylene perks up in her chair.

"There's no way of knowing if someone is telling you everything," Clare says, sipping her coffee. "We all keep secrets."

"Do we? Why would you say that?"

Clare shrugs, uncertain herself. She'd figured that playing the part of Sally's friend would allow her to ask questions, to integrate. That she could fill in the blanks if people dug deeper, work around inconsistencies by claiming a faulty memory, difficult circumstances under which she and Sally met in the first place.

"She wrote Clare a few weeks ago," Helen says. "E-mailed her. When Clare heard she'd gone missing, she came."

"Why did you wait?" Raylene asks. "Why didn't you come as soon as she wrote?"

"It's complicated," Clare says. "I can't—"

"Yeah, well," Raylene says. "Now you're too late."

Raylene squeals her chair along the floor as she stands. She returns the uneaten breakfast to the refrigerator and cupboards, opening and slamming each door with a flourish. Her figure is curvy, and as she reaches for a high cupboard to return the unused teapot her T-shirt lifts. Clare spots the scarring snaked along her belly, the white crisscrosses of faded stretch marks. The marks of a pregnancy with no mention of a child. When the table is cleared Raylene leans on the counter, blowing her hair from her eyes, jaw pulsing. Livid.

"You just show up here, making snide remarks? Some random long-lost friend."

"I'm not random," Clare says.

"You are to me. To us."

"She's Sally's friend," Helen interjects.

"I didn't mean to anger you," Clare says. "I'm sorry."

"Aren't *you* angry?" Raylene asks. "Your friend and her kid are gone."

A sharp ache jolts through Clare's shoulder. She rests her palm over it. She can't tell if she's sweating from the heat or from the feverish spell that comes with the long stretch without anything for the pain. Withdrawal.

"I *am* angry," Clare says, her voice low. "Really angry, actually. More than you can know."

"It's been devastating," Helen says. "Just devastating. We're doing everything we can to find them. To figure this all out. I have hope. I do. I really do."

"I'm here to help," Clare says. "Honestly. That's all I want. I'll speak to the police. I'll search the river myself. I'll do whatever I can."

In a flash Clare's eyes fill. The tears are strangely authentic. Maybe she need only think of her own regrets to invoke this emotion, to think of her own departure, all that she left behind. She need only imagine Grace, imagine her oldest and only friend coming for her, coming too late just as she has pretended to do here. Clare presses her fingers to her eyes. Helen reaches across the table to squeeze her hand.

"We appreciate that you're here," Helen says, standing. "I know Sally would appreciate it too."

Raylene is watching Clare from her perch at the counter, arms crossed.

"We can go for a walk," Helen continues. "Have a chat. Get some fresh air. Would that be okay, Clare?"

Clare nods, sniffling, scooping the crumbs from her muffin over the edge of the table into her cupped hand. These are women among whom trust must be earned. Is it a great stretch for Clare to play this part? No, Clare thinks, swiping away the last of the tears. She could have been friends with Sally. She could have tried to help her friend when everything went awry. So it isn't a stretch that Clare might be the one to make things right.

C lare waits for Helen on the porch. Across the river is a smaller house, a cottage with clapboard painted white. A man chases a child on the lawn. A game. The little girl toddles and squeals and loses her balance. Had Clare noticed the house across the river when she'd gazed out last night? It is set back far enough from the river, small enough that the willow tree might block it from view.

When she closes her eyes, Clare imagines Jason leaning against the willow tree that lined their driveway at home, smiling as he used to when he was waiting for her to return from work. How clearly her mind renders him these days, a depiction more intact than it was in the weeks after she left. He is reappearing, his letter arriving in Blackmore hours before Clare left. *I don't know why everyone here is so willing to forget about you.* The words come to her in perfect order, memorized. *It's like that's what you wanted. To be forgotten.*

A woman emerges on the porch steps across the river. She descends the stairs and says something to the man. He picks up the girl and carries her inside, taking a wide berth around the woman who must be his wife. Even from this distance Clare can see the sighing heave in the woman's shoulders as she stares blankly ahead before turning back to the house herself. Since her own wedding years ago, Clare has become adept at looking for even the smallest fissures in other people's marriages. The undercurrents.

"That's Markus's house," Helen says, sidling up to Clare. "My brother."

"Is that his wife?"

"Rebecca. And that's their daughter. My niece, Willow."

"As in the tree?"

"As in the tree." Helen tugs at the bottom of her T-shirt. "Ready?"

Clare nods and allows Helen to guide her down the porch steps across the lawn. The grass is still moist, the dew cooling Clare's feet through her sandals. Helen turns downstream and for a few minutes they walk in silence along a riverside path. A hundred yards south, the river narrows and churns a frothy white and they enter a grove of trees. Clare looks back over her shoulder to the two houses on either side of the river, facing each other like soldiers at attention.

"This path is well worn," Clare says.

"I've been walking it since I was a kid."

The day's heat is less oppressive under the canopy of trees. Along the riverbank Clare notices a red ribbon tied to a stake. About thirty yards downstream, another one. The path is gone and they now weave around the felled logs and saplings. They come to an eddy, a small pool. Helen circles to the far side so she is facing Clare. She crouches then dips her hands to cup the water.

"It's so calm here compared to the river," Clare says.

"It's man-made," Helen says. "My father dug it out. Dug a huge hole and connected it to the river so it stays full. A swimming pool, but with frigid river water."

"Pretty smart."

"We used to feel these tiny fish nipping at our legs when we swam. Markus hated it. They never bothered me. They weren't trying to draw blood. I think they were just curious."

Clare slips off her sandals and dips her toes in the water of the eddy.

"It's so cold."

"It moves too fast to catch the sun," Helen says.

"I don't know much about this place," Clare says. "About High River. Sally didn't tell me much. You grew up here?"

"It was my family home. My parents died when I was young. After they were gone Markus and Jordan and I left for a while to live with friends of the family."

Though Clare knows exactly how Helen's parents died, the file full of news clippings, she will not ask Helen about it yet. She will mete out the questions.

"Who's Jordan?"

"My youngest brother. He was only a baby when our parents died. He's younger than Markus by ten years. Me by thirteen. When I was old enough to take care of things on my own, we came back here. We had some money. There was a big insurance payout. And I had this idea. To give women a place to stay when they needed it."

"Like a shelter?"

"It's not a shelter. It's just a . . . place."

A place. Helen picks up a stick and circles it in the dirt, writing her own initials then scratching them out. She seems childlike to Clare, cross-legged at the water's edge, her dark hair in a mess of a ponytail.

"How would Sally have found you?"

"The right people know about us," Helen says. "I have connections in the city. Jordan does a lot of pro bono work with local shelters. He's a lawyer."

"So it runs in the family, doing this work?"

"Maybe. But it doesn't matter anymore. It's over now."

"What's over?"

"This place. High River. It functioned on secrecy. And now people know about it. We've been in the news. Sally's name. My name. They might as well have blasted our GPS coordinates. In the few days after she disappeared I had about a dozen people show up at the door. None for the right reasons. Mostly just curious. Even the women I thought might genuinely need a place to stay. What can I do for them now?"

The question is rhetorical, Clare knows. The safety is in the secrecy. The ground beneath her fingers is soft enough that Clare's hands sink in when she leans back on them. She looks up. Many of the trees along the riverbank are leafless, their trunks hollow near the bottoms. Dead.

"I appreciate you letting me come."

"What would Sally think if I turned her friend away?"

With a sigh, Helen gestures onward and they stand and continue along the path. Clare kicks at deadheads with her bare feet, her sandals in hand. Soon they come to a narrow dirt road with a wooden one-lane bridge that arches over the river. They stop halfway across. The railing gives slightly when they lean against it.

"What has happened to them?" Clare asks.

"I wish I knew," Helen says.

Peering down at the river, Clare guesses that an adult caught in its swirling caps would struggle to keep her head above water, and a small boy would have no chance, the force sucking him under at once.

"Could she have jumped?" Clare asks.

"You knew her," Helen says. "Do you think that's something she would do?"

Clare shakes her head. "Well, no. Maybe. You never know what someone is capable of. What they might be driven to do."

Watching the current makes Clare light-headed, the water racing around rocks and twirling in funnels. She must breathe through her mouth to account for the dizziness that comes.

"It's hard to believe they haven't found the bodies," Clare says.

"Searchers were here for a few days," Helen says. "Today's the first time I don't see them."

"It's shallow in places," Clare says. "I feel so certain they would have snagged. They couldn't have just washed away."

The morning sun now lines up with the river, high and hot and untempered by cloud. Clare picks a long sliver of rotted wood from the railing and drops it in the swirling water below. It takes a moment for Clare to notice that Helen's shoulders are shaking. Her head hangs. Clare reaches out and rests her hand on Helen's arm, but she feels only annoyance at her tears, the flinch of impatience.

"It doesn't matter what my intentions were," Helen says.

"What do you mean?"

"It doesn't matter if I was trying to help."

"Yes it does," Clare says.

"Sally was conflicted. She was angry. There was a life she wanted and a life she had and she struggled to reconcile the distance between them. William was the first child we've had here in years. He was angry too, in his little way. Biting, pinching. Wound up the way toddlers sometimes are. But I loved him. We all did. As best we could."

Clare frowns. As best we could? An odd choice of words.

"Sally needed help. She needed somewhere to go. You offered her that."

"And what good did it do her? She should never have told you about High River. She broke the sacred rule."

"There's something I should tell you." This is the hard part, Clare thinks, looking to the water to avoid eye contact. Balancing her truth with this ruse, filling in the story with what she knows to be true about Sally. Authenticating.

"I'm listening," Helen says.

"Sally told me about this place because she thought I might want to come too." Clare pauses, allowing Helen to register her meaning. "Sally and I knew each other distantly growing up. But we met again around Christmas. I left my husband in December. We landed at the same women's shelter. I didn't stay long. I hated it. But Sally and me, we connected. It felt like a real friendship. But she wanted to stay still. To build a new life. I just wanted to move. So I left. About a month ago I stopped in one place for a bit. In this mountain town."

"And your husband caught up," Helen says, not a question.

"There was this event in the town. Like a gathering party. I went. It felt so far from home, so I thought I'd be safe. My picture ended up in the newspaper. Only my first name, but I guess . . . I don't know. He found me. He sent me flowers, if you can believe it. A letter."

There is an entire side to the story Clare does not tell. The story of her own escape, never a shelter but always motels, months of zigzagging westward from her marital home. And then the story of Malcolm Boon, hired by her husband, Jason, to find her, tracking her in expanding circles until he caught

21

up to her somewhere in the flatlands east of the mountains, pressing his way into her motel room and binding her to a chair when she tried to run. Clare will not mention the strange agreement that emerged between them, how he'd offered her a job in lieu of turning her in to Jason. Her job: to search for missing women. Their first case in Blackmore, a missing woman whom Clare risked her own life to find. And it worked. She found her, alive, rescued her. The gunshot wound in Clare's shoulder still aches, her photo in the news because the town hailed her as the hero who disappeared from her hospital bed after taking a bullet to save the woman she was meant to find.

"Now you're on the run again," Helen says.

"I am." Clare pauses. "Sally felt safe here. That's what she said in her e-mail. I guess she wanted me to feel that too."

"You never knew her husband?"

Clare thinks of what little information the file gave. Gabriel Proulx, an insurance salesman from the suburbs, a photograph from the company website, the collar of his shirt too loose, cheeks ruddy, goatee. A man aged out of good looks. A few family photos taken from social media. And then a mugshot from a bar fight only days earlier, the goatee gone. The news articles all said he refused to speak to the press about his wife or son.

"I didn't know him," Clare says. "She didn't talk about him much."

"He was in jail the day Sally and William vanished," Helen says. "Got into some drunken brawl and hit a guy over the head with a beer bottle. Quite the alibi."

"Indeed."

A swarm of aphids circles in a cloud overhead.

"The bugs are terrible this year," Helen says. "It's the heat. The rain."

"The water drowns out all sounds," Clare says. "You hear nothing else. It's like there's nothing else here."

Helen aligns Clare so she faces downstream. Through the distant break in the trees, Clare can see the shadows of low buildings, the tall signs of gas stations and fast-food rest stops poking up at the sky.

"Wow," Clare says. "I thought we were in the middle of nowhere."

"Used to be," Helen says. "Twenty years ago. Ten, even. But the city's flooding outward. Last year a developer bought four thousand acres of farmland just north of us. Plans to build fifteen thousand houses. A whole new suburb. A new town. And they need an expressway to connect it to the city. If all goes well for them, the bridge over the river will be right here." Helen gestures to where they stand. "A six-lane monster destroying everything in its path."

"If all goes well for whom?" Clare asks.

"These men come to the door. Just open up the gate and drive right up to the house like their grandmother lives here. They want to buy the land. They come on behalf of the developer. One came on behalf of the township. Everyone in cahoots. Some of them nice enough, making promises of big money. Others a little more menacing. Reminding me of all the power they have, that it's a matter of when, not if, they get their hands on my land."

"How do you feel about that?"

"I thought I'd be here forever. But I see now that this place is stained. It always has been, I guess. Now I wonder why I took so long to see it. Jordan handles it all for me now. He knows how to navigate these things. And it's so much money. It would set Ginny and Jordan up for life."

Ginny and Jordan, Clare thinks. No mention of Markus.

Three men appear on the shore downstream, two in police uniform and one in a tan suit Clare figures must be a detective. They confer in a tight circle, the man in the suit pointing downstream. Clare feels her heart bang in her chest. Why did she agree earlier to speak to the police? She squints at the detective, his features hard to make out at this distance. He hasn't spotted them.

"That's Detective Rourke," Helen says. "Here on a Sunday."

"Doing his job," Clare says.

"He'll be over to the house later to talk to you." Helen stares ahead. "We should get back. You must be hungry."

Before Clare can speak Helen has moved on, leaving Clare behind on the bridge. The detective's back is to Clare. He gestures at the water, the officers nodding, as if they all know it: They should have found the bodies by now. They have to be in there somewhere. They must still be in the water.

Clare leaves the bridge before they see her. Whatever sadness Helen expressed in words does not reveal itself in her gait. There is almost a spring in her step as she follows the path, disappearing into the woods before Clare can catch up.

The upstairs hallway is wide and dark. Clare stands at its center, not entirely certain which of the four closed doors leads to her room. She runs a hand along the wallpaper ballooned outwards by the crumbling plaster behind it. This house, grand but decaying, creaky with every step Clare takes. A poster-sized photograph of a woman standing in a field hangs in a gilded frame on one wall. There is a wicker basket of corn husks at the woman's feet. She looks like Helen, that same untapped beauty, her hand shading her eyes from the sun. Clare turns to the sound of running water. A far door opens and a young woman steps out, toothbrush dangling from her mouth. She is tall and slender in a tank top and pajama shorts, her hair shorn to a dark and boyish pixie. Ginny Haines.

"What?"

"Nothing," Clare says. "Hi, I mean. I'm Clare."

"You're staring, Clare."

"Sorry."

Ginny looks bored, hip jutted out as her toothbrush stirs up a froth at her lips. She returns to the bathroom and kicks the door closed behind her. Clare absorbs the heat of the still air, taking note of the beads of sweat that trace a path down her chest. There is a window in the hallway, but Clare cannot pry it open. The frame has been painted shut.

Clare orients herself at the window. South. To one side is the field, to the other, the river. She cannot see the bridge where she'd stood with Helen, and from this vantage the only sign of the encroaching city is the pixelated cloud of smog that hangs in the distance. Clare rests her hand on her belly. It is flat and taut. This time last summer she'd been round with pregnancy. She can remember standing at the window of her upstairs hall, watching Jason slide in and out from under his truck in the driveway below, dusty and handsome and streaked with motor oil. She can remember the constant symmetry between hope and despair she'd felt then, each sentiment leaving just enough room for the other. She can remember the sensation of her finger swollen around her wedding ring, but for the life of her, Clare cannot summon the sensation of the baby roiling in her belly, the pressure of its little feet against her flesh. That sensation was washed away when the pregnancy ended.

The window's glass is hot to the touch. Clare imagines Sally Proulx on the bank of the river with her son. The blue light of clouds backlit by the moon. Clare pulls the cell phone from the pocket of her shorts. She has memorized Malcolm's number. She keys it in, about to type a message, then deletes it, keys it in again. What would she say but announce her arrival?

Here I am, she could type. As if Malcolm might expect her to be anywhere else.

"So you're Sally's friend," says a voice from behind her.

Clare startles and spins to face Ginny. "I am. Sorry. You scared me."

"What's with the ancient technology?"

Clare drops the cell phone in her pocket. "I never liked smartphones."

"Old-school," Ginny says. "That's cute. The cops are coming to see you later."

"Yes, Helen told me that." Clare pauses. "We haven't met. Sorry."

"Is everything that comes out of your mouth an apology?"

Clare straightens and drops all hints of a smile. In her hometown she could hold her own easily enough against this brand of prickliness, the sharp edge of her reputation always preceding her. If any nemeses weren't afraid of Clare, of her recklessness, they knew enough to be afraid of Jason. Clare steps closer to Ginny and offers her hand, her look firm with warning.

"Like I said, I'm Clare. I believe you're Ginny."

Ginny takes hold of Clare's hand and shakes. Her complexion is fair and flawless, the only blemish the crescents of leftover mascara under her eyes.

"You slept late," Clare says. "It's midafternoon."

"Yeah, well, it's Sunday. And this place bores me into a coma."

"I guess there's been some excitement lately," Clare says.

A nervous laugh escapes Ginny. "That's a weird way of putting it. She was your friend."

"She was," Clare says. In the silence that follows she feels a shift between them, Ginny fidgeting, nervous. If you want people to believe who you claim to be, Clare has learned in her short time on this job, it is better to be assertive than to demur.

"Who is that?" Clare gestures to the photograph on the wall.

"That's her mother," Ginny says. "Helen's mother, I mean."

"Your grandmother?"

"Yeah. Her name was Margaret Haines. She's dead."

"Did you ever meet her?" Clare asks.

"No," Ginny says. "I didn't."

Of course Clare knew the answer wouldn't be yes. She thinks of the newspaper clippings, this story splashed across the headlines, the police file, the grim history of High River Clare studied before arriving. The murder of Margaret Haines was a case so prominent that Clare remembers it even from childhood, her own mother glued to the television watching this farmland horror story unfold thousands of miles away. Clare shivers at the thought of standing, of sleeping, of living in the very same house as that news story that transfixed her mother so many years ago.

"Your grandmother looks a lot like Helen."

"She'd be the age Helen is now. That picture was taken in the field behind the house. Back when they grew corn. She farmed the land all by herself. Or oversaw the workers who farmed it, at least. My grandfather was a lawyer. Had this big practice in the city."

"That would've been a unique setup at the time," Clare says, prodding. "The woman farming, the man at work."

"This was the eighties. Not the fifties."

"Still," Clare says.

"Totally feminist setup, right?" Ginny offers Clare a cocked grin. "Except one night my grandfather chased his wife outside and shot her in the back as she tried to run away."

"Oh no," Clare says, hand to her mouth for effect. "I'm so sorry. I didn't—"

"Helen and Markus watched it all through the kitchen window. My uncle Jordan was just a baby. Asleep upstairs."

There is something almost giddy to Ginny's telling, the way she shifts her weight and crosses and uncrosses her arms. The way she calls her own mother by her first name, Helen, no *mom* to endear her.

"How old were Markus and your mother?"

"Fifteen and twelve, I think? Markus went and found his father's other gun. When his father came in through the kitchen door, Markus shot him in the heart."

"Yes. Yes. I know the story. I mean, I remember this story. It was big news at the time." Clare allows her real memories to seep through. "I was a little kid. My mom was obsessed with the news reports. The hero boy who killed his evil dad. I can remember my mom telling my dad about it in our kitchen."

"Yep," Ginny says. "I've Googled it. I've seen all the articles. If you dig deep there are even pictures of the crime scene."

The crime scene. Clare's file held the black-and-white photographs, the snow in the field stained black with blood, the mess of the kitchen. Her heart flips at the thought of children within that scene, Helen and her brother cowering in the terrorizing stretch between phoning the police and their arrival, the littlest brother oblivious in his upstairs bed. The thought of this young woman next to her now searching these details online, her family's history laid out for her not in tidy albums but in gory crime scene photos culled from the bowels of the Internet.

"Does Helen ever talk about it?"

"Hell, no!" Ginny says. "Helen's of the 'dig the deepest hole you can and stick your head in it' variety. That's how she copes."

"Who took in your mother and her brothers?"

"They have one random uncle who wanted nothing to do with them," Ginny says. "So they moved to the city to live with the Twinings. Philip Twining was my grandfather's law partner. He and his wife, Janice, took them in. Lived the city life for a while, but I guess Helen hated it. Got knocked up in her first year of college with yours truly. Thanks to me she had to drop out and moved back here. Took her brothers with her."

Ginny stands close to Clare, eyes to the photograph, the thaw between them incited by her chance to tell this story. Clare can see Ginny teetering on that verge, an adult in body but still so young, her history still too full of the stories of others. There had been a few details about the Twinings in Malcolm's file, a news piece about them on the twentieth anniversary of the killing, Jordan Haines starting law school with plans to partner with Philip, to do right where his father had done so wrong. Another story about Philip and Jordan and their plans to open a women's shelter in the city in memory of a mother Jordan surely can't remember. MARGARET HAINES HOUSE. Not a refuge like High River. A brick-and-mortar shelter with Margaret Haines's name on the door.

A phone beeps. Clare rests her hand on her own phone through her shorts, but Ginny pulls one from her waistband, face to the screen. She thumbs a response.

"Jordan's coming," she says. "He'll be here in an hour."

"He lives in the city?"

"Yeah," Ginny says, now scrolling through an app, distracted, double tapping photos at random. "Hot young urban lawyer man."

"You mean your uncle."

Ginny scrunches her nose without looking up. "Oh, I know he's my uncle. He reminds me of that daily. Uncle Babysitter."

Clare leans against the wall and faces Ginny head-on.

"How old are you?" Clare asks.

"Nineteen." Ginny straightens. "Twenty in November."

"Can I ask you something? Why do you call her Helen?"

"She doesn't like to be called Mom," Ginny says. "I don't especially like calling her Mom either. One thing we agree on."

There is hurt in Ginny's voice. Clare remembers the brief period in her teens when she insisted on calling her parents by their first names, how her mother had railed against it. I deserve that word, her mother would say, I worked hard for it. Eventually Clare had relented. And then years later, after the stillborn birth of her son, as the nurse cooed at Clare that she would always be his mom though he was dead, Clare remembers feeling incensed at her mother for those words years earlier, for claiming that motherhood was a badge to be earned and not a twist of fortune that befell some women and not others.

"What are you going to say to the cops?" Ginny asks, eyes still to her phone.

"I'll just answer whatever questions they have," Clare says.

"One of them . . . Rourke?" Ginny tucks her phone back in the waistband of her pajama bottoms. "He's been around a lot—"

"Hopefully so. They've yet to find anything."

"I'm trying to help him." Ginny leans back in a stretch, preening. "The whole family's clammed up. Helen hates having the cops around. I think Rourke's happy that I'm actually trying to be helpful."

"I'm sure he is. Did you know Sally and William?"

"A bit. The kid was kind of crazy. He literally never stopped moving. A lot of the women who stay here are head cases. Angry or superstressed." Ginny shrugs and lets out an anxious laugh. "William was just a chip off the old block."

"Right," Clare says. "What about the other cop?"

"Oh. Her name's Somers. I don't think she likes me very much."

"I'm sure she's just focused on the job."

"Whatever. They'll be here soon. I should get dressed."

Still, Ginny doesn't move. They stand side by side, eyes up to the portrait of Margaret Haines, Ginny taking in breaths as though she wants to speak.

"I'm sorry about your friend," she says finally. "Honestly? I didn't really know her. Or William. I try to keep my distance, you know? Too much drama. But when she wasn't stressed, she seemed nice."

"She was nice," Clare says. "Thank you."

Clare watches Ginny tiptoe back until she's over the threshold of her bedroom, taking her leave in a childish skulk. Ginny Haines is nineteen, still in the purgatory where she might want to act like a child yet be treated like an adult. Clare looks again at Margaret Haines. She wears jeans and high work boots, their soles caked with hard mud. Even a woman as strong as Margaret Haines could not withstand a bullet. Clare walks the length of the hall and picks the correct door, swinging it open to an empty room. Though her shoulder throbs, though the fingers of her left hand still tingle from the nerve damage, Clare feels a swell of purpose, of strength. She will leave the pills at the bottom of her duffel bag for now, change her clothes, speak to the police. Stay alert despite the pain. Work the case. If she clenches her hand and holds it long enough in an angry fist, the tremor will subside.

The river is so loud that he doesn't hear her approach. Clare pauses ten or so feet behind him. The clouds are low and round, a late-day rain rolling in, and in the heavy light Clare can see the curl of smoke rising over Jordan Haines. Helen's youngest brother. Twenty-seven years old, according to Malcolm's file. The toddler in the crib the night his parents died. He holds a cigarette in one hand and a beer in the other, his back to her. When he releases the puff, Clare stops and inhales deeply to catch its scent. In the early days Clare loved to watch Jason smoke, the way his shoulders would gently rise with each inhale, the tender pinch of his fingers on the filter as he lit one for her too.

"Hi," Clare says.

Jordan looks over his shoulder, noting Clare's arrival with only a glimmer of surprise. She aligns beside him so they are both facing the water. She'd spotted him here from her bedroom window. There are characters in Sally's story and Clare can't know which ones hold the key. And people are far more likely to let secrets slip when you have them alone, so take every chance you get. Clare learned this on her first case. She sighs, unable to read Jordan's body language, uncertain how to begin.

"You're Sally's friend," he says.

"Yes. I'm Clare. You must be Jordan."

He smiles without a hint of good humor. He gestures to his cigarette. "You want one?"

"No thanks," Clare says. "I quit a long time ago. I'm just waiting for the police to show up."

"Right. Me too."

The air is soupy with impending rain. Clare can feel the ooze of her shoulder through her T-shirt. Jordan sips his beer, the bottle glowing amber. His features bear the same basics as Ginny and Helen, the dark hair a shock against paler skin. He is trim and tall and wears a pressed shirt with a thin tie loose at the collar. Young to be a lawyer, Clare thinks. Handsome too.

"Sorry. Am I bothering you?" Clare asks. "I saw you pull up through the window. I'm in one of the bedrooms upstairs."

"No bother."

His eyes are upon her, but Clare watches the rolling water instead, too tired to gauge the nuances of eye contact, afraid she will ramble if she speaks. Apologize for nothing. He takes the last sip of his beer. Clare recognizes the label as the brand her brother, Christopher, favored, the Saturday trips he'd make to the next town to procure it from a specialty store.

"I'm a lawyer," he says.

"Yes. Ginny told me that."

"I'm happy to sit in on your interview with the officers."

"That's a nice offer," Clare says, "but wouldn't that . . . Isn't that a conflict of some kind? Given that you're family?"

"I'm not Sally's family. I'm not your family. And I wasn't

35

here when Sally and William disappeared." He takes a long drag from his cigarette and angles to blow the smoke to the sky. "I can find you another lawyer if you'd rather."

"Thank you," Clare says. "I'll see how I do on my own."

Jordan drops the cigarette butt into the beer bottle and tosses it into the river. Clare watches it bob to the surface, then tracks its speedy trajectory downstream. The clouds swirl more violently now, a wind picking up, warm and strong.

"It feels like rain is coming," Clare says.

"When I was young, we could swim in this river," Jordan says. "Walk from bank to bank with our hands in the air." He points to a pile of rotted wood on the shore. "That used to be a dock. We'd fish from it. You could look down to perfectly still water and see fish darting around rocks. But the water has been rising year over year. Last spring the current ripped the dock right off its footings."

"What changed?"

He shrugs. "A lot of things. Storms all the time. They built a dam upstream. Too much water. Some days it feels like the bank isn't going to hold."

By his body language, turned away from her, Clare can't tell if Jordan is arrogant or shy.

"Did you ever meet Sally?" Clare asks.

"I met her. A couple of times. I live in the city. I'm not here much anymore. She was only here a few months."

"A few months is a long time," Clare says.

"It's hard to keep track of the comings and goings."

The comings and goings. Something in his tone nudges Clare, the indifference. Clare thinks of Ginny's story, the news clippings, Jordan sleeping in his crib as his father shot his mother, as his brother shot his father. She studies him as he draws the pack from his breast pocket and curls inward to light another cigarette. Clare watches him inhale and blow the smoke upward again. Is there a small tremble in his hand? It feels like a persona, Clare thinks, the aloofness laid on too thick.

"Sally was quiet," Jordan says. "Seemed worried whenever I saw her. Sad."

Of course she was worried, Clare thinks. Of course she was sad.

"Her son was a handful," Jordan continues. "Bouncing off the walls."

"Well," Clare says. "He was a little guy. Is a little guy, I guess I should say."

"She spent a lot of time with Markus. You know, both of them home all day with little kids."

It isn't hard to detect the scorn in Jordan's tone, the pursed frown he wears to offset it. Clare thinks of Markus chasing his daughter in circles along the river's edge. A stay-at-home father, Clare thinks. In the awkward pause that follows, Clare feels herself edge away from Jordan. She glances to Markus's house across the river, its windows bright. She points to the willow tree, the cross.

"That cross is strange," Clare says. "Isn't it?"

"Markus is strange. He put it there to mark the twenty-fifth anniversary of my parents' death. Which happened to be a few weeks ago. Bad timing."

"It looks like a grave marker."

"Yeah." Jordan unbuttons his shirt cuffs one by one, rolling up the sleeves. "It does."

"It seems implausible," Clare says. "To just disappear without a trace in a river. No bodies found. The police must wonder."

"It's their job to wonder," Jordan says, pausing for effect. "In law school you learn pretty quick that anything is plausible.

About ten years ago a farmer's wife up the road got swept away in the river too. She chased after a bedsheet that flew off her clothesline in a wind. It was right after they built the dam. People weren't used to it. The fast water, I mean. She was never found either."

A navy-blue sedan appears in the driveway and pulls into the space between the house and the river. A man emerges from the driver's side and leans against the open door, surveying, sunglasses despite the clouds. When he closes the door Clare can see a gun holstered to his belt, a badge on a lanyard around his neck. He waits until a woman gets out from the passenger side and comes around before closing his own door. The woman wears a tailored jacket and slacks, dark boots despite the searing heat. She is black, as tall as he is, sunglasses and lanyard too. Next to the car they lean in so that their heads almost touch, a huddle before the play.

"Between them, she's the boss," Jordan says. "Though he'll work hard to have you think otherwise."

Once they are done conferring the female detective smiles and clasps her hands, leading the way towards Clare and Jordan. Clare shifts her weight uncertainly as they approach, swallowing hard when the male detective stops short and removes his sunglasses, squinting at her. Colin Rourke is muscular and good-looking, eyes too bright against his tanned skin, hair buzzed short. He is trying to place her. Clare rubs the back of her neck in nervous reflex.

"You must be Clare O'Brien." The female cop extends her hand, dry against the clamminess of Clare's. "I'm Detective Somers. This is Rourke."

Rourke says nothing. His gaze is so unrelenting that Clare must counter it by lifting her chin in defiance, smiling falsely, her jaw clenched with the effort to stay poised.

"Do you want me to leave?" Jordan asks.

"Not at all, Mr. Haines," Detective Somers says. "We're just here to introduce ourselves." Her eyes shift to Clare. "You arrived last night?"

"Late. Yes."

"And you'd heard from Sally, we hear."

"A few weeks ago. Maybe a month. It was an e-mail. Before she . . ." Clare hesitates.

"Do you have a copy of it?"

"Sally asked me to delete it."

"And you did, I presume," Somers says.

"I did."

No electronic trail. This is Malcolm's rule. Delete all conversations as soon as they happen. Store no numbers or addresses. By the quizzical look Somers is giving her now, Clare isn't sure how well her response will hold up under true scrutiny. The four of them turn to watch Ginny as she approaches from the house, limbs loose as she walks, her expression locked in a smile aimed at Rourke. She wears jean shorts and a black tank top, her lips circled in lipstick a deep red.

"You stole my cigarettes," Ginny says playfully to Jordan, sidling up to him, her elbow pressing into his ribs.

"I borrowed them."

"I hate it when you go through my stuff!" Her giggle is shrill.

Clare feels mortified on Ginny's behalf, certain she detects a look exchanged between Somers and Rourke. Jordan lights a cigarette for Ginny and she inhales without grace. It is difficult to gauge their dynamic. Uncle and niece close enough in age to be siblings.

"You *still* haven't found the bodies?" Ginny says.

"Are we looking for bodies?" Somers asks. "We don't know what we're looking for yet."

"Raylene could have stopped them," Ginny drawls. "She was there. There's no way he would have survived. Will, I mean. A toddler? That's basically a baby. There's no way he'd survive that river."

Jordan clears his throat and takes Ginny gently by the arm. Raylene could have stopped them. Clare processes this detail, avoiding eye contact with Rourke, focusing on Somers instead. A drop of rain lands cool on her head. She reaches up to touch the wet spot at her crown. Rourke hasn't stopped staring at her since walking over from the car and it is making her too anxious to stand still much longer.

"We'd like to ask you a few questions," Rourke says.

Is there something familiar in the low rumble of his voice? His is a face Clare is certain she'd remember.

"Now?" Clare asks.

"Sure. Maybe we can find a quiet place to talk?"

"I'm actually not feeling very well," Clare says. "I might need to sit down."

"You know what?" Somers says. "The sky's about to open. And you must be exhausted from your long trip. Why don't we come get you in the morning? Drive you to the station. We can talk there. A little more formally. Privately. Make you some coffee. We've got *a lot* of questions. It suits us that you're feeling good enough to answer them."

"Okay," Clare says, her voice tight.

"We'll come back at eight?"

"I can drive her in," Jordan says. "I'm staying the night here. I have a meeting in town at nine thirty. I'll drop her at the station."

"That works out well," Somers says.

The cigarette's filter is rimmed with the red of Ginny's lipstick. She makes no effort to mask her irritation, weight shifting, eyes bouncing between them as they speak past her.

"I'll come too," she says. "Not to the interview, obviously. I have stuff to do in the city. To get ready for school."

"School?" Somers asks.

"Ginny's nearly a college grad," Jordan says. "For engineering, remarkably. One more year. She heads back to campus this week. She's smarter than she looks."

"Law of averages." Ginny punches Jordan's shoulder. "If you can be dumb and ugly, then I can be pretty and smart."

"Ha," Rourke says, smiling. Ginny lets out a sharp laugh, then lifts her hand to bite her nails. Despite the tension, Clare detects the affection between Jordan and Ginny, the way he edges closer when he senses she's embarrassed. Clare recalls that even as children it always felt fraught with her brother, Christopher, always felt like he was admonishing her. You'll get hurt. Try harder. Why would you do that? His love presenting only as chiding worry. When Ginny looks up to the sky, a drop of rain hits her square on the nose. Somers raises a hand in a fruitless effort to shield herself.

"Tomorrow," she says to Clare. "At nine sharp."

"See you then."

Rourke reaches into his breast pocket and hands Clare a business card. She takes it without meeting his gaze. As the detectives walk back to the sedan Ginny's face transforms into a pout. Perhaps she'd been expecting more engagement from Rourke, a detective who must be fifteen years older than she is, who may have planted a seed in Ginny that grows without tending. Clare stands with Jordan and Clare and watches the car reverse to turn around, then disappear down the driveway, Somers at the wheel this time.

"How far is the city from here?" Clare asks.

"Thirty minutes if the traffic's light," Jordan says. "Triple that on a Monday morning."

41

The city, Clare thinks. A land still foreign to her, vast and concrete. Malcolm. She will text him. See if there is a way to meet.

"How will I get back?"

"I'll drive you," Jordan says. "And you? Miss Noon Riser. We'll leave without you if you're not ready by seven thirty."

Ginny groans and flicks her still-lit cigarette into the river. The rain begins in earnest. The three of them break for the house, the earth instantly saturated and muddy under Clare's feet. A flash, then the rumble of thunder. Clare pauses on the porch and turns out to watch the storm. The branches of the willow trees sway too wildly, the house across the river now dark in every window. Clare looks down at the smudged business card in her hand. DETECTIVE COLIN ROURKE, it reads. There is nothing familiar in that name. There was nothing familiar in his face, either. And she is too many miles from home, from the last place where anyone knew her, knew who she really was. So why, Clare thinks, crumpling the card in her fist, has Rourke stirred within her that familiar dread?

I n their shared room Raylene lies
on her bed, staring up at the
ceiling, catatonic. The rain clat-
ters on the porch roof. Clare sits on her own bed, her hands
worried between her knees, waiting for Raylene to speak.

"Are you hungry?" Clare asks. "I could get you something
to eat."

The shake of Raylene's head is almost imperceptible. Clare
knows this pose, the numb immobility that comes from con-
taining grief or rage. Clare reaches for the duffel bag stuffed
under her bed. It takes her a moment to call up the combina-
tion to the small lock binding its zipper. She collects her cell
phone and tucks it under her pillow.

"You sure you're okay?"

This time Raylene doesn't answer at all. When she blinks,
a tear runs down her temple and hits the white pillowcase.

"We can talk about it if you want," Clare offers. "They come
at me sometimes too. Thoughts, memories. I don't know.
Whatever's troubling you." Clare pauses. Nurturing is not a

natural instinct to her. The coaxing makes her edgy. "I spoke to the cops just now."

Raylene blinks again.

"They're bringing me in tomorrow for a formal interview," Clare says.

With movements so deliberate they seem in slow motion, Raylene sits and swings her legs over the side of the bed. Her hair is matted. The shirt she wears is tailored but stained, her sandals expensive but worn, her shorts the white sort you'd wear to play tennis. Raylene might have had money once, the tattoo of two cherub angels on her ankle the only anomalous feature about her.

"You stare," Raylene says. "That's a bad habit."

"So I've been told," Clare says. "Sorry. I've been alone a lot the past few months."

"And you forgot basic social norms?"

Clare allows a small smile. "Hopefully not."

"I don't like it when people ask me a lot of questions," Raylene says.

"Neither do I."

"I knew Sally well," Raylene says. "Better than anyone here did, at least. And she never said anything about some friend she met at a shelter. That's not a question."

It rises in Clare, the option to adapt the truth. To mingle her story with Sally's, cross their paths just enough so that it rings true. To imagine Grace Fawcett, her only real friend at home, the scorn they'd often reserved for each other where kindness should have lain.

"We knew each other before the shelter," Clare says. "Distantly. But I wasn't very good to her after we reconnected. She really needed a friend. But I had my own troubles. I couldn't help her."

"What kind of troubles?"

"That's a question," Clare says.

Raylene cocks her head, expectant.

"Well," Clare offers. "The same kind as Sally. The same as you, I presume. The kind that led you here. Like you said earlier, I didn't respond when she first e-mailed me. Now I just want to make amends."

"Right."

"I met Ginny earlier today," Clare says. "We talked in the hallway. She told me that you were there when Sally and William went into the river. Is that true?"

"You think I'd just let them jump?"

"No," Clare says. "Of course not."

"Ginny and her stories," Raylene says. "She's quite the little bitch."

Bitch. Clare thinks of her mother standing over them at the kitchen table, her hand raised in a threat to swat Christopher for calling Clare that very word. How easily it fell from Jason's lips at every turn, even playfully, even in front of friends. *You bitch*, he would say, taking her by the wrist, squeezing until it ached. Clare kicks off her shoes and slides back on her bed to rest against the wall. A clack of thunder startles them both.

"I don't want to talk to the police," Clare says. "The whole idea makes me want to vomit."

"I hear you," Raylene says.

What Clare doesn't say is that her fear is grounded in the way Rourke appraised her earlier, how he and Somers might work together to peel back the layers of her cover. The vigilance it will take to keep ahead of them. There had been no police work to speak of on her first case in Blackmore, no detectives milling about asking questions, a luxury she hadn't fully appreciated until now.

"I don't want to talk to them about my past," Clare says.

"Are you married?" Raylene asks.

"I was. Then I left. Right around the same time Sally left her husband. I've been on the move, mostly. But my husband wrote me a letter recently. Sent it to the place I'd been staying. Like a taunt. He knew where I was. I've been carrying the letter around."

"Isn't that just great?" Raylene says. "Same thing happened to Sally. Her husband wrote her a while ago too. Told her he missed her. As if."

"How did Sally feel about that?"

"To my face she'd insist the prospect disgusted her. That she'd never go back. But then she found out he was moving on. He wrote to say he wanted a divorce. He'd met someone else. She went kind of ballistic. I'd come in here at night and find her red-faced, staring at the wall. Breathing through her nose like a bull, like she was going to blow. It wasn't even about wanting him back. It wasn't about that. It was about . . . family. What she was forfeiting. She loved the idea of one big happy family. Hated the idea of another woman with the man she'd run away from. She knew it meant he was abdicating William. Letting her have him. That made her mad."

"I get it," Clare says.

"William was sweet," Raylene says. She drops her head and breathes against the crack in her voice. "He was wild. Full of beans. But lately he was sick. Weird sick. Throwing up. He had these terrible dark circles under his eyes. Then this fever. Helen made Sally take him to the hospital a few weeks ago. But they couldn't find any cause. Said it was probably just a bad virus."

"Did you see them go into the river?"

"No," Raylene says. "Honestly? It was one of those nights when I had my own shit to deal with. I ran into her in the hallway. She was crying her eyes out about something. Practically frantic. I didn't engage. I went into my own room. Heard her go downstairs. She didn't come back."

"Where was William?" Clare asks.

Raylene shrugs, catching her breath to stem the tears. "I never saw him. I don't know. Then they were just fucking vapor. Gone. I don't even know how it's possible."

So often Clare has wondered how her own disappearance has haunted those she left behind. Her brother, her father, Grace. The questions or regrets that might plague them. Worse, she's wondered if they've been afflicted at all, if instead they've felt only relief to have her gone.

"Where's your husband?" Raylene asks, reading Clare's expression.

"Home, I assume. But I don't know for sure."

"Do you ever ask yourself why? Why Sally ended up here? Why your husband is still at home?"

"It was always his home. It was never mine."

"You lived there, didn't you?"

Clare nods.

"It doesn't anger you that he's still there and you're not?"

"I don't actually know that he is," Clare says, calm, her heartbeat steady.

"But he stayed, right?" Raylene asks. "You're the one who left?"

"Right," Clare says.

"What is it about the world that makes women have to run away?"

"I don't know. It felt like the only way out. For me. For Sally too, I guess."

"Do you see the flaw in that?" Raylene asks. "Grown women forced to run away?"

"I do."

"You never had any kids."

"No," Clare says. "I was six months pregnant around this time last year and—"

"Let me guess. He threw you into a wall. Knocked you down then kicked you and you lost the baby."

The accuracy of Raylene's guess takes Clare aback.

"He pushed me down the stairs," Clare says. "The cellar stairs. But I—"

"Don't. Don't you dare say 'but.' What 'but' could there possibly be?"

"I had a lot of problems. I'd been drinking. I was using. I was a user. Most of my adult life, I was a bad user. You know what? I'm not even sure he pushed me. I might have just fallen."

Something in the confessional breaks Clare open, a sob rising fast in her throat. She drops her head to her hands, body quaking. It takes several minutes for the tears to abate.

"It amazes me," Raylene says.

Clare's voice is still too cracked for her to speak.

"You actually blame yourself."

"What about you?" Clare asks, wiping at her cheeks. "Do you have kids? I noticed the tattoo on your ankle."

"I did," Raylene says. "I had two kids. Twins. A boy and a girl."

Had, Clare thinks. Past tense.

"I was a doctor. I am a doctor. I used to work in a really busy ER."

Clare nods to mask her surprise. She could tell by small details of her clothes that Raylene was probably not completely destitute, but a doctor? The posters on domestic abuse plastered around the hospital where Clare used to work would declare that it knew no boundaries, but Clare hadn't figured that to be true. She hadn't figured the doctors working on the floor where she was a cleaner could be living the same vicious cycle that she was. She used to figure she could spot the women. The ones in the same boat. The accidents they'd claim, a tumble, a scald while cooking dinner. How they averted their eyes at the question, smiled in their answers as though apologizing for the lie. But maybe there'd been women among her just better at hiding it.

"My husband was a banker," Raylene continues. "Big-time banker. Born into money. His mother was fifth-generation rich. His father was a judge, so he knew the system. I was at work one evening and he found a card in one of my jacket pockets. I had no idea he made a habit of going through my pockets. It was a card for a family lawyer. A lawyer who specialized in helping women escape shitty situations."

"When was this?" Clare asks.

"Four years ago. Five days before Christmas."

"What happened?"

"He drowned them in the bathtub. Our children. The night he found the card." Raylene scrunches her eyes closed, clenching her teeth against the wave that comes. "He tried to make it look like an accident. Said he'd heard a noise downstairs and left them alone for just a minute and when he came back, they were . . . He called an ambulance and had the paramedics bring them to my ER."

"No," Clare says.

"Yes. After they were declared, they left us alone with their bodies. 'You did this,' he said to me. 'You did this to them. You made me do it.' And then he lied. To everyone. Called it a tragic accident. Took his eyes off them for a minute or two. Some people believed him. Some of my closest friends. Believed it was an accident. Friends. But an orderly from the ER testified that he'd heard him threaten me, that he'd heard him admit what he'd done, and there were bruises on their arms from fighting him, and it threw his story into question just enough to warrant an arrest. But my husband's parents stood by him. Paid for the very best lawyers. His mother even testified that the orderly had tried to bribe them. The jury was hung in the first trial. He was acquitted in the second."

"Jesus," Clare says. "What did you do?"

"I left. I just left. Buried them and abandoned everything. My parents, my siblings—I have four siblings I haven't seen in two years—my job, everyone. Moved here. To the city, I mean. Found an apartment on the outskirts and got a job working in a factory that makes . . ." Raylene pauses, staring at the wall. "Clocks. If you can believe it. Went from an ER doctor to making clocks. Lived like that for two years."

"What brought you to High River?"

"I met Jordan. I never officially got divorced. When I searched online for lawyers who help women in my situation, he and his partner, Philip Twining, they were the first names to come up."

Clare thinks of the photograph in the file, the news story. Jordan Haines, the lawyer on the mission to do right by the mother he never met.

"He brought you here?"

"He gave me the option to come while we figured out a plan. I took it. Got here around Valentine's Day, about two weeks before Sally and William."

Raylene lies back on her bed, eyes to the ceiling again. For a long moment they listen to the receding storm, the low and distant rumble of thunder. Clare stands and turns off the overhead light, then lies on her bed too.

"Why should they get to live?" Raylene asks.

"What do you mean?"

"Why should our husbands get to live?"

The weight of this question, Clare thinks. The what-ifs debated too many times. It is too much, her own past swirling into Sally's. She thinks of the pill bottle at the bottom of her duffel bag. The dullness she would welcome.

"I thought of killing him," Clare says. "Many times. Sometimes I wondered whether I was inventing it all. He could be so convincing. People loved him. I couldn't be sure anyone would believe me."

"Few would have," Raylene says. "I learned that the hard way."

Sometimes, at night, in the many motels since leaving, Clare would lie awake and wonder if aspects of her life, of her marriage, were not memories but a series of muddled dreams. She'd told no one her story while it was happening, not the whole truth, anyway. And so after she left, the only account that remained was her own. Clare was never one to trust herself. What proof did she have that any of it was true?

Raylene clears her throat. "I wasn't lying when I said I didn't see her go in," she says.

"I didn't think you were," Clare says.

"I heard a scream. I looked out the window. I'm not sure, but I think I saw something. Someone in the river. I do remember that. I think I saw her. I think so, but I'm not sure."

See? Clare thinks. The trick of memory.

"I know for sure that I never saw the boy," Raylene says. "There was just one person."

"What did you do?"

"I went downstairs. I couldn't find Helen. I went outside and there was no one there. I called Jordan. Then he called the police. And I looked myself. I searched along the river until the police arrived."

"You did what you could," Clare says.

"The funny thing?" Raylene says. "When Jordan got here, he told me to just tell it that way."

"What way?" Clare asks.

"He told me to tell the police that I'm sure I saw Sally go into the river. He said it might be helpful even if I'm not totally sure. He said that way we could be sure the police would check the river thoroughly, not give up too soon. You know how police are with missing women. With women like us."

"I do," Clare says, thinking of Jordan by the river earlier, the aloofness, the offer of counsel. "I guess that makes sense."

"I heard her," Raylene says again, fidgeting, eyes ahead as if trying to conjure a clear picture. "I heard a scream."

"Okay, but—"

Raylene holds up her hand to stem the questions. It is dizzying, the way their conversation jumps, both with too many secrets, too many stories to tell. Lies and omissions replaced by strange truths as the conversation wears on. Versions. Clare closes her eyes and presses her head into the heat of the pillow. All she wants is sleep.

"They'd be six by now," Raylene says, a whisper.

Who? Clare thinks to ask, but realizes Raylene means her children. Clare says nothing. There is no answer that will help.

Tomorrow morning Clare will speak to the police. She must sleep now, steel herself for their questions. She must breathe against the unease tomorrow incites. The rain sweeps sideways, the wind picking up again. Clare knows she should be sending a message to Malcolm, setting a meeting time for tomorrow if she can sneak away. It is remarkable how distant he feels from her now, as though it weren't him who hired her. As if she were working entirely on her own. When she closes her eyes she can barely recall Malcolm's features, stranger to her now than he's ever been.

MONDAY

The water slaps around her, dark and foamy and cold. She pops out at the surface and manages a gasp. She can see that it is night, that the stars are clustered in milky swarms above her. There is no shore in any direction. A wave comes at her, a hand around her ankle, then an arm around her waist. Clare can't crane, can't kick, can't turn. Instead, tethered to his weight, she gives in and lets herself sink to the bottom.

When she wakes Clare is thirsty, her shirt soaked through with sweat. Raylene's bed is empty. She slides her hand under her shirt to the moisture of the wound. Only when she turns does she see the figure in the doorway.

"Jesus!" Clare says. "You scared me."

"You were calling out," Helen says.

Helen enters the room and sits on Raylene's bed. She hands Clare the glass of water she holds. Clare gathers the sheet over her legs, then accepts the glass and drains its contents.

"You were calling a name," Helen says. "You were calling for Malcolm."

The room is too dark, Clare knows, for Helen to read any shift in the expression on her face.

"Who's Malcolm? Is that your husband?"

"No," Clare says, looking down to evade the questions. Even if it were a story she could tell without blowing her cover, how would she explain Malcolm Boon to anyone when she doesn't understand him herself? He is not my husband, she might say. He searches for missing women. That is his job. My husband hired him to find me after I left. And when he did find me, he hired *me* instead of turning me in. Clare's head shakes slightly at the thought of it, the implausibility of their arrangement, her inability to summon words to define it. She thinks back to her mother in the hospital, flipping through a photo album Clare had made her, her life story laid out in caption-free pictures. The unlikely friendships, the heartbreaks, the losses, the mistakes. The turns she didn't see coming. *You can't make up a story stranger than the one you live*, her mother said after snapping the album closed, not a hint of nostalgia in her voice. Clare sighs and looks up.

"I'm not prying," Helen says.

"I'm sorry," Clare answers. "It's the heat. It makes me so light-headed. Malcolm is . . . He's from another life. He's no one to worry about. What time is it?"

"Three."

"Where's Raylene?" Clare asks.

"She might be downstairs. She's often up at night."

"I don't usually call out in my dreams. I'm sorry I woke you."

"You didn't. These days I'm not sleeping more than an hour at a time." Helen pauses. "Dreams are funny. They're the brain's way of telling us something we need to know. Don't you think? I've had many premonitions in my sleep and I wasn't always one to trust them. I regret that now."

"I've never really thought about it."

In truth Clare has thought of it many times, the dreams of running she had for months, even years, before she actually left Jason. And then after she was gone, the dreams of Jason chasing her. Clare hands the glass back to Helen. She imagines Helen opening the bedroom door, watching her as she tossed and turned. It distresses Clare to realize she didn't wake when Helen came in. When she first married Jason, Clare would sometimes be gardening or chopping wood outside, absorbed so fully in her task that Jason would have to whistle to catch her attention from the porch. I've been standing here watching you for five minutes, Jason would say, and you never noticed.

"Can I get you anything else?" Helen asks.

"No. Thank you. I'm fine."

"Sally's son used to wander at night."

"Oh," Clare says. "I didn't know that about him."

"He was already out of a crib even though he'd just turned two. He'd wake up at night and wander. I guess Sally slept like such a log that he'd slip by her."

"Where was their room?"

"Across the hall. Facing the back field. I keep it locked now. Sometimes I'd hear him out in the hallway or making his way downstairs one step at a time. I'd intercept him and we'd go downstairs and share a glass of warm milk. He didn't speak much. A handful of words, but he had this way of telling you exactly what he . . ." Helen quiets and looks down the hall as if expecting to see the boy there.

A tight grip takes hold of Clare's chest. In the low light Helen looks defeated, sad. She stands.

"I had a clear vision for this place," she says, repeating her own words like a chorus, as though forgetting their riverside conversation this morning. "My intentions were good. For every woman I've had here. My intentions for Sally and little William were good."

Clare nods. "Of course they were."

"Maybe I can still help you," Helen says.

"How?"

"Give you some options. To get away."

"I want to find Sally," Clare says.

Helen gazes at nothing, her hand closing tightly around the glass. Without another word she turns down the hall. Clare listens to her footsteps and the open and close of her bedroom door. She digs through her bag for her cell phone, then tucks it in the elastic band of her sleep shorts and tiptoes downstairs, stalking the perimeter of the main floor. Where is Raylene? Clare sits in an armchair, its fabric warm with absorbed heat. This house feels ghostly in the dark, rotting, spots on the ceiling plaster peeling open like gaping wounds. Clare closes her eyes. The dream comes back to her in a flash. Underwater, a pull on her leg, a hug around her chest, the last bubbles of air leaving her lips. What if her instincts haven't been honed at all these past months? What if Jason is right behind her, ready to pull her under?

Calm down.

Clare sits up, eyes open, fishing for the cell phone fallen loose into the folds of the chair. She listens.

I'll handle it.

Voices. Clare stands and adjusts herself behind the drapes to ensure she's in full darkness. Out the window she sees Jordan, the bright white of his shirt. She cannot see who is with him. He's lowered his voice so he speaks in pantomime, arms in vivid gesture. He reaches out and draws the person he's addressing into a hug, wrapping her. Raylene. She is crying, her hand in a fist against his chest. Jordan takes Raylene by the wrists to calm her. Then he startles, pausing to look around, as if aware someone is watching.

He doesn't see Clare in the window. She tiptoes away and climbs the stairs. In her room Clare sits on the bed and tucks her head between her knees, dizzy with exhaustion or anxiety, her palms hot and dry on her face. She peels back the sleeve of her T-shirt and examines her shoulder. The scarring is purple, flared, the skin warm. It hurts more than it has in days. She fumbles through her bag for the bottle of pills, only a few left.

My intentions were good, Helen said. Clare pulls her cell phone out and punches in Malcolm's number.

Coming to city in AM. Might be able to get away for an hour. Can u meet? Somewhere central.

Wherever he is, Malcolm is likely sleeping. Still, the phone seems to pulse in her hands as she cradles it. When it vibrates only a minute later, Clare jerks.

Sentinel Park. Benches by the pond. Easy to find. I'll be there 10AM.

Then, after a beat, **Will wait. Txt if you can.**

Clare can't be sure why she feels such relief in reading his message. She thumbs a reply.

Ok.

From her vantage point, the porch roof blocks Jordan and Raylene from Clare's view. Beyond, the river roils madly. Clare can envision Sally Proulx on the dock with her son, whether she went there on her own, whether she'd been led there by someone else. The versions. Sally's son sleepwalking, a terrible accident, her scream as he wandered off the river's bank, her terror as she jumped in after him. The version where someone leads Sally there, her son too, where she pleads, promising to keep some secret, to undo some terrible wrong. Clare pictures Sally placing her son in the water, then going in after them, provoked by despair. Or someone chasing her, chasing them both, Sally's scream loud enough for Raylene to hear it from this room even over the din of the river.

Jordan told me to just tell it that way, Raylene said.

Clare imagines the eroding soil of the riverbank giving way beneath them, tossing Sally and her child in, or the two of them tumbling in a push. Sally Proulx would have clawed at the surface, called for help, reached for her baby boy. The cold of the water. There would be nothing to grasp but each other, and Sally might have held on to her son for dear life. But the current would have been too strong. She could not have kept hold. In no time, it would have ripped them from each other's arms.

A light comes on in the house across the river, and then another, and Clare can track the shadow of someone moving room to room. She thumbs at the lid of the pill bottle. Three in the morning in this house, yet no one here seems to be asleep.

The sensation is a perfect one. It kicks in all at once, a balm across the skin, her pain numbed, her thoughts clear. Clare stands under the willow tree, watching the river. Her hair drifts up in the gentle wind. It still smells of salt from the ocean. She can almost feel it, the lightness of her body floating in the calm of low tide, the salt water stinging her shoulder. Was Malcolm there? She can see two chairs on the sand, the rocky path to the motel. But Clare cannot see him. She bends and lowers her hand to the river's current, allowing the water to slap hard at her fingertips. A river colder than the ocean.

After Helen left the room, Clare could not sleep. She'd feigned it when Raylene came back, eyes pressed closed until she was certain Raylene was asleep, her hand gripping the prescription bottle under the pillow. Then she'd tiptoed to the kitchen and swallowed one. Two. Now she stands here, the sky still black with night, her muscles relaxed and happy. She sidesteps to where the cross is nailed to the tree. Globs of dried paint hang from its ends. On closer look Clare can see initials carved into the wood. *I hate that cross*, Helen said. *Markus put it up.* A gesture of remembrance, Clare thinks, for a murder committed decades ago.

Clare leans against the tree and listens. For what? Any sounds above the roar of the current. When her mind is open like this, when the pain is gone, every sound is distilled. The first time she'd experienced this sensation was a dozen years ago, the single pill stolen from her mother's cancer stash. Clare remembers the coolness of the autumn late afternoon as she walked to the far end of her family's wheat field, the pill pinched between her fingers, the burn as it dissolved on her tongue. And then came the washing over, the calm, her vision so sharp that she could discern the dusk colors overhead as if she'd painted the sky herself. The next day she woke up with a headache, the hours between the pill and bedtime a strange blur. Everything is exactly right at the moment, Clare remembers confessing to a disapproving Grace, but then you come down and you remember almost nothing.

Across the river the light comes on again. This time Clare can see into the kitchen through the sheer curtains, a man at the sink. Markus. He disappears briefly, then emerges on the porch and descends the side stairs to cut across the lawn. Clare watches the flashlight beam bounce ahead of him until the trees swallow him up. Ten minutes must pass before the beam bobs again, this time on her side of the river. It flashes in a strobe. He is moving through the distant trees, away from the river. Clare follows it, cautious in her steps. Now the beam seems to shoot up from the ground, washing the trees above in yellow light. Clare can make out two small trapdoors flipped open from what looks like a hole in the ground.

The river is far enough away that Clare catches the small sounds. A click. A shuffle. She tucks herself behind a tree. It makes you reckless, Clare, her brother used to say once her addiction had fully set in. You do things you'd never do sober. Like, Clare thinks, follow a stranger's flashlight into the woods at night. She calls a hello and moves even closer.

"Hello?" she says again.

Markus pops up between the trapdoors.

"Oh dear," he says, lifting himself out of the ground. "Hello?" He squints. "Sorry. I can't see who you are!"

"Oh." Clare steps into the ambient light. Maybe she should be nervous, but she isn't. She is calm, her nerves numbed, her arms dangling heavy at her sides. "I'm Clare. I just arrived here yesterday. I'm sorry. I couldn't sleep. I was getting some air. I saw the light through the trees."

"Clare. Right. Clare." He scratches his head. "Helen told me you'd arrived last night. You're Sally's friend."

"Yes," Clare says. "I don't mean to bother you."

Markus bounces on the spot and draws his hands in and out of his pockets. "This probably looks strange to you."

Well, yes, Clare thinks, but she won't say it. Instead she leans over the opening to the underground room and takes in the wooden stairs that descend to it.

"What is it?" she asks.

"It's a bunker. My father built it thirty years ago. He was a paranoid guy."

In their own yard Clare's father had dug one too, a hole formed into a room with beams made of used barn boards. The bunker stood a hundred feet from their house. Not paranoid, he would say to Clare's mother as he lined its shelves with canned goods. Just realistic. Prepared.

"I get it," Clare says. "My father had one too."

There is a bed of dead pine needles and leaves built up around the open doors. She thinks of the cellar off the kitchen at the home she ran away from, Jason bolting her in, trapping her under her own house. She thinks of the mine egress in Blackmore, its heavy doors pierced by bullets, all the clues that led her there. These dark places.

"I know it looks strange," Markus says. "Ha. I'm repeating myself. But it's funny, you know. Because the only other person to catch me here in the middle of the night was Sally." He shifts on his feet again. "I'm sorry for your loss, by the way," he adds.

It strikes Clare, his use of words. *She spent a lot of time with Markus,* Jordan had said by the river. *Both home all day with little kids.*

"I'm hopeful she'll turn up," Markus says. He presses a finger into his eye.

"Are you all right?" Clare asks.

"Fine." He lets out a high-pitched laugh. "It's the middle of the night. I'm tired. What am I doing out here?"

"Sally caught you here too, you said?"

"She sure did. She had a smoking habit she was trying to hide. Trying to kick. She'd walk over to the eddy in the middle of the night for some peace. Smoke her way through half a pack in one go. And she caught me on my way here. We caught each other, I guess." In the faint light Markus's features aren't fully clear, but Clare can see he looks earnest and boyish, an older and paunchy look-alike of his brother, Jordan, his T-shirt untucked and his jeans spotted with stains. "It's been a terrible week. Devastating. Rebecca and I have been beside ourselves."

"I'm sure," Clare says.

It feels impossible to read his body language. In gauging his jumpiness Clare cannot figure what questions to ask, how to possibly make sense of the scene before her. A scene that might scare her in any other state of mind. Markus backs up and gestures for Clare to approach.

"Do you want to check it out?" he asks.

"No," Clare says. "My mother taught me never to enter a bunker with a stranger."

"Ha," he says. "Ha! Right."

"I'll just head back. I should try to get some sleep."

"Right. I'm sorry. I don't even know what to say. I know it's preposterous. Skulking around here at night. Sally thought so . . ." Markus draws a closed fist to his mouth to stifle a cry. "I hide baby formula down here."

"Sorry. Did you say 'baby formula'?"

"One whole shelf lined with it," Markus says. "Rebecca—my wife—she's very keen on holistic measures. We both are. She shuns western medical practices. But our daughter, Willow, she's been losing weight. They call it 'failure to thrive.' Really unusual for a two-year-old. They tend to gobble up anything in sight. But she's so picky, and a lot of foods make her sick. So I bought her some formula out of desperation. I give her a bottle at night when Rebecca's sleeping."

His expression is so somber that Clare must bite her lower lip to avoid any reaction he might misread. His eyes are puffy. A man in mourning, she thinks. A man in pain.

"Once Sally knew about this place she'd come here too. Like a refuge within a refuge. Ha. I'd let her smoke in here even though it made me want to puke."

Clare decides to prod a bit further. "Helen told me you two were friendly."

Markus nods, raising a hand to stop Clare from saying more, another effort to keep his tears in check. "I'm sorry," he says after a minute. "It's been a lot. William is my daughter's age. The sweetest boy. So full of life."

"The cross next to the river. Helen says you put it there." The words spill from Clare before she thinks better of them. Markus nods.

"I meant it as a memorial." He pauses, scratching his head. "But now it just looks like . . ."

"A grave marker."

Markus frowns. "Yes," he says.

Clare peers over the opening again.

"Actually," she says, "do you mind if I go down? I'd like to see it."

Markus rubs his eyes, then waves her to the stairs. Even when she grips the shaky handrail, there is no pain in her shoulder. It feels healed for the first time since Clare was shot. An illusion produced by the pill, she knows, but a relief nonetheless. The bunker is a squat and square room much larger than Clare expected, its walls lined with sheeted metal, each with a caged lightbulb so bright that Clare cannot look at them directly. There are shelves lined with boxes and canned goods along two walls, at least a dozen cans of baby formula, a couch with faded patterns straight ahead. A gun rack high on the far wall. Markus hovers at the bottom of the stairs.

"My dad was convinced we'd be taken out by a bomb, or a meteor, or a tornado or electrical storm that would wipe out the grid," he says. "This was his means to escape the end of the world." He pauses and scratches his head again, a tic. "I was away from High River for a long time. Years. When I got back I only remembered vaguely where it was. Took me weeks to actually find it. That's how well it's hidden."

"Do the cops know about the bunker?" Clare asks.

"Nope," he says. "But that's just because no one else does. I promised Helen I'd fill it in years ago. But I never did. You'd have a very hard time finding it in the light of day even if you knew it was here. It's always been my little hideaway. I guess lying about it in the first place is not the kind of thing you can backtrack on."

"Even the search party never found it? The ones looking for Sally?"

Clare can tell the question has provoked Markus despite his efforts to hide it. He coughs.

"They've stuck to the river," he says. "I'm as surprised as you, to be honest. I keep waiting to get caught."

The trapdoors mustn't be more than a quarter mile from the house, however set back in the woods. Hiding from the people closest to you. It seems implausible, but then, Clare thinks of the hunting cabin Jason built at the far edge of their property, a hole in the roof to release the smoke from the fire pit he'd laid at its center, the supplies he'd collected on hooks and plywood shelves. By the time she'd finally discovered it on a spring jog she could tell it had been there a long time, years, even, by the way the earth had already started to reclaim it.

Markus collects a can of formula and sits on the couch, sinking low into it, the look of a lost boy.

"I know it's bad," he says, his voice shrill. "Keeping it a secret. Hiding it from my wife. From Helen. Squirreling away cans of formula."

"You're trying to do right by your child," Clare offers.

"Rebecca would say I'm poisoning her."

"Surely she'd understand if—"

"Every morning Rebecca gives her a tincture of echinacea and almond oil. She thinks that's what's helping. Meanwhile, I'm hiding baby formula in a bomb shelter and giving it to my daughter behind my wife's back. It's working, though. Willow's gained five pounds."

"Well, there are certainly worse things you could be giving her."

A shadow passes across Markus's face. Clare can't read it. She feels wobbly on her feet, the air in here too stale despite the open doors. Markus stands and straightens. It amazes her how quickly a man's demeanor can change, how a perceived slight can shift his body language, alter him physically.

"We're all very sorry about Sally and William," he says, monotone.

"I am too," Clare says.

"But like I said, there's reason to hope, isn't there?"

"I think so," Clare says.

"Helen told me you're going in for questioning tomorrow," Markus says. "Or today, I should say."

"I am," Clare says. "Any tips on what I should expect?"

"Don't let the detective run you in circles. Rourke. Detective Rourke, I mean. He's not one to follow procedure. He likes to throw his weight around."

"I think interviewing a friend of Sally's is pretty standard procedure, isn't it?"

"Of course. We just want him to respect the process. Follow the obvious leads."

"What obvious leads?"

"Sally was unwell," he says. "There's a whole side to this story that doesn't seem to interest him."

"Unwell how?"

"How well do you think you knew her?" Markus asks.

"She was my friend," Clare says, her voice low, her pulse picking up pace. The light in here feels too bright.

"Are you settling in okay otherwise?" Markus asks, the change of topic so abrupt that Clare shakes her head.

"Yes," Clare says. "Fine. Thank you."

The wayward questions and answers are muddling her. Why did she come here? Why did she take those pills, her wits fogged as they wear off? Clare's instincts draw her to the gun rack. Markus follows her gaze.

"Rebecca won't let me keep them in the house. The guns, I mean. She hates them."

"Where does she think you keep them?" Clare asks. "If she doesn't know about this place?"

Markus ignores the question. "Helen and I are the last of

the country people. Our parents were country people. They never would have dreamed of the city closing in the way it is now. Ginny and Jordan, they're city types. Even Rebecca. They don't understand how country people live. Guns are only evil if you have no practical use for them."

"My father felt the same way," Clare says.

"Did he? These belonged to my father. Not much else around here did."

Did you use your father's own gun to kill him? Clare thinks to ask. Instead she takes his cue and ascends the stairs to the wet ground of the surrounding woods. When he flicks off the light the blackness is so deep that Clare cannot see her hand when she raises it to her face. Is it not morning yet? When will the day break? Markus switches on a flashlight and hands it to her along with the can of formula. She watches as he closes the trapdoors, pulling thick carpets covered with dirt and leaves on top as camouflage.

"See?" he says, standing and wiping the earth from his jeans. "Gone. Like it was never there. A secret isn't a secret unless it's well kept."

Markus tucks the bottle of formula under his arm and takes her by the elbow, his palm clammy against her skin.

"I need to get home," Markus says. "I'm pressing my luck at this point."

"Of course. Your daughter is waiting."

"She is." Markus looks to the sky. "An hour to sunrise? Maybe we'll sleep yet."

A wave of deep exhaustion hits Clare as they pick their way through the trees. How quickly the effects of the pill have come and gone, Clare thinks. They cut through the trees in silence, then Markus stretches the beam of the flashlight to allow Clare a path back to Helen's house. She turns to wave in thanks before sliding into the darkness, grateful to be away from him at last.

T he police station is a squat
old building, the gargoyles
of its stone facade a mis-
match to the glass condo towers that surround it. The drive
in from High River had been full of stilted silences, Jordan
offering one-word answers to Clare's questions, Ginny on her
phone in the backseat. And Clare had been too foggy coming
down from the pills she'd taken, too anxious to prod beyond
setting an agreed meeting time at Jordan's office. Now it's been
ten minutes since Jordan dropped her at the police station
and she stands frozen on the sidewalk in front of its heavy
doors, her backpack between her feet, her pulse in her ears.
How long did she sleep after leaving Markus and the bunker
and returning to her bed? Two hours?

Just play the part, Clare thinks, her fists in tight balls, eyes
blinking back tears. They have no way of knowing who you
really are.

"You okay?"

A hand rests on Clare's shoulder. She jolts and turns to see Somers holding a tray with three coffees.

"Yes," Clare says, the break in her voice betraying her. "I'm early, aren't I?" She pauses. "Sorry. I'm nervous."

"Listen," Somers says. "We all want the same thing, right? To figure out where your friend's gone?"

"Yes."

Somers raises the tray. "I got you a coffee. The best in town. We'll just sit and have a chat. See what we can find out together."

Clare nods. Somers yanks open the doors and waves Clare in. Inside, a uniformed officer sits at a large wooden desk, his chair reclined at a steep angle, grinning at the screen of his cell phone. Only when Somers clears her throat does he bolt to attention, setting the phone down and sliding it away from him.

"Quiet morning?" Somers asks.

"Yes," he says, eyes to the desk. "So far. So far."

Above him is an analog clock: 8:55 a.m. This young officer can't be twenty-three, the skin on his cheeks pink and free of stubble, the shift in his demeanor telling Clare that Somers is not a detective to be trifled with.

"This is Clare O'Brien," Somers says. "Can you log her in and call Rourke to say she's here?"

The young officer lifts the receiver of the phone on his desk. He makes a show out of punching at the keys, all business on Somers's behalf.

"I'll see you inside," Somers says to Clare. "Just need to grab a few things. Rourke will get you settled."

And then Somers turns a corner before Clare can protest. She remembers this from the cop shows she used to watch with her mother, the divide and conquer, two detectives playing characters for their witnesses, tag-teaming, a way to poke holes in their story. Clare breathes against the tightness returning to her chest.

"Yeah." The young officer speaks into the receiver. "There's a woman here to see you. Somers just brought her in. Clare Brien? No. O'Brien? Okay. Yep." He hangs up and gestures to a stone bench along the far wall. "Wait there. He's coming for you."

He's coming for you. In five years of marriage, Clare only ever visited a police station once. Not to report her husband, but to spring him after a drunken brawl outside his favorite bar. The officer who'd helped her with the bail forms was the same one who'd arrived at her home months earlier when she'd called 911 on Jason. If that officer remembered Clare, if he had any notion that he and his partner had not arrested Jason but instead convinced her not to press charges, to let him sleep it off in his own bed instead, he pretended otherwise as they sat at his desk and settled the conditions of Jason's bail.

Now the bench is cold against Clare's legs. When Rourke appears, Clare stands and hikes her backpack onto her good shoulder.

"Very punctual," he says.

"I try to be."

"Come in." Rourke props the door open with his foot. "Somers is just grabbing some paperwork. She'll join us in a minute."

In the station proper a few officers sit at desks laid out haphazardly around the room, some plain-clothed and others in uniform. The air-conditioning blasts so forcefully from the vents that it lifts the ends of Clare's hair, goose bumps coating her arms. Rourke places his hand on her high back and weaves her through the desks and down a hall to an interrogation room.

"We're not trying to be intimidating," he says, showing her to her seat. "It's quieter in here. We can talk in private."

We'll just sit and have a chat, Somers had said outside. *The good cop.*

"Do you want to wait for Somers?" Rourke says.

"Do you?"

Detective Rourke frowns and looks around at the bare room. "I'll go see what's up. Give me a minute."

When he leaves, Clare adjusts herself in the hard-back chair and tucks her backpack under it. It feels like a movie set, the spare gray of this room, this metal table and two facing chairs, a third chair ghostly in the corner, the rectangular window on one wall, its mirrored glass. Is someone on the other side, peering through? Clare glares into it to meet the invisible gaze.

Rourke returns and sets the coffee tray Somers had been carrying on the table, removing two of the cups and setting one in front of Clare. She lifts it and inhales its scent. Rourke searches his pockets for a pen. Once ready, he takes a sip of his coffee and looks up.

"Can I have your full name?"

"Clare Anne O'Brien."

First and middle name the same. Last name picked by Malcolm, this time a more common O name. *O'Brien*, he'd said.

"And you know Sally Proulx."

Clare recites the details for him, the times and places turned over and over so that they'd feel rote under this line of questioning. Rourke writes in point form, dabbing a hard period at the end of every line, underlining with silly flourishes. The fabric of his sports coat is pilled at the elbows and collar. He is handsome, Clare thinks, olive-skinned and sandy-haired, an athlete's build.

"You're close friends with her?"

"I was. For a brief time."

"Let's not use past tense," he says, scrutinizing her. "Until we know—"

"No," Clare interrupts. "I meant I *was* friends with her. And then I wasn't. We knew each other distantly growing up. We connected again later."

"Right." Rourke rubs at his chin, tapping his pen to the page. In how many of those cop shows did this very scene play out? The detective shifting in his seat, a coy exchange across the table.

"And what are you doing here now?" Rourke asks.

"You asked me to come."

"No," he says. "Not here. I mean, why did you come to High River?"

"Sally reached out. By e-mail. As I mentioned yesterday."

"When?"

"A while ago. A month? I'm not sure exactly."

"Do you have a copy of the e-mail?"

Clare makes a point of sitting up straight in the chair. She knows her lines. She will not get flustered.

"No," she says. "I told Somers yesterday. I deleted it. Sally asked me to."

"Why? Did she say she was in trouble?"

"Sally was always in trouble," Clare says. "She told me where she was." Clare thinks of her conversation with Raylene. *He'd been getting sick a lot.* "She told me William had been having some health issues. She said she was sorry for how we left things. That she wished her life had taken different turns. That she hoped we'd see each other again someday."

"Did you reply?"

"No."

"Why not?"

Clare shrugs. She thinks of the skills gleaned on her first case in Blackmore. The tricks. Keep your false identity closely aligned with your true one. Never evade questions. Stay vague. What if it was Grace sitting here, answering questions about Clare? After Clare left she had written endless notes to Grace, narrating the whole story of her departure on motel pads, sometimes repentant and other times full of accusations, adaptations she'd scribble out, then rip up and flush down the toilet. It wasn't that she didn't want Grace to know, it's that a part of her felt certain Grace didn't care, that her oldest and only friend was glad she was gone.

"Friendship is complicated," Clare says. "If I'd known this was going to happen, I would have answered her."

"How old are you?" he asks.

"Twenty-seven," Clare says. She offers him the date of birth on her fake ID, three years younger than her actual age of thirty to line her age up with Sally's. Clare wonders whether the fine lines around her eyes make that gap implausible to Rourke. No. Men don't think of women in terms of age, her mother used to say, only in terms of era. Girl, woman, old lady.

There is a depth to Rourke's frown that disconcerts Clare. He is no longer writing down her responses. When the door swings open, Clare jumps. Detective Somers enters and grabs the extra chair from the corner. She sits not across from Clare but sidelong to her, the three of them in a triangle.

"Were you on the other side of the glass?" Clare asks.

Somers laughs. "You watch too many cop shows. We use that room for storage."

"We're just covering basics," Rourke says. "Clare already told us that she heard from Sally by e-mail about a month ago. Telling her where she was."

"Reaching out to an old friend." Somers nods. "You mentioned that yesterday."

"Why are you two on this case? It can't be within the city's jurisdiction."

"They called us in for help," Rourke says. "Don't exactly have trained homicide detectives out there in the sticks."

"Not that this is a homicide," Somers says, eyeing Rourke.

"Right," Rourke says. "You said Sally was always in trouble. What do you mean by that?"

"She courted it," Clare says, thinking of the profile article from Malcolm's file. "That's what I knew about her. That was her reputation, I guess. She loved excitement, drama. She was always looking for action. For exciting things. We had a lot of mutual friends. They'd tell me stories about her climbing the highest in the trees or playing chicken with the cars on the road. As you get older, those stakes get higher, you know? She was the first to start smoking. The first to steal liquor from her parents and bring it to someone's party. She married right out of high school just to be the first to do that too. And she married the best-looking guy in town, the most exciting. But he was also the most reckless. And the meanest."

Clare watches as Somers slides the pad away from Rourke and resumes the note-taking with her own pen. Her handwriting is smaller, neater.

"Why did you and Sally lose touch?" Somers asks. "Or stop speaking, as the case may be."

"We weren't really friends back home." The tears that spring to Clare's eyes feel too real. "We ran in different circles."

"We're talking about a small town," Somers says. "It would have been tough to avoid each other."

"When you know every corner of a place, it's easy enough."

"Tell me about her husband. Gabriel Proulx."

There was a family photograph in Clare's case file that struck her, Sally's husband leaning into a tree, newborn William weightless in the crook of his arm, Sally next to him at a strange distance, a portrait of marital strife. Though Gabriel Proulx looked nothing like Jason, Clare had seen a resemblance between them anyway. Something in the callous eyes, the smirk. The file had also held a single police report from years ago, a domestic incident where the neighbors called the police. *No charge filed*, it read at the bottom.

"I didn't know him," Clare says.

"You didn't like him, you mean?" Somers says.

"No. I didn't know him. I'd heard stories."

"Did you ever see any evidence of—"

"Bruises? Abuse? Not directly."

Clare thinks of Grace stopping in the cafeteria line at the hospital where they both worked, yanking up the sleeve of Clare's uniform to reveal a cluster of purple thumbprints on her forearm. I banged it on the door, Clare said without making eye contact. And though Grace clearly didn't believe her, though she shook her head in sad disapproval, it seems to Clare now that her friend could have pushed harder, could have done more.

"I think she hid it well from the people around her," Clare continues. "She clearly made a point of hiding it."

The detectives nod in unison. Clare knows she must retain these answers, commit this persona and these new details to memory.

"Was Sally a drug user?" Rourke asks.

"What does that matter?" Clare says, too loudly.

"It doesn't," Somers says. "We're just trying to build a full picture."

"I don't know. Maybe. She functioned well enough. She would have stopped when she got pregnant."

It feels easy to superimpose, to make sense of this story by imagining it to be her own. Clare was never good at playacting. In childhood Grace would compel her to pretend they were sisters despite the divergence in all their features, lying even to the teachers at school. How confident Grace could be in the lie.

"I never really realized things were so bad for her," Clare says, thinking of the interviews with Sally's former teachers in the articles about her disappearance. "She was smart. Things came easily to her."

"Easily. Huh," Somers says. "Do you have a family?"

"I did," Clare says. "I do, I mean. My mother died of cancer a few years ago. I have a father and a brother."

"No husband, no kids?" Somers asks.

"Do *you* have a husband and kids?" Clare asks, her cheeks hot.

"I do," Somers says. "One husband. Three kids."

"I tried it once." Rourke smiles. "Didn't last long. No kids, thankfully. Cops and marriage don't mix very well. At least that's what the statistics say. Somers here is the exception."

"Anyway," Somers says. "As far as we know Sally bounced in and out of foster care and was cut loose on her eighteenth birthday. One sister she doesn't speak to anymore."

The most striking feature of Sally's life, revealed by all the articles and news pieces and bits from social media, was how everyone she knew saw her in their own way. Clare remembers sifting through the file in the motel room after taking the case, trying to paint a picture of this missing woman. But everyone interviewed gave a unique account of Sally Proulx. To the teachers, she was the gifted straight-A student, to her friends, the careless risk-taker. A foster child who'd grown up with no stability, and then a doting wife and mother to William until her marriage became untenable. It struck Clare in poring over the articles that Sally was a chameleon of sorts, each person in her life describing her differently.

"Hard to imagine she had it easier than anyone," Somers continues.

"That's not what I meant," Clare says.

The detectives say nothing, allowing space for Clare to continue. But she only sighs.

"She left her husband in late winter," Rourke says. "Have you seen her since then?"

"No," Clare says.

With the way Rourke watches her, Clare can't bring herself to give them the same story she'd given Helen, to tell them that she'd reconnected with Sally at a shelter. Clare knows too well the line of questioning that might incite.

"Did she have any other troubles you can think of?" Somers asks. "Enemies? Debts? Family troubles?"

"Probably. She was very good at keeping secrets." Clare frowns for effect. "Listen. Sally went into a river. You know that much, don't you? There was an eyewitness, wasn't there?"

"Eyewitnesses are unreliable," Somers says. "Especially in the dark."

"Still," Clare says. "Shouldn't the focus be on finding the bodies? Maybe it was just an accident. William was a sleepwalker. Maybe he went into the river and she jumped in after him."

Rourke chews the end of his pencil. "Maybe."

"We're looking for the bodies, believe me," Somers says. "And it's pretty damn weird that we haven't found them. Makes you wonder if—"

The sharp ring of a cell phone cuts through the room. Rourke reaches into his pocket and swipes the screen with his thumb. After a few curt words, he stands and collects the writing pad from the desk.

"I'll finish up here," Somers says before Rourke can speak. He nods grimly at Clare before leaving.

"I don't think he trusts me," Clare says once the door closes behind him. "The way he's watching me is making me nervous."

"He's new to the precinct," Somers says. "He's got something to prove. You know. Alpha males."

Clare smiles. "I do."

"Pretty sure he's never had a female partner before either. Not sure he can handle it."

They laugh. Clare feels a kinship forming with Somers, the calm lilt in her voice reassuring. They both want the same thing. They are both looking for answers.

"What can I do to help you?" Clare asks. "That's honestly what I want to do. Help."

Somers leans back in her chair and crosses her hands over her stomach, watching Clare.

"We've been trying to get a search warrant for High River since the morning Sally disappeared," she says. "For the house. The houses, actually. Both of them. Helen's and the one across the river. Her brother's."

"They won't let you in without a warrant?"

"No," Somers says, her face set tight. "They won't. And the rule of law is pretty strict. For good reason. You can't just ransack someone's home without excellent cause. Most judges won't touch it with a ten-foot pole. A woman's gone, her kid too, but there's no evidence to show it's suspicious. But I think I've found a sympathetic judge. She's got a thing for missing kids and maybe a thing or two against certain citizens of High River."

It makes sense to Clare that Helen Haines hasn't thrown

the doors wide open. Who knows what secrets she keeps in that old house, or on behalf of the women she's taken in. Clare knows she could tell Somers about Markus's hole in the ground, the bunker, about Markus skulking there at night on his bizarre mission. In the dark hours of this morning it had seemed plausible that Markus was just using it to hide his formula, a getaway amidst the chaos of High River. But now Clare's head hurts and she wonders if she'd just been pliable, if the pills had made her prone to belief. Clare knows she could buy herself some goodwill by telling Somers all she knows, giving her the best coordinates she can remember. She opens her mouth to speak, then bites her lip. No. Markus would know it was she who gave it up. She will keep it to herself for now.

Somers reaches into her back pocket and fishes out a card to match the one Rourke gave Clare yesterday. The embossed letters bumpy under her thumb.

Hollis Somers. Senior Detective.

"No one at High River is too keen to talk to us. We could use someone with her ear to the ground. Listening."

Clare gestures to the lanyard around Somers's neck. "It's the badge," she says.

"What about it?"

"These women have no good reason to trust it. That's why they won't talk to you."

Somers sighs. "I guess you're right."

"I'll do what I can," Clare says.

"I'd appreciate that," Somers says. "We just want to find them, your friend and her son. You don't know what the clues are until you solve the puzzle, you know? Is there a number where I can reach you?"

Despite herself, despite her pact to use her phone only with Malcolm, Clare gives her the number. Somers jots it down, then stands and walks her chair back to the corner where she found it. Clare is aware of her gun, the scratched leather of its holster, the tools Somers would have at her disposal to dig into Clare's true past should her cover be called into question. When Somers opens the door Clare stands too, smoothing her jeans with her hands before bending to grab her backpack.

"Do you need a ride somewhere?" Somers asks her in the hallway.

"I'm headed to Sentinel Park. Meeting a friend. I think I'll walk."

"That's about ten blocks due north up Young Avenue. Twenty minutes if you're a slow walker like me."

"Thank you," Clare says. "Good luck getting that warrant."

This time as Clare passes through the maze of precinct desks all heads pop up, the room quieting. Clare spots Rourke across the room leaning over to read from a colleague's laptop. He smiles at Clare. His eyes remain upon her until she is through the foyer and out the front door.

Outside the police station the pedestrian current absorbs Clare and carries her northbound. Men in suits, women in sunglasses, tourist families in tight packs. Already Clare's lungs burn from the smog. Her shirt clings wet under her backpack.

After she left home, Clare saw him everywhere. Jason. He was every man peering out to the road from a chair on the porch, every man crouched over a laptop in the corner of a coffee shop. He was every man on the street corner waiting for the light to change. As she walks up Young Avenue to Sentinel Park, Clare's eyes flit from face to face, searching for his features, the lumber of his gait. In a crowd like this he could be upon her before she noticed it was him.

The blocks are short and Clare reaches the south end of the park in only minutes. Though it is a weekday, the paths are crowded, the grass patched with blankets and bodies angled to the sun. Clare follows the signs to the pond, then comes over a rise that overlooks it. She scans its perimeter until she spots Malcolm on a shaded bench, eyes to the phone in his lap. From a distance he looks almost fragile, lost. She circles along the path behind the trees and stops just out of view.

Barely six weeks ago she'd known nothing of Malcolm Boon. This crisp, detached stranger and the unexpected offer he made. *Come work for me. Help me find a missing woman.* Now she studies the rise and fall of his shoulders as he sighs and thinks how inscrutable he remains, in part because this Malcolm before her now seems nothing like the one she first met. This Malcolm is fraying at the seams. Clare crosses the last stretch of lawn to the bench.

"Hey," she says.

He looks up and offers a wary smile. She is still unaccustomed to his smile.

"I have an hour," Clare says, leaving a small void between them on the bench when she sits. "I have to meet my ride."

"You were able to get away."

"I had an interview at the police station this morning. One of the Haines brothers gave me a ride in. The lawyer."

"Jordan," Malcolm says. "How did the interview go?"

"I handled it."

A duck lands in the center of the pond, its wing tips rippling the water. They both watch it, unwilling to face each other.

"Why would someone hire us for this job when the police are working the case?"

"Because a lot of people don't trust the police," Malcolm says.

"And you're not going to tell me who it is?"

"I actually don't know," Malcolm says. "Sometimes the call is anonymous. They wire money, hide their identity. I have no name."

"That doesn't worry you?"

"No," Malcolm says. "It doesn't. It makes sense to me. The anonymity. The police mistrust. These things make sense to me."

Clare clears her throat.

"You seem calm," Malcolm says.

"I'm detached. I learned my lesson last time."

"They believe you're Sally's friend?"

"For now they do. I'm playing the part."

"You were supposed to touch base with me yesterday morning."

"It's not easy to just pull out my phone, Malcolm. What am I supposed to say? 'Excuse me while I text the man I'm working for'?"

His laugh is small, as though he tried to catch it before it escaped him. He pinches a clover leaf and rolls it between his thumb and forefinger. What's changed in Malcolm? Clare can't exactly pinpoint it. He looks too casual, almost disheveled. Unshaven, his hair long enough to curl behind his ears. The circles under his eyes are a shade darker. He blinks more. It could be that these changes have been too gradual for Clare to notice. It could be that she doesn't remember, that the past few weeks are less clear than she realizes. The fog of the pain and the pills.

"What do you need?" Malcolm asks.

Clare reaches into her pocket and passes Malcolm a scribbled list. "There's a developer trying to buy up High River to build a new expressway."

"Yes. That's all in the file."

"There were some basic details in the file, but I need more. Anything you can find. Any companies linked to the applications. Names. People who work in the township who might have a vested interest in seeing Helen Haines ousted."

"Okay," Malcolm says, again the hint of a smile. "You think that's related to Sally?"

"Everything is related to Sally." Clare taps at the list Malcolm holds. "There's a woman there named Raylene. She arrived at High River a few months ago. I don't have her last name. She says she used to work in a downtown ER as a doctor. I don't have any specifics on the city. She says her husband drowned their kids in a bathtub but got off after several trials. She's friends with Sally, they seemed close. I don't know if any of this is connected, but . . . Raylene is not a common first name, so—"

"If she knew Sally well, it's worth a look."

"There's a bunker," Clare says. "Markus Haines, the middle brother. He has a hole in the ground about a quarter mile from the house."

"That's odd."

"It *is* odd." Clare will not give Malcolm the details she knows will exasperate him, that she'd found it late last night after taking a few pills, that she'd accepted Markus's invitation to descend its rickety stairs. "One more thing," Clare continues. "The Twinings. The couple Helen and her brothers moved in with after their parents died."

A man and woman stroll by arm in arm. The woman wears a summer dress and throws her head back in laughter at something the man is whispering to her. They take no notice of Malcolm and Clare. When the man leans to kiss the woman, Clare feels herself shift farther away from Malcolm on the bench.

"We left Blackmore nineteen days ago," she says.

"We did."

"My memory's a little spotty. Until a few days ago, it's spotty."

"You weren't yourself," Malcolm says.

"Myself? I'm not sure you know—"

"You'd been shot and you were on heavy medication," Malcolm says. "You slept a lot. I weaned back the pills and I imagine that's when things got clearer. There isn't much to remember."

Clare feels her teeth clench in anger. "What were you doing the entire time we were at that motel?"

"Tending to you."

Tending to you. Clare remembers driving straight to that motel after the last case ended, Malcolm securing supplies to clean her gunshot wound before springing her from the Blackmore hospital to avoid any scrutiny as the media circled, as the police arrived to take credit for the work Clare had done. She remembers her motel room, the beach down the path from the parking lot, the small grocery store up the road that Clare would walk to once her strength began to return. She remembers hour after hour of television, Malcolm changing her bandages, supplying her pills right on schedule. But what bothers her, Clare realizes now, are the long stretches when Malcolm was gone. When she was alone. What bothers her are the muffled phone calls she could hear through the wall that separated their rooms, the urgency in his voice. What bothers her is the notion that Malcolm is using the gaps in her memory to omit, to keep his own secrets secure. Secrets about his past, about his own wife gone missing, secrets he's so far refused to share with Clare.

"You must have been doing other things too," Clare says.

"I was lying low. Tying up loose ends. Waiting for the right case to come up."

"Right," Clare says. "Sure."

"How is the shoulder, anyway?" Malcolm asks.

"It hurts. I have one pill left."

"You shouldn't need them anymore. The pain should be receding by now. Maybe it's infected."

"It's not infected. It just hurts. The pills help."

"You were out of sorts for a while there, Clare. It's better if—"

"Do I seem out of sorts to you now?"

"No. But we agreed, Clare. You promised."

Agreed on what? Clare wants to shout. She presses her clamped fists between her knees. Promised *what*?

The couple now sits on a bench adjacent to them, the woman's head bent to rest on the man's shoulder. For years Clare has taken note of this sort of happy coupledom in her midst with both awe and resentment. The way her brother, Christopher, poured his wife's morning coffee as soon as he heard her descending the stairs. The gentle ribbing between Grace and her husband at the dinner table or in the car, even the barbs a form of endearment. That easy devotion was entirely foreign to Clare. Malcolm folds Clare's note and tucks it into his back pocket.

"You really know what you're doing this time," he says. "You're on it."

"Please don't do that."

"Do what?"

"Condescend. 'Good job, kid.' You know I can get those pills anywhere, right? I don't need to get them from you."

"You would do that?"

Clare doesn't answer. On the far side of the pond, a father chases his squealing toddler as she veers close to the pond's edge. She sees Jason even in him, a doting father. Even in the men nothing like him.

"Have you heard from him?" Clare asks.

"From your husband?" Malcolm sighs. "No. He's dropped all contact. I told you that. After I e-mailed him to say I'd had no luck finding you, that I was returning his fee. That was it. I've heard nothing since Blackmore."

"I don't believe you."

"Why would I lie to you?"

Because you refuse to tell me the truth about your life, Clare thinks. But she says nothing.

"He's not here," Malcolm says.

"I keep thinking I see him. Everywhere. I see him everywhere."

"The mind can play tricks," Malcolm says.

"It's more than that. It's more . . . like a sense. I can sense him. Getting closer, or something. Approaching."

"Listen," Malcolm says. "There's no way for him to know where you are. You're a thousand miles from the last place he knew you to be."

"He hired you," Clare says, shrugging. "He could have hired someone else too."

"I doubt that."

How clearly Clare can picture Rourke across from her at that steel table, the badge on a lanyard around his neck. How far will he dig? A dog approaches the bench, sniffing at their feet. Malcolm reaches out with an open palm, allowing the dog to pick up his scent before the owner arrives to retrieve it. Can Malcolm see the tremor in her hands? Has it worsened since she sat down?

"Where are you staying?" Clare asks.

"Here," he says. "In the city. I've got some other things I'm looking into."

"Like what?"

"I can't discuss them."

"Anything to do with your wife?"

"Clare."

"What? Don't you think it's time you told me?"

"Told you what?"

"Let me think," Clare says, raspy. "Who you are. What you want. Why you're protecting me. You name it. I could go on."

"I've told you everything you need to know."

"So I'm working this case alone," Clare says.

"You were alone last time too, weren't you? We agreed you're better off that way."

The words sting Clare. The phone in Malcolm's pocket beeps. He takes it out and holds it on his lap until it beeps again. She watches Malcolm closely as he lifts the phone to read the message, resisting the urge to snatch the phone and read it herself. His eyes dart across the screen.

"Listen." Malcolm tucks his phone back into his pocket. "I have to go."

"I want more than half the money this time. You get a cut, but not half. You get twenty percent."

"That's fair," Malcolm says. He stands and steps to the edge of the pond, his back to her, his mind so clearly elsewhere. "Anything else?"

"One other thing," Clare says. "Don't call him my husband."

"Sorry?" Malcolm pulls out his phone again and clutches it in his hand.

"Don't refer to Jason O'Callaghan as my husband. That's what you called him. He's not my husband anymore. I'm not his wife."

It feels impossible to interpret the look Malcolm gives her, the steadiness of it. He mouths the word *okay*. To Clare's relief, a family cuts through the path between them, breaking the gaze. Malcolm's phone beeps again.

"I really have to go," he says. "I imagine you'll keep in touch."

Clare shrugs, her jaw tight. The couple watches Malcolm as he walks away, perhaps trying to appraise what his relationship to Clare might be. What is different about Malcolm's gait? Then it comes to her: he's not carrying his briefcase. By the time he reaches the far side of the pond, Clare can see his face in profile. He pulls his phone out again. That frown. Clare remembers it. She remembers the frown. The slam of a car door, lifting herself carefully from her motel bed. She remembers parting the curtains to see Malcolm standing shirtless next to his sedan, frowning down at his phone just as he does now, some kind of package tucked under his arm. The motel sign behind him flashed: VACANCY. It must have been dawn.

Now, when she closes her eyes she can see him as he was, standing there shirtless in gym shorts, his hair messy with sleep, his body lean. *I really have to go*, he had said, just as he did now. In watching him then through the curtains of her motel room, in watching him walk away now, she feels an intense stab. Not of longing, not of kinship or hope or fear. Not even of anger. It is something else almost indiscernible. Grief.

I *needed some air.*

This was the line Clare always offered Jason upon returning from a run, even on November nights frigid with rain, her cheeks stung crimson as she peeled off her layers in their front hall. Jason always asked where she'd gone but never questioned this response, never even looked up from the television, never noticed her run growing longer and deeper into the evening. But after the death of her unborn son in September, all Clare could do was run morning and night, figuring her resolve to escape would grow stronger as her body did. Now she sits across from Jordan Haines in his office, the large desk between them, offering him the same answer to the same question.

"I needed some air," Clare says.

"Pretty warm out for a walk," Jordan says. "Did you get far?"

"Sentinel Park," Clare says. "Lapped it, then headed back here. Too hot for me. Where's Ginny?"

"Her class just ended. She'll be here in a few minutes. We'll

94

hit the road before traffic snarls us up. How did it go with the detectives?"

"Straightforward," Clare says. "Obvious questions."

"I have a lot of questions for you too," Jordan says.

And I you, Clare thinks. "Maybe give me a breather," she says. "I might be questioned out for the morning."

Jordan angles his head to study Clare. He wears a full suit and tie, his dark hair clean cut with just enough curl left on top. The resemblance to Markus is striking, as if Jordan were a photograph of his older brother in better days, his suit tailored to his lean build, versus the washed-out T-shirt and stained jeans Markus wore at the bunker. Clare looks around to shake his stare. The wall of glass behind her faces a converted loft space, windows to the street stretching ceiling to floor. A fishbowl.

"Used to be a garment factory," Jordan says. "We converted it into an office a few years ago."

"It's a beautiful space. Quiet for a Monday."

"The August holiday," Jordan says. "Easier to just shut down and give everyone the same two weeks off."

"And you don't take a break?"

"There's no holiday from the work I do."

Something in his tone irks Clare, a smugness, his expression solemn in anticipating her next question.

"Helen told me that you do a lot of pro bono work with shelters," Clare says, taking the bait.

"I do." He points to a framed set of building plans hanging on the wall closest to his desk. MARGARET HAINES HOUSE, it reads across the bottom. "We acquired the empty lot next door to this building last year. We've been raising funds to build the city's biggest and newest shelter. I don't even think of it as a shelter. It's a place for next steps. A launching pad. To help women in a real way. Give them real options."

"Like what Helen does."

"Right," Jordan says, his smile tight. "Except Helen can only take in a few women at a time. This shelter would have dozens of rooms."

"Helen said yesterday that the land might be taken to build a highway to a new subdivision. What's the word for that again?"

"Expropriation," Jordan says. "I don't think it'll get that far. We've been negotiating with the right levels of government. With the developer. I think Helen will just sell it."

"You don't have a say in whether it gets sold?" Clare asks.

He leans into the desk, considering the question. "I was ready to let that place go a decade ago. My life is here now. Downtown. My focus is on the shelter we're trying to build here. I think Helen is ready to move on too. But Markus and Rebecca are rooted there. Markus has this grand notion of turning the fields organic. They have this whole vision. An urban farm. Closest one to the city. They're big into wellness stuff." He shakes his head. "Obviously an expressway isn't part of that vision. And Helen . . . She wants Markus to be happy too. I think it's hard for her to let go. I keep telling her she'll have a big role here. Any role she wants. Out there she just doesn't have the resources we'll have—"

"Who's *we*?" Clare asks.

"Philip Twining and me," Jordan says. "He's my partner. Not really a partner. I'm taking over the practice. He's on the exceptionally long road to retirement."

"Why do I know that name?" Clare asks, playing along.

"Maybe Helen's mentioned him. He and his wife, Janice, took us in after our parents died. I was a baby. They raised me, pretty much." Jordan pauses. "You're not from near here?"

"No."

"Right. Of course you aren't. Sally wasn't. I'm sorry."

"It's fine," Clare says.

"I just asked because Janice and Philip were both very big on the civil rights scene. Then women's rights. Philip has this knack for taking up the cause of the day and making his way to the front lines."

Clare must fix her expression to mask her annoyance, the tension she feels at his words. "The cause of the day?" she repeats.

"Not like that," Jordan says, catching her tone. "He genuinely cares. He and Janice both. They instilled that in me. The desire to help. The desire to be on the ground as change takes hold—"

"They clearly instilled it in Helen too."

Jordan's body language is quiet, the way he pinches the edge of the desk to adjust his posture or sets his hand to the back of his neck. He is used to eyes on him. Modesty does not come easily to him, Clare sees. It takes effort to keep his vanity in check.

"Listen," he says, face somber again. "I'm sorry about what I said last night."

"What did you say?"

"About the comings and goings. About Sally. Implying I barely knew her. I mean I didn't know her well. But I'm doing whatever I can to help with the search efforts. I know this must be hard for you."

"I haven't slept much since I got here," Clare says, the truth. "I was in the kitchen last night getting some water. Middle of the night. I saw you outside with Raylene. I guess you couldn't sleep either."

If there's a shift in his expression, Clare doesn't catch it.

"I stay over sometimes on Sundays," Jordan says. "To keep Helen company. And Raylene is a mess. I've been offering her some legal counsel. Sometimes I think she goes out to the river to cry just so that no one will hear her. I caught her out there last night."

"She looked upset," Clare says.

They watch each other in a showdown across the desk. Neither of them notice the older man outside the room until he swings open the glass door to Jordan's office. The man grabs a chair and pulls it to sit in close conference with Jordan and Clare.

"Phil, this is Clare O'Brien. She's a friend of Sally Proulx's. Arrived the other night. Hoping to help. Clare, this is Philip Twining. My partner."

Philip extends his hand. "Sorry to meet you under these circumstances."

"Thank you," Clare says.

Philip Twining is short, a round belly stretching his golf shirt, his gray hair combed over. He slumps in the chair and grips its armrests.

"You missed the meeting," Jordan says. "The JJ & Sons lawyers were all here and you weren't."

"I couldn't find a clean shirt," Philip says.

"Christ, Phil. You heard of a dry cleaner?"

"I'm a pathetic bachelor divorcé," Philip says to Clare. "I can barely keep myself fed, let alone dressed."

The smile Clare offers hardly masks her distaste at his comments, but Philip takes no notice.

"I read through the memo you e-mailed," he says to Jordan. "What did I tell you? You don't hire a bunch of highway pavers to put up a building, no matter what the deal might be."

"Let's talk about this later," Jordan says.

"These guys don't know what they're doing. Have you looked at the inspection report? The whole foundation might need to be redone."

Clare can't gauge the look Jordan gives Philip, whether it's impatience or even a twinge of disgust. Anger. They all turn at the bang announcing Ginny's arrival through the front door. She lifts her sunglasses and offers them a cute wave through the glass. Philip rises from his chair and meets her at Jordan's office door, lifting her off the ground in a grandfatherly hug.

"How's my girl?" he asks, setting her down. "You need some money?"

"Don't give her any money," Jordan says, rolling his eyes.

"Says you!" Ginny extends a flat palm to Philip.

Philip fishes his wallet from the back pocket of his shorts and hands Ginny a fifty-dollar bill. She snatches it with glee, planting a kiss on Philip's cheek and raising her eyebrows to Clare. At his desk, Jordan gathers his things, packing up the laptop and checking his pockets for keys.

"We should go," he says.

"We should let Philip take us to lunch," Ginny says.

"I'd love that," Philip says.

"Helen wants you home," Jordan says. "And I promised Clare a lift back. I don't want to sit in traffic."

"Blah," Ginny says, pouting.

They leave the office in formation and walk the length of the hallway towards the back of the building, passing an even larger office that must be Philip's. At the end of the hall Jordan presses open a fire door that leads to the parking lot. In the brief time Clare's been inside it has clouded over, the light dulled, the air heavy with coming rain. Beyond the lot is the construction site, men in hard hats gathered in a circle in the shade, one dousing himself from a water bottle. FUTURE HOME OF THE MARGARET HAINES HOUSE. JJ & SONS. The heat makes Clare unsteady, the events of the morning already too much to process. *You don't hire a bunch of highway pavers to put up a building,* Philip had said, and Clare cannot shake the look Jordan gave him when he did.

"I'll be back in a few hours," Jordan says to Philip. "Will you be here?"

"Yep," Philip says.

He opens the back door for Ginny, then the passenger door for Clare. She arches as his hand slides up her back to guide her in. They don't mean anything by it, her mother used to say about the men who'd squeeze the younger Clare's shoulders or reach out to tug the curls of her hair. The older men especially. They just feel it's their right, Clare's mother used to say. Philip might intend his touch to be gentlemanly, old-fashioned. But Clare never believed that they don't mean anything by it. She's grown to sense a man's intention through his touch. His audacity. Something is always meant by it. It said something about Jordan that he struggled not to boast at his own goodwill. And it says something about Philip Twining, Clare thinks as she watches him round the car to the propped door of the office, that he'd place his hand so intimately on a woman he just met.

In the backseat Ginny's thumbs dance madly on the screen of her phone. The road narrows from eight lanes to six, tall buildings giving way to warehouses and subdivisions, roadside fast food. Clare watches the changing landscape with her mind on all that transpired this morning, the interview with Rourke and Somers and the scrutiny she felt under Rourke's regard. And after that, Malcolm's voice in her head. *We agreed. You promised.* His appearance, the anxious air that surrounded him. Then the hour in the glass case of Jordan's office, her skin bumpy with the cold of its air-conditioning, the exchanges between Philip and Jordan too cryptic to decipher.

"So what'd the cops ask you?" Ginny asks.

"Routine stuff. About Sally."

"Did they ask about me?"

Clare shifts to face Ginny in the backseat. "No."

"What questions would they have about you?" Jordan asks.

"Who knows?"

Ginny's cheeks have reddened. She lifts her palm to one as if expecting to find it hot.

"How long did they interrogate you for?" Jordan asks.

"An hour, maybe," Clare says.

"Then you went to the park," Jordan says.

This had been her story, but now Clare registers that Jordan might have means of knowing her true mission. Might have had her followed. There were so many people at the park that someone watching would have easily blended in. Or, Clare thinks, Jordan might know of Malcolm because he might be the one who hired him to take on Sally's case. She has to measure every word.

"Like I told you," Clare says. "It was too hot at the park. I didn't stay long."

"It's disgustingly hot," Ginny says. "Did you walk up Young Avenue to get there?"

"I did," Clare says.

"Did you shop? I really need a new jean skirt."

Something in the banality of the question makes Clare queasy. To imagine a life so unencumbered as to be about trying on skirts in stores when a woman has just disappeared. But with Ginny the nonchalance seems forced. She is working hard to detach herself from the terrible things unfolding around her.

"No," Clare says. "I didn't have time to shop. I was trying to get my bearings. I'm not used to cities, really."

"That's pretty obvious." Ginny unlocks her seat belt and pulls herself forward, one elbow on each of the front seats.

"Do up your seat belt," Jordan says.

"I feel left out back here," Ginny says. "Just don't crash, okay?"

It is striking how flawless Ginny is up close, how young, her hair swept aside on her forehead in a perfect pixie. She studies Clare too from only inches away.

"You're kind of . . . boyish," Ginny says.

"My mom used to say the same thing."

"Nice hair, though. Eyes too. You're actually really pretty."

Clare flushes. She can sense Jordan glance her way.

"Stay away from Markus," Ginny says.

Too late, Clare thinks, the details of their encounter at the bunker blurry in the haze of the pills wearing off. But she clearly remembers his agitation, the way Markus fidgeted, the stains on his clothes. The look of a man coming undone.

"Why stay away from Markus?" Clare asks.

"Rebecca has serious jealousy issues. She thinks every woman who shows up at High River is after her man."

"I'm not sure that's true," Jordan says.

"Oh, it's true," Ginny says. "She's like a crocodile. Eyes above water, quietly watching. Ready to pounce. Even me, and Markus is my uncle. Don't mess with her perfect little life." Ginny claps her hands flat to mimic the snapping mouth. "Or she'll snatch you by the legs and break your neck."

"Ginny!" Jordan scolds.

"They met on some new age dating site," Ginny says. "Got married after about a week."

"It was two months," Jordan says.

"Yeah, well. Not quite enough time for Rebecca to pick up on what a doozy she was landing."

"I assure you," Clare says. "I'm not interested in anyone else's husband."

"It doesn't matter. You're prettier than Rebecca and that'll make her insane. Trust me." Ginny puckers her lips in a whistle. "What about Rourke? You interested in him?"

"What? No. Why would you ask that?"

"He's hot, isn't he?"

"I wasn't paying attention to how he looks," Clare says.

"Come on. He makes you pay attention to how he looks. And you're pretty. As if he didn't notice that."

Clare shakes her head, bewildered. Ginny's boldness astounds her.

"Don't tell me you never cared about that stuff," Ginny continues. "Pretty women always know they're pretty."

Of course. In high school it followed Clare like a scent, and she feigned indifference in part because it seemed to heighten it. Any time Grace would mention a boy's name Clare would feel herself circling, however subtly, laughing a little harder at his jokes as Grace hovered shyly nearby. Be careful, Clare's mother would say as she combed out her hair. Those looks of yours will bring you trouble. You don't realize it. They're a weapon you're not trained to use. Now Clare thinks of the long hold in Rourke's glances. Could it be only that? That he finds her *pretty*?

"You must have been a hotshot in high school," Ginny says.

"I don't know," Clare says. "I was more into—"

"Please don't say sports," Ginny says.

"I was going to say guns."

Ginny squeals. "What? Tell me more!"

They turn off onto a four-lane road. For years, Clare's mother called her boyish because of how well she took to her father's shooting lessons, outdoing her older brother in no time at target practice, her father encouraging her despite her mother's protests. Clare's muscle memory can still call up the feeling of her father's shotgun in her hands, the barrel pressed into her shoulder, cheekbone resting close to where her finger grazed the trigger. She will paint this picture for Ginny and Jordan, their own histories marked by guns, a telling of Clare's truth that may incite them to share.

"I grew up on a farm," Clare says. "My dad taught me to shoot when I was young. I took to it. I'm good at it."

"A markswoman. That could have come in handy."

"What do you mean?"

"You were Sally's friend," Ginny says. "You knew what she was up against. Why didn't you just sniper off her husband for her?"

"Ginny!" Jordan cranes to her, the car reacting with a small swerve.

"It's okay," Clare says. "It's actually a very valid question."

"She could have claimed self-defense." Ginny swats Jordan on the shoulder. "You need to watch the road!"

"Maybe," Clare says. "But there's more to it than that."

"Listen," Ginny says. "A lot of the women who show up at Helen's house seem perfectly normal. I know it's supposed to be about empathy. I took Psych as an elective and the prof was always waxing on about not judging people's lives, because you never know the whole story, examine your own position first, blah blah blah. And this is a terrible thing to say, but part of me just wanted to yell at them. The women. Why didn't you just leave? Or fight back? I'm practical that way, you know? That's why I'm studying engineering. Why I can't handle things like Psych. Because if it's not working, fix it."

Clare looks to the roof and blinks fast.

"You were her friend," Ginny continues, quieter. "Why didn't you help her?"

"I don't know. I didn't. I couldn't."

"You could have gone in and shot him when he was sleeping or something. The two of you could have hatched a plan. When he wouldn't see it coming. Like poetic justice. You could have helped her out. Helped her fight back. You don't even need to be a markswoman to shoot someone when they're sleeping. They would have made a movie about you."

"It'd be pretty hard to claim self-defense," Jordan says.

"I'm sure you'd figure out a way, Jords. That's your thing."

Tension hangs between them as they wait for Clare to speak. She takes a few controlled breaths.

"Can I give you some advice, Ginny?" Clare asks. "I get the impression that you care about seeming older than you are. Mature or worldly, or whatever. So what you just said? About fighting back? Don't say things like that. Because your Psych prof was right. Empathy isn't about feeling sorry for people. It's about recognizing that you don't always understand what people are going through. That sometimes you can't possibly know. And you, Ginny? You really, really don't get it. What you just said about killing Sally's husband? You sound naive at best. At worst, catastrophically stupid."

Ginny recoils to the far side of the backseat, burned. Her face sours when she notices Jordan nodding.

"You said yourself it was a valid question," Ginny says.

"You're young," Clare says. "You can't possibly understand."

"I hate it when people say that."

"But you *can't*," Clare says. "I remember exactly what it's like to be your age. You look at the adults around you and swear you'll never end up like them. I used to do that with my parents all the time. It never occurs to you that your own life might turn out worse than theirs did."

In Jordan's profile Clare is certain she catches a wince, a frown he quickly corrects, gripping the wheel tightly. The road narrows again to two lanes, bare fields marked by billboards heralding future development. Clare breathes deeply and turns to look out the window, squeezing her eyes shut. How different life had been the summer Clare was twenty-two, her mother in remission, her bags packed to leave for college. The early days of Jason. The drugs and the drinking still at the edge, encroaching too quickly. No wonder that era remains so clear to Clare. Everything that's unfolded since can be traced to a handful of choices she made that summer, at Ginny's very age. A life laid out by choices she was too young to make wisely. She opens her eyes. More billboards. PAVING THE WAY TO YOUR FAMILY'S DREAM COMMUNITY, one reads. JJ & SONS, the developer's name at the bottom, the same one Clare remembers from the sign for the Margaret Haines shelter. She peers over to Jordan but his eyes are locked to the road.

"It only turns out worse if you make the wrong choices," Ginny says, flopping into the backseat. "You don't have to be so dramatic."

"No one makes the wrong choices on purpose," Clare says.

"You don't think so? You should talk to Rebecca."

"Ginny," Jordan says. "Stop it. You have no idea what you're talking about."

"Don't I? Willow is always sick. Markus wants to take her to a real fucking doctor and Voodoo Rebecca, the nature freak, won't let him. Or maybe it's the other way around. Don't you think *that*'s a wrong choice?"

"It's just not true," Jordan says. "Any of it."

"How do you know? When's the last time you and Markus actually spoke?"

They pass the gas station where Malcolm dropped Clare off days ago. Ginny opens her backpack and pulls out a travel mirror, circling her lips with a shade of lipstick to match her nails. Clare shifts in the seat to watch her. The lipstick makes her eyes pop.

"You know what, Clare?" Ginny says. "All I meant to say is you'd be pretty if you put in a little effort."

"It doesn't matter," Clare says. "It's fine. I didn't mean to be so harsh with you. The stress is getting to me."

"Whatever," Ginny says. "Is Rourke going to be there when we get back?"

"You need to find friends your own age," Jordan says. "And no. He isn't going to be there."

"Friends." Ginny drawls the word. "Who said anything about friends?"

Jordan sighs, exasperated. They turn down the High River driveway. Jordan parks and gets out of the car, heading to the house, eyes on his phone. Clare goes to open the door, but Ginny has already bounded from the backseat. She blocks Clare's exit from the passenger side, lowering close to whisper.

"You might think I'm naive." She points to the bend in Clare's elbow. "But I'm not that naive."

"Excuse me?" Clare says.

"I know where those kinds of scars come from."

Clare crosses her arms, resting her palms on them to cover the tiny dots. "I quit a long time ago."

"Did you quit? Really? Because some of those holes look pretty fresh."

"That's from an IV. I was in the hospital recently." But as Clare runs her fingers over the scars, she can't be certain the freshest one is from the IV they'd given her in the Blackmore hospital before Malcolm sprung her. Could it be more recent?

"I know how hard it can be to kick it," Ginny says. "I have friends, you know. Who are into it. I'm not beyond the odd recreational dabble myself. So, if you needed a little something, I can get you anything you want."

"Like I said, I quit."

"You have the shakes. Your hands are trembling like an old lady's."

"My friend is gone," Clare says. "I just finished interviewing with the police. I'm tired. I'm worried. You're blocking my way. My nerves are a little worn."

"Well, either way. There's a guy in my program. We'll be in

108

the same dorm this semester. He's got a thing for me. I can get anything you could ever dream of."

"No," Clare says.

The car is sweltering but Ginny has not cleared the way to let Clare stand.

"I'm good at keeping secrets," Ginny says, finally backing up. "I swear. I'll keep it between us."

There is a squeeze in Clare's chest as she watches Ginny turn and bound to catch up with Jordan on the porch. *I can get you anything*. It always amazed Clare, the abundance of supply. In Blackmore it was too easy. It was always too easy. What good reason does she have to abstain, to endure the pain in her shoulder, the steady flow of all these revelations, too much coming at her at once? There must be a good reason. Clare slams the door behind her and looks to the house where Ginny and Jordan have gone inside. In the strong light of midafternoon she sees it, the layer of decay blanketing this place, the garden around the porch lifeless despite so much rain, the house large and eerie next to the rage of the river.

Clare and Raylene sit side by side on the porch swing, silent in the sticky heat. Clare found Raylene here after spending hours alone in their bedroom, fighting sleep, the events of the day so far swirling. Raylene bites her fingernails, the gnawing sound grating on Clare. As the sun sets the sky is awash with pink, the river silver against the earth it carves through. If not for its tragedies both recent and old, Clare thinks, High River would be a beautiful place.

A woman exits the house across the river.

"Who's that?" Clare asks.

"Rebecca. Markus's wife. Helen's sister-in-law."

Rebecca walks to the edge of the water and waves to them. Raylene drops her hands to her lap and exhales a long breath before waving back. Then Rebecca turns and heads towards the bridge, the same path Clare had watched Markus take with his flashlight before dawn.

"Oh God," Raylene says. "She's coming over here."

"You're not friendly with her?"

"She's . . . fine. She tries. But she's hard to like."

"Are they both home all day?" Clare asks.

"Not normally Rebecca. She's a teacher. She commutes to the city every day to teach high school Latin. Latin, for chrissake. She's just off for the summer."

"What does Markus do?"

"Good question. He's full of big ideas, I hear. Plans to make himself rich. His next big push is organics."

Clare thinks of the bunker, Markus standing at its center, hapless and nervous.

"They met online and married in short order," Clare says. "That's what Ginny told me."

"What I heard is that Markus took off for the coast in his twenties. Invested in some real estate with his share of the family money. Then the crash came and he lost everything. Showed up back here with nothing but the shirt on his back, begging his big sister to bail him out. She let him build that house on the property. Paid for it too, I'm sure. Now he stays home with his kid, making plans to rule the world while his breadwinning wife schleps ninety minutes each way to teach a dead language to teenagers."

"Who told you all this?"

"Ginny. Helen. Rebecca." She pauses. "And Sally. You hear lots of stories. You piece it together."

They sit in silence and watch the line of trees until Rebecca emerges from it. As she approaches Clare can see what Ginny meant about her plainness, Rebecca's hair a straggle down her back. In the photographs from the file Clare had been struck by Sally's beauty, her face luminous even when unsmiling. Rebecca reaches the porch and climbs the stairs halfway.

"I wanted to introduce myself," she says to Clare. "I'm Rebecca Haines. You must be Clare."

"I am."

"I'm so sorry about your friend," Rebecca says. "Sally, I mean, of course. And her beautiful son. He was a wonderful playmate for Willow. Will and Willow. Like they were meant to be."

Past tense. Some people here still speak of Sally and her son in present tense, Clare thinks. Like Helen. Somers. And then others speak as if they are gone.

"I'm sure Sally was grateful that William had a friend," Clare says.

"Would you two like to go for a swim at the eddy?" Rebecca says. "It'll cool us all off."

Clare and Raylene can't help but exchange a look, both confounded by the suggestion.

"I don't have a bathing suit," Clare says.

"You don't need one. You can just dip your feet in if you prefer. Or go in your undies."

"Undies," Raylene repeats.

The screen door swings open and Ginny skips out. "I'll go for a swim!" she says.

"Oh, great," Rebecca says, her smile false. "What about Helen?"

"She's already asleep."

"Okay, then. Shall we?"

It takes a few minutes for them to scramble for towels and reconvene on the porch, Clare following the rest of them dumbly, unable to find a reason to extract herself from this plan. They descend the porch and walk in single file along the bank of the river. Clare trails behind Raylene, trying not to trip over tree roots. If she musters enough focus, Clare thinks, this could be a chance to ask questions. Soon they reach the small eddy that juts off the river, round like a pool, its water dark and calm. Homemade, Helen told her yesterday, by her dead father. The group fans around it, four of them in a circle: Rebecca, Ginny, Raylene, Clare.

"It'll be cold," Rebecca says, lifting her dress over her head. Her bathing suit sags at the belly, the fabric worn to reveal the shadow of her breasts, her skin glowing pale in the dark. She sits on the edge and lowers her legs into the water, then retracts them at once. "Oh my Lord. Forget cold. It's frigid. Come on, girls."

Girls, Clare thinks. How it used to madden her when Jason used that term, referring to everyone—from the waitress pouring his coffee, to Clare's mother, even to Grace, an accomplished doctor with ten years more education than he had—as a girl.

Ginny takes off her T-shirt. She wears a bikini top underneath, thin and tall, a thorny tattoo across her lower back. Clare finds herself studying Ginny's arms for telltale signs, the tiny holes. She spots none. Ginny slaps her arms to her side, still wearing her shorts, and leaps into the water like a dropped pencil, gone.

"How deep is it again?" Raylene peers over the edge.

"Ten feet," Rebecca says. "Maybe twelve."

They watch the small funnel formed at the center of the pool, waiting.

"Where'd she go?" Raylene asks.

Ten seconds must pass before Ginny breaks the surface with a yelp. She hoists herself easily from the water and shakes her head, her short hair in spikes. They sit in a semicircle. Side by side the differences in their bodies are stark, Ginny stretched long and tall next to the rounder Rebecca, Raylene's skin an olive brown next to Clare's paleness.

Raylene nudges her. "You're staring again."

"How's Willow?" Ginny asks, gazing at her fingernails before raising her eyebrows to Clare. She is making a point.

"Better," Rebecca says. "She's had a good week."

"Has your daughter been sick?" Clare asks.

"She's very sensitive," Rebecca says. "She has a lot of environmental triggers."

"Maybe it's something in the water," Ginny says. "William was sick too."

If Ginny's tone is edgy, Rebecca pretends not to notice.

"You never know," Rebecca says. "This farmland. Pesticides. Children are very susceptible to these things. We've been thinking a lot about toxins. Markus and I."

"Toxins," Raylene says.

Clare thinks of Markus in the bunker, cradling the bottle of baby formula, an act of rogue parenting that should seem benign enough. *A secret isn't a secret unless it's well kept*, he'd said.

"What we put into our bodies," Rebecca says. "Into our children's bodies. I've been reading up."

"In Latin?" Ginny says.

With a jolt Rebecca snatches her dress and fumbles to pull it over her head. She stands to shake it down over her body. Despite the stoic expression Rebecca still wears, the wrath is palpable in the way her eyes dart between them. Clare feels Raylene edge closer.

"Sit down," Ginny says. "I'm only teasing you."

"You're joking about my sick child."

"I know." Ginny casts her eyes downward, contrite. "She's my cousin, Rebecca. I'm sorry. I shouldn't be so gross. Sally was always talking about that stuff too. She couldn't understand why Will was sick all the time."

Rebecca sighs and sits again at the greatest distance from Ginny she can manage. "I'm telling you. It's these toxins."

"Speaking of toxins." Ginny digs for a pack of cigarettes and a lighter. "Does anyone mind?"

"I don't want—" Rebecca begins.

"That was actually a rhetorical question," Ginny says. She takes a long drag from the first cigarette and passes it to Raylene before lighting another. Raylene inhales and coughs.

"I forgot how disgusting these things are," Raylene says, handing it to Clare.

The smoke in her lungs makes Clare feel light-headed. She imagines Jason at the kitchen table, the depths of his inhales, the stench that permeated everything in their home, from the dish towels to the wallpaper. How sometimes, after a few drinks or a pill on her tongue, she'd beg him to give her one too, the sting of the smoke as it traveled down her airway, the look of lust on his face as he watched her. Clare takes another long drag, then mashes the lit end into a rock.

"Let's hear all about you, Clare," Ginny says.

"Ask me anything," Clare says, readying.

"How'd you meet Sally?" Rebecca asks.

"We've known each other since we were younger. We went to school together. We weren't friends, but we knew each other. We reconnected later."

"She moved around a lot," Raylene says.

"I know she did," Clare says, thinking of the children's services documents from the file, Sally and her sister removed from home as children and separated. Sally bouncing through foster care until her mother sobered up enough to reclaim them, how they'd jumped from county to county as her mother looked for work, Sally in a new school every fall, reports from the teachers, her coaches. "I'm not sure she had many friends back then, but she was still good at a lot of things. A star on the swim team. Everyone knew who she was. We reconnected again . . . later. As adults."

"I thought Sally couldn't swim," Ginny says, dipping the butt of her cigarette into the water to extinguish it. "She would freak out any time William went near the river."

"She would have been afraid for his life," Clare says. "The water isn't exactly still."

"Are you a swimmer, Clare?" Rebecca says. "Think you'll take a dip?"

"It's too cold for me," Clare says, thinking of her shoulder, the scar still red and aching around the wound, the marks on her arms Ginny noticed earlier, a living history dabbled across her skin, the chance to share some truth. "I have a shoulder injury. It's not quite healed."

"What kind of injury?" Ginny asks, her voice a singsong.

"A gunshot wound," Clare says.

At this revelation Rebecca's and Raylene's brows shoot up in quiet surprise. Ginny slaps her hand to her face with a gasp.

"You have to show us," Ginny says.

"You have to tell us," Raylene says.

"I was in some trouble before I came here. I got tangled up with the wrong people. And I got shot." Clare takes a deep breath. She will adjust the truth just enough. "It was an accident. I wasn't the intended target."

"Who was the target?" Rebecca asks.

"Like I said, I got tangled up. And I ended up in the wrong place at the wrong time. But I got out."

"And made your way here," Rebecca says.

"Please can we see it?" Ginny asks.

"It must be some scar," Raylene says.

Some scar. Clare remembers sitting in a chair facing the setting sun, a blanket draped over her legs, a constant wave of sleep, her eyes open then closed. Clare had never thought of wind as exhausting, but here it was, the ocean breeze a sedative whipping her hair, the drone of the water curling to and from her feet. Painless warmth. She remembers lifting her hand to her shoulder, her palm covering the wound, this gesture a tic newly formed. His voice. Where was he? Malcolm. Was he standing in the ocean? Can she see him there? Yes. He stands in front of her, blocking the sun. He is speaking. *That's some scar*, he said. *Don't worry. It'll fade.*

The three women watch her expectantly. Clare uses her good arm to lift her shirt over her head, her bra loose against her frame, its cotton ragged.

"Jesus Christ," Ginny says.

"That looks really fresh," Rebecca says. "I hope whatever trouble you're in doesn't follow you here."

This place was troubled enough before I got here, Clare thinks, hugging her T-shirt to her chest.

"I thought that was the point of this place," Raylene says. "To help those of us in trouble?"

"Only a certain kind of trouble," Rebecca says. "Helen's very clear about that."

"Shut up, Rebecca," Ginny says. "Don't speak on my mother's behalf."

"I have the right to feel safe here," Rebecca says. "This is my home too."

"No it isn't," Ginny says. "This is Helen's home. She only lets you live here because she feels sorry for her deadbeat brother."

"It was Sally's home too," Raylene says. "And now she's gone. You know anything about that, Rebecca?"

"Jesus, no!" Rebecca cries. "And this *is* my home. Don't say it isn't. How do we know Clare isn't making all of this up?"

The clench in her teeth makes Clare's jaw throb. She notices that Rebecca changes the subject every time Sally's name is mentioned, redirecting the focus. *Don't mess with her perfect little life,* Ginny said on the drive home.

"Why would I lie?" Clare says.

"Why do we lie to each other about anything?" Rebecca asks.

The question hangs in the air between the women for a moment.

"We lie to protect ourselves," Raylene says.

"No," Rebecca says. "We lie to get what we want."

"Isn't that the same thing?" Clare asks.

"It depends," Rebecca says. "What do you want, Clare? Why do you lie?"

"Give it up, Rebecca," Ginny says. "She's Sally's friend. What else do you want?"

"It's a simple question," Rebecca says. "Sometimes we're not even sure when we're lying. You know? How does the saying go? There are three sides to every story? Yours, mine, and the truth?"

"Your story's pretty clear-cut," Ginny says to Rebecca. "Meet a cute entrepreneur online, marry him after, like, a week. He fails to mention he went bankrupt selling oceanfront condos. But your biological clock is ticking and he's such a dashing catch that you don't think to ask how much money he's got in the bank."

"I can't imagine what it's like to be you," Rebecca says. "So mean-spirited for no reason at all. Taking pleasure in hurting others."

"Yes you can," Ginny says.

This dynamic feels impossible, Clare too tired, too ill-equipped to navigate it. Rebecca scrambles up and smooths her dress with her hands.

"It's late. I need to make sure Willow is asleep."

"You're way too sensitive," Ginny says. "I'm just a kid having some fun."

"I'm not sensitive," Rebecca says. "I'm tired of it. I get that it's hard. But you don't need to be so nasty. We should have each other's backs in times like these. And you're not a kid any more than the rest of us." Rebecca pulls a small flashlight from the pocket of her dress and twists it on. "I thought this would be nice. Maybe take our mind off things. But you can't help yourself, Ginny. You just can't. You pounce on everyone who comes anywhere near you."

They stay silent as Rebecca disappears into the trees, the sounds of her footsteps fading.

"She's probably still breastfeeding," Ginny says.

"What's wrong with you?" Raylene asks. "You took that too far."

"I hate her," Ginny says. She lights another cigarette. A shimmer of tears rests on her lids as she blows the first exhale to the sky. "She's so fake. You know what? Last week I was smoking on the porch and I saw her come out of her house. She was going crazy on Willow. Yelling at her. I couldn't hear her across the river but her face was basically purple. The way she yanked Willow by the arm made me want to puke. Don't talk to me about toxins when you go psycho on your two-year-old for throwing a ball in the river, you know? How two-faced can you possibly get?"

"No one said she was a good person," Raylene says. "I'm just telling you not to bother with it. Stay out of her way."

Ginny is careful to wipe away the tears before they breach and fall. Rebecca collects a pile of pebbles and lines them up into small pyramids next to her. Clare sucks in a deep breath, then pushes off so that her body slides into the icy water. Under the surface her head throbs from the cold, and though her eyes are open she sees nothing. She pops back out, the air too warm in contrast.

"See if you can touch the bottom," Ginny says.

"It's freezing," Clare says. "My body feels heavy."

"Perfect. That'll make it easier to sink."

Despite the bite of her words, there is a playfulness to Ginny's tone. Why is it that Clare feels kinship with Ginny, this caustic girl? Treading water, she thinks of Grace. The hours spent at the swimming pool in town, Grace's gliding backstroke, Clare always lagging, her long legs like dead weights behind her. Clare dips her head back to look up to the sky, the cold water a balm on her shoulder. Raylene is watching her, Ginny too. In another life, Clare thinks, they might all be easy friends.

"If you don't come up in five minutes," Ginny says, "I promise I'll come in after you. I'd never let you drown."

Clare points her toes and propels downward. It takes three strokes until her feet hit a sandy bottom. She plugs her nose to release the pressure, then treads to maintain her depth. Clare opens her eyes to the blackness. She thinks of her dreams, someone grabbing at her legs, pulling her under, the ache of her chest as the air runs out. She thinks of Sally Proulx, grasping to hold on to her son. She thinks of Jason, unable as he was to swim, how he would take hold of her when they waded in together, as though he'd rather drown them both than die alone. Clare kicks and her left foot hits something. It moves. She presses hard into the ground and shoots herself upward, breaking the surface with a terrified gasp.

"You were under for a good minute," Raylene says. "I was about to dive in."

"There's something down there," Clare says, breathless.

"What?" Ginny says.

"I kicked something. It moved."

"It could be anything," Raylene says. "A deadhead. A rock."

"It wasn't a deadhead," Clare says. "Or a rock." Her limbs are numb with cold. Clare pulls her weight onto land, wincing, and accepts Raylene's arms around her. Her teeth chatter wildly. "I swear. My foot touched something."

They exchange glances.

"You losers," Ginny says. "You're such chickens. I'll go." She stands and steps off the edge into the water. After a minute Ginny emerges, takes a deep breath, then goes under again, this time diving, her feet kicking into the air and splashing them. Clare shudders against the warmth of Raylene. When Ginny breaks the surface again, she lifts one hand out of the water, holding the object aloft, terror on her face. Raylene raises her hand to her mouth to stifle a cry. Though it is wrapped in stringy weeds, the superhero figure on the side still glows a bright red. A child's running shoe.

TUESDAY

In the kitchen Helen pours Clare a coffee and offers Clare a plate of fruit. They sit opposite each other at the table. A fly dives in and away, its buzz disconcerting Clare. Even overnight, the heat has not broken.

"Jordan called this morning to say the police have their warrant," Helen says. "He's got a friend at the precinct who tipped him off. The shoe. It was the shoe. That's what got them the warrant. They'll be in before noon."

If Helen is anxious or distressed, she goes to great efforts to mask it.

"What does that mean for you?" Clare asks.

"You may want to remove your things before they arrive," Helen says, evading Clare's question. "We'll all have to leave once they get here."

What does Clare have to hide? There is the folder in her bag, an obvious giveaway, and then the letter from Jason, stuffed among the small collection of ill-fitting clothes Malcolm procured for her after they left Blackmore. What would that letter tell someone if read out of context? The story of a jilted husband begging his wife's return? An ordinary enough tale. One with the worst details left out.

"Raylene is out on another walk this morning," Helen says. "I don't know what she thinks she's looking for."

"The shoe," Clare says. "That was upsetting to her."

Helen flinches ever so slightly. Her capacity for composure is remarkable, Clare notes as she watches her across the table.

"What about Ginny?" Clare asks.

"I'll get her up in a minute. We can send her to campus for the night. Her room there is ready."

"Ginny is quite something," Clare says.

"Don't call her a firecracker," Helen says. "She'll skin you for it."

What an odd thing to say, Clare thinks. Helen sips from the juice in front of her.

"Ginny's smart," Clare says.

"She is," Helen says. "She doesn't get that from me."

"You raised her alone?" Clare asks.

"She doesn't know her father. He's not on the scene."

"That must have been hard for you. Going it alone, I mean. Especially given . . . this place. The work you do."

"I was young when I had her," Helen says. "It never occurred to me to adjust my life to make things easier for her. I started taking women in when she was just a baby. There was always a lot of grief around. A lot of struggle. Women at their lowest points staying in our home, eating their meals with us, crying in our living room. But it didn't used to matter. She was this gorgeous and precocious little light of a child. The women here just wanted to take care of her. Jordan, he was always ambivalent to this place. He did his thing. Made friends, played lots of sports. School was a breeze for him. Markus was a homebody. He loved the attention he got here too. He tried college, but couldn't manage it. Doesn't like to be told what to do. But Ginny. She was always the light. Always. Even in her teens, she always wanted to be helpful. Now she says she resents living here. But ironically, I think having her around was the thing that helped me keep it going."

"What do you think changed?"

"She went off to school. I think the world opened up to her and now she thinks this place is small. Hopeless. And Markus moved back and took up with Rebecca. Ginny hates them both."

"That's pretty clear. Why?" Clare asks.

"I don't know," Helen says. "Markus isn't a perfect man. He's got big ideas but can't seem to follow anything through. He likes the thrill of the plan and the prospects, but doesn't love the actual work, you know? Ginny's never had any time for him. I think she's mad at me for letting him move back here, build that house. Even when she was a little girl he made her edgy." With a start Helen sits erect in the chair, tracking the fly. When it lands on the table she slams her palm down hard on it, lifting her hand to reveal its twitching corpse. "You know, I can give *you* options too. Next steps."

"What do you mean?"

"I've been thinking about what you confided to me at the river. About your background. There are options we can provide."

"Okay."

Clare takes a napkin from the dispenser on the table and rips tiny pieces from its corners. She pictures Ginny at the center of the eddy, holding the small shoe aloft, a look of horror on her face. The confusion that followed as they returned to the house with it and woke Helen, the look on Helen's face when Ginny handed her the dripping running shoe. It hadn't been a look of fear or distress, but instead of something quieter. Disappointment. From there Helen had insisted they go to their rooms while she dealt with the police. And now, Clare thinks, Helen seems almost hell-bent on speaking of anything else but what transpired last night.

Helen refills their juice glasses. "I don't believe in coincidence," she says. "People like to talk about good luck and good timing, or bad luck and bad timing, about things working out or going awry because of fate. Pardon me, but I think that's all bullshit. Just an excuse not to take the reins. Take control of your life."

"I agree," Clare says. For years she'd excused away the specifics of her existence to these very things, the poor luck of her mother's cancer, the fated pills in the cupboard, meeting Jason at that bonfire party she'd tagged along to last minute. It was always easier to blame chance and fate. *No matter what your circumstance*, Clare's mother used to say, *you always have a choice. It's always your choice.*

"There are more ways out than you realize," Helen says. "We try to make plans for women here. It's not just a place to sleep and hide out for a while. I want to provide real options."

"Okay," Clare says again, puzzled by the turn in conversation, by Helen's shift in demeanor, so businesslike.

"You said the other day that you left in December."

"I did," Clare says. "About eight months ago, give or take. Right before Christmas."

"What was your plan?"

"My plan was . . . to leave. I saved money. My mother left me a bit of money too. When she died. Enough to survive for a while. To be honest, I didn't plan very far beyond the escape."

"What have you been doing for the past eight months?"

"I've been on the move. Place to place." Clare recalls her

confession last night, her wound revealed to the other women, her true story and this invented one mingling in unruly ways. She must keep track. "I got into some trouble where I stayed last. I stopped for too long in the wrong place. Then I heard from Sally. It took me a while to gather myself up and get here."

"Do you keep in touch with anyone at home?"

"No," Clare says. "I figured they thought I was dead. But I now know they don't think that. I heard from my husband. He said everyone knows I'm alive and I ran away. He said they're all mad at me."

"But you don't know for sure that he's telling the truth," Helen says.

"No. I guess I don't."

"He might say anything to lure you back."

"Yes," Clare says, her eyes instantly brimming. "He might."

"We used to try to help women prosecute. My father's old law partner was big into the justice route. He would help. He'll work pro bono."

"Philip," Clare says. "I met him yesterday."

Helen's chin lifts at the sound of his name. "He doesn't do much anymore."

"Jordan said the same," Clare says. "He said he's semi-retired."

"Right. Jordan's mostly taken over since he finished law school. Do you know what the conviction rate is for domestic assault?"

Clare shakes her head.

"Let's just say it's grim. Most cases don't even make it to court. We stopped even trying. We started looking for a more permanent solution."

"What do you mean by permanent?" Clare asks.

Helen's fingers rap the table. "Jordan works with connections in the city to get the paperwork in order. You cut your hair, dye it, like you see in the movies. We give you a new name, a new passport. Clothes, everything. We can even provide some employment references, based on skills you might have."

"How do you do that?"

"You need to know the right people. Once everything is in place, you go wherever you want and start over."

"I tried that," Clare says.

"Right, but we can provide a death certificate too," Helen says. "On paper you're dead. Your next of kin is contacted. We kill you off first, then we turn you into someone else."

Clare straightens in her chair. How could it be so simple? "What did Sally choose?"

Helen's face clouds over. "Are you implying we'd put a child in a raging river?"

"God, no. Of course not. But you could say that's what happened. They can't find the bodies. Give Sally a way out."

The other day at the river Helen had cried. Clare hadn't realized then that those tears might have been a rarity, because Helen's poise hasn't faltered since. Even now, the only sign of her effort to stay composed is the beat of her breaths in and out.

"I understand why you might assume this based on what I've just told you," Helen says.

"Assume what?" Clare prods.

"That Sally's disappearance was part of a plan. But, no. It wasn't. I don't know what happened. She could have just left on her own. She might have just left on her own."

"We all know Raylene saw the whole thing," says a voice from the hall. Ginny stands in the doorway in a short and loose nightgown. She joins them at the table, setting down the phone in her hand with its screen facing up. "She woke everyone up to search, right? Someone obviously called the cops. It was an accident. That's what you said, Helen. I hope you're not lying."

"Of course I'm not lying," Helen says.

"Were you here that night?" Clare asks.

"No," Ginny says, studying her fingernails. "But I was here last night. With that fucking show."

"Ginny," Helen chides.

Side by side the resemblance between Ginny and Helen is striking, their expressions perfectly matched. Ginny angles herself daintily towards Clare.

"Does Helen want to kill you off too?" Ginny asks.

"Ginny, please," Helen says. "You don't know how this works."

"Oh, yes I do," Ginny says. "Jordan and Philip break the law is how it works. I know you think I'm in the dark about your antics, but I'm not. Pay off a shady coroner and get your hands on a nice little death certificate. Then another woman shows up and you do it all over again. Eventually some starlet makes a movie about you." Ginny slides Helen's glass of orange juice over and drains it. "If I was going to start over I'd move to the East Coast. Change my name to Claudia."

"Don't be ridiculous," Helen says.

Ginny slaps her hand hard to the table, the juice glasses dancing at the impact. "You basically locked me in my room last night!" she screams.

"The police had work to do here," Helen says, ever steady. "We needed to stay out of their way."

"I found the fucking shoe! You don't think they'd want to talk to me?"

"It's up to them who they talk to," Helen says. "They spoke to Raylene. They have a search warrant now. They'll be here soon."

"I'm not leaving," Ginny says, slouched, her arms crossed.

"You won't be allowed to stay," Helen says. "They've offered to put us up in a hotel for a few days. You can go to your dorm. It's open. Your roommate won't be there, but you can still—"

"I don't want to go!" Ginny yells.

The flush of Ginny's cheeks, the fear on her face, tells Clare that maybe she knows more than she's let on.

"What if I come with you?" Clare asks. "If your roommate's not there?"

But Ginny isn't listening. She has fixed her hearing on a sound in the distance. A whining.

"What is that?" Clare asks.

"Probably just an animal," Helen says, frowning.

When Clare goes to speak again, Helen lifts a finger to silence her. The wail comes again, this time louder. Clare runs to the door and outside, Ginny and Helen following close behind her. Across the river Markus and Rebecca appear on their porch, Willow on Rebecca's hip with her thumb in her mouth, the three of them focused on the sound too. It is louder now and Clare can tell it's coming from the trees downriver. Not a wail but a distinct word. *Help!*

Clare's feet feel cemented to the ground, her body searing hot. Everyone around her, frantic. Though she sees their lips moving, she can't make sense of their words with the ringing in her ears. A scream. *Help!* She watches Raylene, emerged from the woods, her face twisted, her gait labored under the weight of a small body. Then they are all on the grass by the river. Markus. Helen. Ginny. Raylene. Markus takes the boy from Raylene's arms and sets him gently down. Ginny collapses next to him. No! she is wailing. No!

"He was so heavy," Raylene says. "Too heavy."

The boy wears cars-and-trucks pajamas and one shoe to match the other they'd found last night. The skin is blue-gray. Clare can't bear to look at his face.

"Where did you find him?" Helen asks. "Raylene! Where did you find him?"

"Across the river. There was a catch of dead branches. I saw from this side, but he was over there . . ."

Raylene's clothes are caked with mud. Clare cranes to see Rebecca seated on her porch, her hand pressing Willow's face into the crook of her neck. Her lips are puckered, shushing her, but her face is otherwise devoid of expression. Take that child inside, Clare wants to scream at her.

"Raylene," Helen repeats. "Where? How far down?"

"Past the bridge. I don't know. Half a mile?"

"Was he underwater?"

Ginny screams again, this time so piercing that Clare feels it stab in her ears. William, she is saying. She is screaming his name.

"Take her back to the house," Markus says to Helen. "I can't listen to her!"

Helen works to bring Ginny to her feet, angling her so that she cannot twist to look down at the boy again. Ginny pries herself free and links arms with Clare, shaking Helen off when she tries to take hold of her again. They watch as Raylene adjusts the body in precise ways. She presses the flat of her hand to the chest, then bends the neck back to open the mouth.

"We should leave him," Markus says. "You shouldn't touch him."

But Raylene doesn't listen, reaching for the boy's arms and placing them gently at his sides. Markus cups Raylene by the armpit and attempts to pull her to standing.

"Stop it," he insists. "Don't touch him."

Raylene wrenches free and closes to within a few inches of Markus's face.

"Don't you touch *me*!" she says, a violent hiss.

"Raylene," Helen says. "Let's go. We'll go back to the house and wait. You, me, and Ginny."

"I'm not leaving him here," Raylene says.

"You can't move him," Markus says.

"He's already been moved."

"Well, we're not moving him again," Helen says.

"Then get a sheet to cover him!" Raylene screams, her body jolting with rage.

"I'll go," Helen says. "I'll call the police. I'll call Somers directly."

Clare feels Ginny's weight lean into her as they watch Helen jog back to the house.

"There was no water in his mouth," Raylene says.

"What do you mean?" Clare asks.

"His chest felt—"

"No," Markus interrupts, waving his hand to shush her. "No. Please. Let's not speculate."

"She's an emergency room doctor," Ginny says. "It's not speculation when you're a fucking doctor."

"She has no authority—"

"Shut up," Ginny screams. "Shut up right now. You think I don't know about you? You're a fucking pig!"

Clare tugs on Ginny's arm to retract her. She keeps her chin held high to avoid looking down at the boy, his lifelessness too eerie. When Helen returns she and Clare flap the sheet open and drape it over the body. They stand in a line looking down at the small features that take shape as the sheet settles over him.

"Jesus Christ," Helen says. "When will it end?"

"When will what end?" Clare asks.

"This." She gestures to the boy. "This."

The corners of the sheet flap in the breeze. A heave of bile comes to Clare's throat. How could no one have spotted the body until now? The police have been searching for days, Somers told her. Divers trained to find a penny on the ocean floor. Clare thinks of Sally on the dock, screaming, jumping in after this boy, a scene she's pictured dozens of times since arriving at High River. Of course a mother would jump in after her child. But Clare knows the story doesn't begin or end there. Everyone else here knows it too. Clare stumbles to the riverbank and vomits into the churning water. She sits, light-headed. In the distance she hears the whirl of overlapping sirens. She drops her head between her legs and reaches under her shirt to rest her hand on her shoulder wound, sticky with new flesh. The others form a semicircle around the body, each staring ahead, no one speaking.

On paper you're dead, Helen said to Clare earlier. There is one version of Sally's story where she took that option, killed herself and her son off on paper, and began a new life else-where. But here is the boy, dead, to tell Clare that can't be what happened. *She could have just left on her own*, Helen said. On her own. Without her son, who ended up in the river one way or another.

The bathroom door is open. Clare stands out of view in the hallway, the air so warm that it burns on the inhale. The only sound is the lilt of Helen's voice shushing Ginny as she cries. Clare strains to hear the whispers.

"She said he was too heavy," Clare hears Ginny say. "What does that mean? He's so small. Why was he so heavy?"

"I'm going to get you a towel," Helen says.

Before Clare can duck into the bedroom she is face-to-face with Helen in the hallway.

"I didn't want to interrupt," Clare says. "Is she okay?"

"No. She's not. Are you okay?"

"Yes," Clare says, flustered. "I'm sorry. I don't know what to say. It's horrible."

Helen blinks at her, expressionless. The unwavering composure.

"Can I do anything?" Clare asks.

"Clare?" Ginny calls from the bathroom.

"Sit with her," Helen says. "I need to go speak with the police. With Markus."

Clare nods. Her chest and neck tingle with heat, her shoulder pulses with pain. Helen descends the stairs.

"Clare?" Ginny says again, her voice broken. Clare peeks into the bathroom. Ginny sits in the bathtub, her knees to her bare breasts, hair in dark spikes. She picks at the faucet with her long fingers. Her skin is pinked by the warmth of the water.

"I'm so sorry," Clare says in the doorway.

"You saw him?" Ginny asks.

"I did. Remember? I was with you."

"He wasn't breathing, right?"

Surely this isn't a question. The gray of the boy's skin won't leave Clare's mind. She swallows to catch the lump working up her throat.

"He wasn't," Clare says.

"They'll check for a pulse, though. Right?"

"They will. The ambulance is here. The detectives will be here any minute. They'll take care of it."

"He was heavy. That's what Raylene said."

Clare edges herself fully into the bathroom and lowers the lid on the toilet to sit. "I'm so sorry," she says again. Ginny turns and takes hold of Clare's hand, pulling at her until Clare must drop to her knees on the floor, their faces close.

"William was Sally's baby."

"I know. He was. I know."

"You know Rourke?"

"Yes," Clare says. "Of course. He's on his way."

"He likes you."

"No. I just met him."

"I can tell he likes you. You need to talk to him. He needs to ask the right questions. He needs to talk to the right people."

"I'm sure he's talking to everyone. That's his job. Somers too. They seem very diligent." Clare pauses and squeezes Ginny's damp hand. "But Ginny? You need to tell them everything you know. If there's something you know. About Markus, or even about your mom . . ."

Ginny leans until her mouth grazes into Clare's hair, whispering. "Sally was pregnant. She *is* pregnant."

"Oh." Clare's heart flips, her mind scrambled. She straightens her leg to ease the bathroom door closed with her foot. "How do you know that?"

"By accident. Sometimes I'd go through her stuff. I found a pregnancy test in her drawer. Positive. Two lines. And there were other signs too. Before she disappeared she refused to eat half the stuff Helen gave her. Even barfed a few times. She was sleeping a lot. You don't have to be a rocket scientist to—"

"Why were you going through her stuff?"

For a moment they watch each other, Ginny's eyes defiant. "I go through everyone's stuff. Except yours. You know, because of the lock."

Clare thinks of her duffel bag under her bed, her phone, the letter from Jason, the file on Sally at the bottom. The lock Clare had picked up at a gas station and looped around the zipper. A lock that would give easily under the force of pliers.

"You shouldn't be doing that," Clare says. "It's not right."

"Your friend was pregnant. Don't you get what I'm saying?" Ginny takes hold of Clare's forearm and squeezes until her knuckles whiten. "Scold me about this another time, okay?"

"Okay." Clare clears her throat. "Sally's been here for a few months. Could she have been pregnant when she arrived? Maybe that's why she left her husband in the first place. No. That doesn't make sense."

"She's been here since March." Ginny gestures to her bare belly. "She would have been out to here by now. And why would she be taking pregnancy tests if she already knew?"

"So she got pregnant here? How do you know that?"

Markus. Ginny mouths the name without saying it aloud. She puts her finger to her temple and forms a gun with her hand, mimicking the pull of a trigger.

"What?" Clare says.

"Markus knew about the pregnancy. Rebecca doesn't. Or didn't, apparently. Maybe she found out."

"How do you know that?"

"I confronted Sally. *Confronted* isn't the right word. I told her I knew she was pregnant. That it had to be Markus, right? They were together all day while Rebecca was at work. I'd come out here for the day to study during exams and they'd be out there by the river, basically frolicking. It was gross. But then William got sick and Sally wasn't coping. So, you know. I'm well connected in the city. Basically half the girls in my first year of college had the same . . . problem. I told Sally I could help her deal with it."

"What did she say?"

"She flipped out on me. Lost her mind. Sally had a real temper. She was all about the father wanting to keep it. About me not knowing shit. That I needed to mind my own business."

"How do you know she meant Markus?"

"Let me repeat: They were always together. Their kids playing. Coffee at nap time. Laughing at each other's jokes while his wife was working. I remember this one dinner we all had maybe a month after Sally and Raylene showed up. It was Jordan's birthday. Helen always wanted to make sure everyone felt included, so Sally and Raylene were there. At the dinner. And Sally and Markus were laughing it up, already with all these inside jokes. It was so awkward. I swear I thought Rebecca was going to take the antique salad tongs and jam them into Markus's eyes. He's so disgusting." Ginny shakes her head. "I don't know why Helen defends him—"

"You haven't told anyone this, not even Jordan?"

"Why would I do that?"

"Because he's your uncle and you two seem close."

"I would never trust him with a secret like that."

"And Rourke? You didn't think to tell him?"

Ginny crinkles her nose. "Rourke thinks I'm a kid. He'd accuse me of making it up. And there's no body to prove she was pregnant. It's not like they can do an autopsy. And Rourke would ask Markus about it, and guess what? All fingers end up pointing back at me, saying I'm a drama queen."

The new spark in Ginny's tone mystifies Clare. A minute ago she'd been stricken, but now she looks at Clare without a hint of sadness. Her nakedness feels like a ploy, Ginny so unselfconscious, Clare averting her eyes.

"You need to tell the police," Clare says. "You can't withhold this. It's not just a gossipy secret anymore. It's evidence."

"Markus knows." Ginny drops her voice. "Did he tell them? I'm pretty sure Helen knows too. Did she?"

As if on cue, the door opens and Helen squeezes in.

"There's tea downstairs," Helen says. "Time to get out. You'll catch a chill."

Ginny buries her face in her knees and cries again, but this time her tears seem feigned. Helen shifts her weight, impatient, yanking a towel from the hook on the door. For someone whose life work is about offering refuge to women, Helen does a poor job of comforting her crying daughter.

"I should go find Raylene," Clare says. "I don't know where she went."

"She's in your room."

In the hallway Clare leans against the wall to catch her breath. When she closes her eyes she sees herself in the bathtub at home, Jason on the floor next to her, his arm submerged in the water, his rough palm cupping the growing roundness of her pregnant belly. She can see it precisely, feel the weight of his hand. The gentle splash as he retracted his arm, the smile on his face. Clare feels a wave of nausea. That might have been exactly one year ago.

"Stop it." Clare can hear Helen through the bathroom door. "Don't even say that."

"You promised this wouldn't happen."

"There's nothing you could have done. Okay?"

Clare stands frozen, waiting for more. But all she hears is the swirl of a body stepping out of water. Before Helen and Ginny emerge from the bathroom Clare ducks into her room and finds Raylene cross-legged on her bed, bent over an open journal.

"Raylene," Clare says. "Are you okay?"

"I'm trying to record the details."

"The details?"

"What I noticed. In case anyone asks."

The pen moves furiously, Raylene's writing in diagonal across the journal's page. Frantic. Clare moves to the window. An ambulance is parked on the lawn next to the body still under the sheet. Next to it Rourke and Somers flank Markus, all three frowning, hands on hips.

"Did Rourke or Somers interview you?" Clare asks Raylene.

"Not yet. They told me to wait inside."

"Did you tell them you're a doctor?"

"They don't care who I am or what I am. The body will go straight to the coroner."

"So what are you writing?"

Raylene puts down her pen and looks to Clare.

"His lungs. They seemed empty."

"What does that mean?" Clare asks. "You said he was heavy."

"He was. But that could have been . . . He was in wet pajamas. But I'm telling you, William was dead before he went into the water."

"What? How can you know that?"

"I know what drowning looks like. How it presents in a body. That boy didn't drown."

When Clare goes to speak, Raylene waves her off, then resumes her writing. Out the window, the paramedics lift the stretcher and set it through the rear doors of the ambulance. From this distance she cannot read the expression on Markus's face. Clare's gaze shifts to Rourke. Behind him, the sky is black with clouds. He looks up and spots her in the window, smiling as hello. A smile though a dead child just lay at his feet. Why does the sight of Rourke tighten Clare's chest, make it harder to breathe?

"You should tell the detectives what you just told me," Clare says.

"I don't trust that guy."

"Rourke? Why not?"

"I guess I should," Raylene says. "But I don't."

Neither do I, Clare thinks. She turns away from the window and lies down on her bed, her body too sore. How can she be so tired? She closes her eyes. There he is. Jason. They are sitting together in a field of shorn hay. Far ahead is the bonfire, its orange flames licking up, black silhouettes milling around it. Clare looks for Grace's form among them, Christopher's too. They were both here a minute ago. Why did they let her walk away with him? Jason takes her hand and pries it open. *Put this on your tongue*, he says. *Let it melt.* Clare does as she's told. The paper tastes bitter. After a few minutes the light of the fire is stronger, higher. Too high. Does it go all the way to the sky? It is too hot. Too many colors. *How do you know what's real?* It feels like a thought, but she must have said it aloud, because Jason answers her.

This is real, he says. *We are real. You and me.*

Her eyes pop open again. Clare sits up, her mouth dry. The room is empty and the light through the window has shifted. A dream. How could she have fallen asleep? Out the window the ambulance is gone, the sheet where the body had been left in a rumpled pile. Rourke and Somers are no longer in sight but their squad car is still parked askew to the house. Clare grabs her phone and wanders to the hallway. The other bedroom door is closed. In the bathroom Clare clutches the sink, afraid she will vomit again. When the wave passes she sits on the edge of the bathtub and stares down at her phone, unsure of what to write.

Boy's body found, she types. **Police here.**

She waits for a response. A swirl of anger hits Clare. His small body, lifeless. A boy dead and too many secrets. What is she doing here?

Can you call? comes his response.

Yes, Clare thinks, but not here. She will have to leave the house. She peers out the window. Though the light has dulled as a storm moves in, it's not raining yet. She will go for a walk.

Give me a few mins, Clare types.

C lare waits in the woods, her grip on her phone so forceful she must be careful not to crush it. When it vibrates she stares at it blankly for a second, her thumb hovering before finally tapping to take the call.

"Hello?"

"Hi."

The swell in Clare's chest takes her aback. Malcolm's voice feels far away, gruff.

"Are you okay?" he asks.

"It wasn't good," Clare says. "It was pretty bad. He was so small. Just a little boy."

"It's already all over the news. I just read about it online."

"What are they saying?"

"That the body of the missing boy was found. Mother still missing. Details to follow." Malcolm pauses and lets out a long sigh.

"I haven't seen any reporters," Clare says.

"Tell me what you saw."

146

Clare leans on a tree and looks back to the lawn where it all unfolded only hours ago.

"One of the women was out for a morning walk. Raylene. I told you about her. The doctor. She found him. She carried him back to the house. He was . . . he was clearly dead."

"I'm sorry you had to see that."

Clare bites her lower lip. She does not want Malcolm's comfort. *Sorry*. How often did Jason utter that word? Often enough to render it meaningless.

"The police have a search warrant," Clare says, working hard to steady her voice. "We can't be in the house while they execute it. I may go to the city with Ginny. Helen's daughter. She has a room on the college campus. A spare bed. Where are you?"

"In the city," Malcolm says. "Not far from the college, actually."

A silence passes between them.

"I could come get you," Malcolm says finally. "We're not obliged to finish the job."

We, Clare thinks. *We*. What are we?

"You're not obliged, I mean," Malcolm says, reading her thoughts.

Clare walks along the path towards the eddy, the phone warm against her cheek. *I could come get you.* She thinks of Helen at the table this morning. The option on offer. The plan. Everything about Malcolm too distant, yet more familiar than anything else right now. A flash comes to Clare of Malcolm on the phone, pleading with someone. Who? Clare was watching him groggily from the motel bed. His voice was hushed and she could make out his words. Just the tone. The pleading. A name.

"Clare? Are you there?"

"No," she says. "I mean, yes. I'm here. But no. I don't want you to come get me. I want to stay. I want to finish the job."

"Okay."

"Just get me the information I asked for."

"Yes. I'm on it." Malcolm pauses. "Clare?"

"What?"

There is another pause. Clare was never one for talking on the phone, never able to dream up the other person as they spoke, never able to endure any silence that stretched on too long.

"What?" she says again.

"Nothing. It's fine. As long as you're sure you're okay."

"I'm fine."

The words come out louder than she intends. When Clare looks up, she is surprised to see Rebecca sitting with her legs in the eddy pool, watching Clare from a distance with a curious frown. Willow sleeps pressed to her chest.

"I have to go," Clare says, ending the call before Malcolm can respond.

"I was wondering whose voice I could hear," Rebecca calls as Clare approaches. "You okay? You sounded upset."

"I just was talking to a friend," Clare says. "Letting them know about . . . about the boy."

"Nice that you keep in touch with your friends. You must miss your life at home."

What a thing to say, Clare thinks. Rebecca's face is locked in a peculiar expression, a blank half-smile.

"Do you worry about holding a cell phone to your ear like that?" Rebecca asks.

"Pardon me?"

"The waves. High frequency. I've read they mess with brain composition."

How can her tone be so blithe? Clare watches as Rebecca swings her legs through the water, the little girl gripping at her mother's shirt in her sleep, her hair wild around her small face. There is a slow gentleness to Rebecca's movements. Clare feels a well of disgust at the scene, the doting mother cooling off in a river from which someone else's dead child has just been pulled.

"We can speak in code," Rebecca says. "In case she wakes up."

"I'm sorry?"

"I see the look on your face. Is there something you'd like to say?"

"No," Clare says.

"Because I can feel the weight of your judgment." Rebecca cocks her head. "Do I seem indifferent to you?"

Clare shrugs.

"What am I supposed to do?" Rebecca looks down at Willow. "How do I explain such a thing? She loved that boy. He was her only friend. What am I to do but carry on?"

"I didn't—"

"Of course it's upsetting. But that kind of showy grief is a luxury I can't afford."

Showy grief? Clare remains silent, mystified. When the girl stirs, Rebecca hugs her tightly and shushes her until she drops slack in her arms again. At two, Clare's nephew had stood as tall as her hip. This girl seems the size of a baby.

"You don't want to sit?" Rebecca asks as though nothing has passed between them, as though it's an ordinary day, an ordinary conversation.

"I should go back. See if Helen needs anything."

"I tried to help her, you know," Rebecca says. "You know who I mean?"

"I think so."

"Will you sit? Please?"

Clare's whole body aches. She approaches the eddy and lowers herself to sit cross-legged at the far side.

"The boy's mother? Your friend. I tried to help her."

"Yes," Clare says, icy.

"I'm a teacher, not sure if you knew that. The only person here with an actual job. But I saw a lot of her in the evenings. Weekends. Our kids played. She seemed to idolize Markus and me, our life. The stability of it, I suppose. But right away, you could tell. From day one. She wasn't right." Rebecca taps her forehead. "And I'm not just talking about the blues. She would . . . see things."

The swirl of nausea returns, Clare's head throbbing. She wants only to get away from Rebecca.

"Was she like that before?" Rebecca asks.

"No. She was not."

"Here it seemed like she was always afraid. Or angry. Very paranoid."

"Did she see a doctor?"

"No," Rebecca says. "It never got to that point."

"Didn't you just say she was paranoid? Hallucinating?"

"I said she was seeing things. And they made her afraid. Aren't you afraid?"

Clare doesn't know how to answer.

"Anyway," Rebecca continues. "We agreed we would try to help her here."

"Who's we?"

The wind presses Rebecca's hair upward, her daughter stirring and opening her eyes. Clare remembers the seething way Rebecca had stormed off last night. How unwilling she'd been to discuss Sally. Now she seems almost giddy.

"Maybe she needed a doctor," Rebecca says finally. "Maybe that's something we'll have to live with. Especially now. Look what she's done."

Clare stands and steps back to lean against the young tree behind her. It bends against her weight.

"It's not uncommon," Rebecca says. "This kind of thing. When a mother goes, she takes her child with her."

The little girl now sits erect on her mother's lap, quiet, looking across at Clare with saucer eyes. Clare feels a drop of rain hit her. She looks up to the dark sky.

"I'll be glad if it rains," Rebecca says, scrambling to stand with her daughter still in her arms. "I can't think straight in this heat."

For a moment they face each other in silence, Rebecca adjusting her daughter on her hip, her expression unreadable, sad or angry or neither. Blank. With a wave Rebecca turns and recedes in the other direction. Over her shoulder the little girl watches Clare as if expecting her to call out to them, as if to urge her back so that more might be said.

Somers stands alone by the willow tree. When she sees Clare, she nods in solemn hello, in acknowledgment of the terrible events that have unfolded since they last spoke. The rain has yet to unleash, only the odd drop threatening.

"I'm really sorry," Somers says when Clare arrives beside her.

"It's pretty horrible," Clare says. "I guess it doesn't bode well for Sally."

"You never know." Somers shakes her head. "I'm not giving up hope. Because that's the weird thing about this job. You really never know."

"I hear you got a search warrant."

"So much for the element of surprise." She shades her eyes despite the lack of sun, looking across the river to where Rebecca climbs her porch. "We might have to start across the river."

"This place is really . . . These people are . . . I don't know," Clare says. "I can't articulate it."

"Weird?" Somers asks.

"It's not what it's meant to be. Not at all."

"That makes me sad," Somers says. "Listen. If you want to get your stuff. Pack up. A little head start before the swarm arrives with the warrant, I won't tell."

"I appreciate that," Clare says. "How would Rourke feel about you helping me?"

"Why wouldn't I help you? Your friend's son was just pulled from a river. I figure you've had enough for one day. And I figure you'd help me too if you had the chance."

A meaningful statement, Clare thinks. A loaded one too.

"Where is Rourke?" Clare asks.

"Around. Doing his thing."

"Have you two been partners long?"

"No," Somers says. "He just transferred in. Maybe a month ago. My previous partner retired after twelve years together, so I was single. Lucky Rourke. He's a good guy, even if he mystifies me. He insisted on taking this case. Beats me as to why. Not even in our jurisdiction. They were shorthanded out here and he jumped on it. And it's a missing persons case. I like to stick to homicide, but that's just me."

"It isn't a missing persons case anymore," Clare says.

"True," Somers says. "Now it's both."

A slight frown overtakes Somers's face as she considers her own words. Her skin is smooth, her hair pulled back in braids. Clare guesses Somers to be in her late thirties. Her children must still be young. Beyond her Clare can see deep into the woods.

"There's a bunker," Clare says.

"Sorry?"

"Like a hole in the ground. The kind of thing someone digs to escape a nuclear war."

"There's no escaping nuclear war," Somers says. "What are you talking about?"

"Markus Haines says his father dug it years ago. It's impossible to spot unless you know it's there. He says he was supposed to fill it in on Helen's order but didn't. Apparently no one else knows about it except him. Maybe Helen too, if she's wise to the fact that he kept it open."

"You've been there?"

"Early yesterday morning. I couldn't sleep. It was still nighttime, really. I went outside for some fresh air and saw a light in the trees. A flashlight. I followed it."

"Don't you watch horror movies?"

"You sound like my mother," Clare says. "She used to accuse me of being reckless. Anyway, Markus was there. He invited me down. Didn't seem terribly upset that I'd come across it. He told me Sally'd found him there too. He hides baby formula. His daughter's not growing well and he's feeding her the formula behind his wife's back."

"Come on," Somers says with a sharp laugh. "This was yesterday? Before you came in to see us?"

"I know, I know," Clare says. "I should have told you then. I'm sorry. I haven't had the best experience with cops in my life."

"Neither have I," Somers says. "What else was down there?"

"Shelves, some canned goods. Bare bulbs, a couch. A gun rack. It was creepy."

"You can't make this shit up," Somers says. "Can you give me any sense of where this thing is?"

"It's inland, in the trees." Clare cranes her head in its direction. "That way. About a quarter mile from the house if you draw a line parallel to the river. I think it's nearly impossible to spot."

"We have our techniques," Somers says.

"I was hopeful until today," Clare says. "I thought maybe Sally had escaped again. Gotten away."

"Nothing makes sense about this case. A team has been scouring the river looking for the bodies. Nothing's been found. To say that it's unusual for the kid to turn up now is a serious understatement."

"I know. He could have snagged, though. You never know."

"Nope," Somers says. "You're right. You never know."

There is much more Clare could confide. The pregnancy test Ginny spoke of, the symptoms. Helen's offer to make her disappear. But the last thing Clare wants is to end up in the interrogation room again. Maybe she trusts Somers, but she can't bear Rourke's scrutiny again. And she feels ownership over this case. If Sally is alive, Clare wants to be the one to find her. She will save the other details for now.

"We've offered to put everyone up in a hotel in town," Somers says. "You'll all have to vacate."

"Ginny Haines wants me to stay at her dorm with her. I could use the company. I think she could too."

"That number you gave me yesterday? The area code's not local to Sally's hometown."

Clare's mind races. "It wouldn't be. I don't live there anymore. I left a while ago."

"Rourke made a call," Somers says. "To some contacts back home. Your hometown, I mean. Sally's hometown. The detachment out that way is doing some groundwork for us."

The river's current makes Clare's head spin. She knows what Somers will say next.

"No one remembers Sally having a friend named Clare."

"No," Clare says. "They wouldn't."

"Is that not your name?"

The lies are knocking up against each other now, Clare thinks. It is becoming too much.

"It's not my real name," Clare says. "Sally and I didn't know each other well back then. Just in passing. But we met again . . . at a shelter. We had similar reasons for being there, if you catch my drift. I changed my name. Sally didn't change hers. Maybe that was her mistake."

"Got it," Somers says, calm. "Okay. You could have told me that yesterday too."

"Like I said, I haven't had the best experiences. Maybe if Rourke hadn't been there I would have told you."

Clare looks at Somers straight in the eye, holding steady. Perhaps an understanding has formed between her and Somers, but Clare can still envision the precise way Rourke sized her up yesterday, as though he knew she was an imposter and was waiting for Clare to slip up. Behind them a car door slams and Jordan Haines makes his way across the lawn. Somers raises an upturned hand to catch the first drops of rain.

"Where's Helen?" Jordan asks.

"Everyone's inside," Somers says. "Rourke and I need to ask you a few questions."

"Right. Okay." Jordan looks to Clare. "Ginny says you're going to stay at her dorm? Is that so?"

"I guess," Clare says.

The rain begins in earnest and the three of them dash to the porch. Jordan goes inside, leaving Clare and Somers alone.

"I've got to get in there," Somers says. "You know how to reach me."

"I do."

"I appreciate your help. The info. I won't let anyone know where I got it from." Somers grins. "Especially Rourke."

Once Somers is inside, Clare sits on the porch and watches

the rain come down in hard pelts. The sheet they'd used to cover the boy is still on the grass, flattened under the weight of the rain. There it is again, Clare thinks, the tightness in her chest. The anxiety. It amazes her how clearheaded she feels since arriving here, how on task. It amazes her too how muddled everything remains from before she arrived. For so long she'd used pills or whatever else was on offer as a means to dull her senses and forget. But now Clare knows she must keep track of every detail here in High River, every conversation and tidbit exchanged. Every lie told, even her own. Somers might be onto her, others too. She must stay sharp. If she is to find Sally, she has nothing but her wits to stay ahead of them.

C lare counts the seconds between the flash of lightning and the crack of thunder. Four. Ginny should be back by now.

The dorm room is dark but for the round light of the desk lamp. Ginny's half of the room is crowded with the objects of youth—concert posters, an open armoire stuffed with crumpled clothes, a new laptop on the desk surrounded by piles of novels and textbooks. The other side of the room is bare. Clare leans in to examine the photos pinned to Ginny's corkboard. Selfies with a mishmash of friends, a shot of her with Markus and Rebecca's daughter, Willow, one of Ginny holding a placard at a protest. Clare startles when the thunder cracks again.

The door kicks open and Ginny falls into the room in playful distress, her clothing soaked through. She cradles two plastics bags to her chest.

"Success," she says.

Ginny unloads the supplies onto the desk. Packaged sushi, cola, a small bottle of rum. Then she peels her clothes off into a wet pile on the floor. Though she'd seen her in the tub yesterday, Clare is still awed by the youthfulness of Ginny's body, her skin creamy and even, the lanky proportions. Ginny digs a blue minidress from the armoire and pulls it on, shaking her short hair dry.

"If it's too crowded in here I could still take Somers up on the hotel offer," Clare says.

"Nope. You're my prisoner. I have a sleeping bag you can use. It's clean. Mostly." Ginny digs through the armoire and pulls out a pair of shorts and a gauzy T-shirt. She throws them to Clare. "Change. You look wet too."

"I have my own clothes."

"Uh, yeah. Army issue. Try on some style." Ginny reaches into her purse and pulls out a baggie of colorful pills. "Oh, and I made a pit stop to see my friend. Remember the friend I mentioned? The one who loves me? I told him I had a special visitor."

"I don't want any," Clare says.

"Oh, relax. You don't owe me anything. He gave them to me." Ginny winks. "For free, kind of."

"Really," Clare says. "I don't want it."

Ginny plops onto her bed and tears open the sushi. "Can we at least smoke a joint? There's a party later and I need something to calm me down." She angles one ear to her shoulder to stretch the tendons in her neck. "Every time I close my eyes I see that baby boy lying on the grass."

The rain slaps against the window. Clare sits on the bed opposite Ginny and watches as she crushes the marijuana leaves between her thumb and forefinger, then sprinkles them onto the rolling paper. Ginny edges to the window before lighting the joint. She takes a long drag and passes it to Clare.

"The river will be bad tomorrow," Ginny says, holding the smoke in her lungs. "Too much rain."

The joint is hot between Clare's fingers. Jason hated smoking joints, and so they rarely did. What Clare would give to feel the heaviness of the high, the dulling of her thoughts. Ginny doesn't seem to notice that Clare passes it back without inhaling.

"What was it like growing up in High River?" Clare asks.

"*So* not my vibe. Maybe Helen will finally come to her senses now. Ditch it. Get a fucking life." Ginny reaches out to tap Clare's knee. "Listen. I'm sorry about yesterday. About being such a bitch to you in the car."

"It's okay."

"You know how they say that men who grow up with strong moms end up, like, hating feminists?"

"Do they say that?" Clare lies back on the bed, her head in the crook of her bent arm. "I don't think anyone has ever said that."

"Whatever. I used to really resent the women staying with us. Like Helen always had something to prove. This revolving door of women and children. These sad cases. My mom being everyone's savior while I'm busy trying to figure out how to make myself a bowl of oatmeal, you know? It basically ruined my childhood."

"You never call her mom."

"No, I don't. Helen's thing was about me being independent. She refused to baby me. It kind of bordered on neglect."

"She was your age when she had you."

"Yeah," Ginny says. "She most definitely didn't care when I stopped calling her mom. It was like she needed me to be fierce, to take care of myself so she could take care of everyone else."

"You might end up thanking her one day," Clare says.

Ginny pinches the remnants of the joint to her mouth, then drops it into a dusty glass of water on her desk.

"Maybe. Jordan says I'm heartless."

"How old were you when your uncle Markus met Rebecca?"

"I don't know. Fifteen? He moved away when I was eight or nine. He became this family ghost. This East Coast high roller who never visited us once. Those were the golden years, I'm telling you. You know that creepy weirdo at the back of class who you think could open fire from a clock tower or something? Markus is that guy. Jordan, on the other hand, is this star. Growing up, he was captain of everything from the basketball team to the debating club. Being his cute little niece was serious currency out there. It still is."

"How long was Markus gone?"

"Five years? He came crawling back to Helen with nothing when I was maybe thirteen. A hobo with a 'the recession stole everything from me' sob story. She built him that fucking cottage across the river. Then he met Rebecca on some website for loser health nut singles and here we are."

"Why don't Markus and Jordan get along?" Clare asks.

"I don't know," Ginny says. "They literally act like the other doesn't exist."

In the expressiveness of her answers it's clear that Ginny is enjoying the line of questioning, the interest in her side of things. It must be, Clare thinks, that she is unaccustomed to being asked her opinion when it comes to family matters. Or that she's high. Either way, Clare will press until Ginny's interest wanes.

"And you don't like Rebecca," Clare says.

Ginny pops a piece of sushi in her mouth. "She's so fake. They're both so fake. Her and Markus. Rebecca will tell you never to judge your fellow human, that we're all walking our own path, blah blah. And she'll say it all in Latin. She'll tell you that she's one with nature. But I swear she'd murder your child if you crossed her."

Clare raises her eyebrows. Ginny slaps her hands to her mouth.

"Sorry. That came out wrong. But Sally crossed her. Obviously."

The rain has tapered, the thunder a low rumble in the distance. Clare thinks of the small body lifted onto a stretcher twice too long for it, the grave look on the faces of the two men loading it into the ambulance.

"To be clear," Ginny says, reaching for the makeup bag at the foot of her bed and unscrewing the cap from a bright pink lipstick. "Rebecca's a bad person and I'm pretty sure her husband knocked Sally up. But she wouldn't actually kill anyone's kid."

"Can I ask you something? What do *you* think happened to Sally?"

Ginny furrows her brow, thoughtful. "Honestly? I don't think she's dead. William is. Obviously. But I still think she's alive. I don't even know why. I just do." Ginny pauses. "You're basically the first person to ask me that."

"Ask you what?"

"What I think happened. Somers and Rourke, they asked me where I was that night. Cursory questions, like they were trying to make me feel included. Rourke gave me his card, told me to call him anytime. But he was just being nice. It's like people don't realize how firmly I've got my ear to the ground. When you're the only normal person in a place like that you really notice the kind of shit people are trying to pull. No one else notices because they're too wrapped up in their own mess."

"Somers and Rourke would hear you out if you have anything to tell them," Clare says. "Like, say, what you told me about Sally and the pregnancy test."

"They should know to ask me."

That makes no sense, Clare wants to say, but Ginny is already standing in front of the full-length mirror on the armoire door, applying the lipstick then patting it and rubbing it into her cheeks. Ginny's phone rings on the desk. She checks it.

"He's picking me up in a cab in five minutes."

"Who is?"

"A guy from my program. He's got a line on some party." Ginny doesn't look up from her phone. "Do you want to come?"

"I'm fine here. If that's okay."

"If you want. There's a sleeping bag in the armoire. A pillowcase too."

"Do you mind if I use your laptop? I need to check my e-mail."

"Go ahead. There's no password. Just don't look at any porn on my account. I swear the campus priest will show up." Ginny twirls. "How do I look?"

"Beautiful."

"I hate that word," Ginny says, rolling her eyes, the hint of a smile. She scribbles two numbers onto a scrap of paper on the desk. "That's my cell phone. And that's Jordan's. Don't wait up." She points to the pills. "And don't OD while I'm out, okay? The last thing I need is another dead body on my hands."

And then she's gone, the door slamming behind her. Is it resilience that has allowed Ginny to recover so quickly from today's events? Or is it something else? The drugs. Indifference. Clare digs a bottle of water from her backpack and gulps it, then piles the remaining sushi rolls into her mouth. She opens the laptop and watches dumbly as it powers on. It's been months since Clare sat at a computer. She hovers her fingers over the keyboard, uncertain as to where to start.

Colin Rourke Detective

The screen fills with news stories. She clicks on a link about a murder case, a younger Rourke standing behind yellow tape, his suit loose on his frame. Down the page she finds more of the same. Deep in the results, she finds an article from ten years earlier. "Promising Local Athlete Granted Ivy League Scholarship." The photo is of a teenaged Rourke in a baseball uniform, squinting in the sun. Clare leans to the screen to study it before typing again.

Hollis Somers Detective

Page after page of news stories, citations and commendations, cases solved, court testimonies. A photograph of Somers at an awards ceremony a few years ago, Officer of the Year, flanked by a beaming husband, a son and two daughters with wide smiles too. The photograph pulls at something in Clare. Imagine, she thinks, arriving on scene to the horrors of a dead little boy, then returning home later to your own family.

Clare clears the search history. *Think.*

Malcolm Boon Wife Missing

A mishmash of stories pop up. Clare switches from news to images as she scrolls. Photos of missing women with fathers or husbands named Malcolm, the sheer volume overwhelming. How many women go missing in a day? She knows Boon isn't his real name. Still, as she clicks randomly from one story to the next, it amazes Clare that it's taken her until now to even try searching. Fifteen minutes pass before she clears the history to try again. She types Clare O'Dey, then deletes it before hitting enter. Then Clare O'Callaghan. Delete. She can't bear to read her own story, or Jason's recounting of it, whatever version is to be found online. She doesn't want to see the faces from Blackmore. No good will come from searching these things. She types again.

Private Investigator Missing Women

This time the results are mostly advertisements with a few news stories mixed in. Each link she clicks reveals an elaborate website, often with a lengthy biography of the private investigator, mostly retired police officers with unsmiling head shots and a long list of specialties and success stories. It takes until the bottom of the fifth results page for Clare to see something that stops her in her tracks. She clicks through to a single home page, black but for a few lines in white at its center.

Has Someone You Love Disappeared?
Private Investigator for hire. Specializes in missing persons.
Discreet methods. Anonymity. Proven record. Guaranteed results.

Clare stares at the screen until her eyes itch. No number is provided, only a generic e-mail address, but in her gut she is certain this is Malcolm's site. She can imagine Jason typing in similar search words and scrolling to this page. She thinks of how Malcolm might have responded. The exchanges between them. Jason providing him with Clare's photograph, copies of her identification. What did Malcolm see when he first looked at those photos of her?

The clock reads 11:40 p.m. Though it feels like only minutes have passed, Clare has been sitting at the computer for two hours. She clicks through Ginny's files, opening essays and assignments, nothing of interest. Then she clears the history and closes the laptop. Her throat aches with every swallow. Outside, the rain has stopped. The campus green is vast and dotted with circles of white light from lampposts along the path that bisects it. At its center is a statue of a man on a horse, a sword high in the air, a bench facing it. Ginny has left the baggie of pills on the desk. Clare steps out of view from the window and changes into the clothes Ginny left for her. The shorts fit, loose silk hemmed to rest high above her knee. Clare stands in front of the mirror. She is surprised by the sensation of her bare legs against the air-conditioning shooting from the grate above her, her thighs coated with goose bumps. Ginny left her lipstick behind. Clare dabs it on her finger, then traces her lips, rubbing the remnants into her cheeks as Ginny had done. Then she digs in her bag for her phone and thumbs a text.

In town, on college campus. I know it's late but can you meet?

Clare wonders where he might be at this hour, whether he's alone. His response comes after only a few beats.

Where?

Clare holds her hand to her mouth. She might not have been expecting him to answer.

Statue at center of main lawn? she types.

OK, comes his response. **20 mins.**

C lare sits on a bench across from the statue and watches the empty parking lot beyond the green, waiting for the double beam of his headlights. She counts her inhales to steady herself. It will be almost midnight by the time he gets here.

The bench is patched wet with rain. Clare sets her hand down in one of the puddles, the water warm to her touch. She sees herself in the bathtub of the motel room, her knees bent, the water not covering her breasts no matter how low she sank. The bathroom door was closed. Why would she have closed it? Malcolm must have been on the other side.

"Clare?"

The voice comes from behind her. Clare jumps to her feet. Malcolm stands, hands in his pocket, a folder tucked under his arm. He wears shorts and an army gray T-shirt, so casual, and he smiles in a way that baffles Clare.

"I didn't mean to scare you," he says. Is that a slur in his voice?

"Didn't you drive here? I was watching the parking lot."

"I walked," Malcolm says.

"From where?"

Malcolm circles the bench and sits. Clare backs up towards the statue, adjusting her posture to account for the clothes Ginny gave her, her legs bare, the shirt cut so that a band of her bare waist is revealed if she lifts her arms. Malcolm studies her, eyes glazed.

"Have you been drinking?" Clare asks.

"I have a folder for you. Full of goodies."

"Goodies? What is wrong with you?"

Malcolm cranes to absorb his surroundings, the empty campus.

"Sit," he says, patting the bench next to him.

"No," Clare says, backing up again until she lands against the granite of the statue's base.

"There were statues like this all over campus when I was in school," Malcolm says. "I never understood it."

"Understood what?"

"Monuments. To war."

There is ten feet between them, Malcolm's shoulders slumped, his skin tanned against the gray of his shirt. Clare wants to be angry with him, but there is a swirl of something else too. There is an ache in her chest. Malcolm looks at her, then gestures towards the dorm on the far side of the green.

"Why are you here again?" he asks.

"They've executed a search warrant at High River. We had to leave." Clare points to the single window lit at the building's center. "I'm staying with Virginia Haines. Ginny. Helen's daughter? She's an engineering student. She had a spare bed in her room."

"You made a friend," Malcolm says.

"What? No. Like I said, we had to leave." Clare sighs. "What's in the folder?"

"I found plenty on your friend Raylene. That Twining guy too, and Jordan Haines. Local heroes. Lots of stuff on the land expropriation. Planning and zoning applications. I can't see how any of it connects back to Sally, though."

"Because you know nothing about the case."

Malcolm sets the folder down, its edges wilting with moisture.

"The boy is all over the news," he says.

"I know. You said that earlier."

Clare waits for Malcolm to respond.

"What's wrong with you?" Clare asks again.

"Me?" Malcolm smiles. "I was just thinking. You're getting better at this job."

"You're drunk."

Malcolm stands and steps towards her. Clare presses back into the statue until there's nowhere else to go.

"Why did you ask me to come?" he asks.

"I found your website," Clare says. "I was searching for you online. Searching for your wife."

Malcolm coughs. "You won't find anything."

"I might if I knew your real name."

"What exactly are you looking for?"

"Whatever it is you aren't telling me."

He steps closer and reaches out to rest his palm lightly on Clare's shoulder. The heat travels right through her shirt.

"Does it hurt?" Malcolm asks.

Don't touch me, Clare thinks to say. She can smell the sweetness of alcohol on his breath.

"Does it?" Malcolm repeats.

"What do you think?"

And then Malcolm is leaning, his hand gripped to the sol-
dier's boot. He is taller than her by half a foot, her eyes level
with his chin, his face angled down to hers. She could sidestep
to get out from under him, but instead Clare remains frozen
in place, this proximity too familiar.

"Do we not make a good team?" Malcolm says.

"We're not a team," Clare says. "I work for you. We're not
a team."

"You're something else, you know that?" Malcolm says.
"You owe me an apology."

There is a chiding to Malcolm's tone, a playfulness.

"For what?" Clare asks.

"You could have killed me."

Clare feels her whole body stiffen. She sees it, a gun in her
hand, Malcolm's face etched in fear. The motel room. *You could
have killed me*. Clare takes his wrist. She pulls her shirt down
to reveal the skin of her shoulder, then sets his thumb into
the crater of scar tissue over the bullet wound. Malcolm tries
to retract his hand, but Clare grips it fiercely in place.

"What do you think this is?" Clare presses his thumb down
harder. "Who did this to me?"

"Clare. Please."

"You did," Clare says. "I took a bullet for you."

"I never would have sent you if—"

"Don't," Clare says, her voice low. "It's way too late for
that. You could have let me go from the very start. You knew
all along. In Blackmore, here. You never cared about the job.
The job is a joke to you! You just want control. Right? Put
me in the line of fire so you don't have to be. You want to
control me. I took a bullet because I was working for you,
doing a job you were supposed to do. And then how long
were we at that motel? Weeks. You doling out the medication

like I'm some kind of child. It's just control. That's all it is. The gun? I aimed it at you to make a point. That you don't control me."

"No," Malcolm says. "You're not remembering clearly."

To her horror Clare feels a well of tears. In her marriage, Clare's memory was so often a jumble, whole days and nights erased by something she'd taken. *Don't you remember?* Jason would say. *You fell. You burned yourself on the pot. You hurt me.* The snippets that came back to her in flashes always contradicted what he'd said happened. Her entire marriage, Clare's memory failed her. Or at least Jason made her believe it did. Clare blinks tightly and allows rage to wash over her instead.

"Don't tell me what I do and don't remember," she says.

"I wanted to help you."

Clare laughs bitterly, swatting his hand away. "Was that the issue with your wife?" she says. "You couldn't control her? I bet you wanted to help her so badly but she wasn't having it! So . . . what? You killed her? Or did she run away from you? Is that why you do this? You're looking for your own wife and figured you'd make a job of it?"

"I would never, ever have hurt her." Malcolm steps back until he hits up against the bench. He sits.

"That's what men always say," Clare says. "I won't hurt you. But the words mean nothing. And now here you are, drunk. Drowning your sorrows. Your guilt."

The distance between them is wide enough for Clare to see the pained look on Malcolm's face. Her shoulder throbs. She thinks of the pills on the desk in Ginny's room, their colorful array, the relief they'd offer. No, she thinks. Stay sharp. Malcolm's eyes remain focused on the ground. Then, with a start, he straightens.

"What do you want?" he asks. "Do you want out?"

Clare shrugs, defiant.

"I offered you an out. At the motel. A straight out. Do you remember that?" Malcolm waits, but Clare doesn't speak. "See? That's the problem. You don't remember."

"I was taking the pills you were giving me. I remember that."

"You were hurt," Malcolm says. "I was helping you. If it wasn't for me you'd have—"

"Stop," Clare says, one hand up. "Stop talking."

"No. You need to listen to me, Clare. The pills made everything worse. You weren't yourself. I felt responsible for that. I gave you a choice. You wanted to come here. You wanted to work this case. You said you were ready."

"I want you to tell me the truth," Clare says.

"I am telling you the truth."

"No. I mean the truth about you. Something changed. At the motel. You were taking calls. I remember. I know they weren't about this case. Or about Blackmore. Something happened. You need to tell me what."

"I can't," Malcolm says, standing. He approaches Clare again, this time stopping just short of her. She follows his gaze upward. The clouds have split to reveal hazy clusters of stars.

"Are you in danger? Am I in danger?" Clare asks.

"I need you to trust me, Clare. I haven't hurt anyone. I'm trying to protect you."

"Come on. You're protecting yourself. Not me."

"You're good at this job. I want you to know that. We've . . . You just have to trust me. I can't tell you anything yet. I need some time to . . ."

Malcolm scratches his head, one hand in his pocket, looking lost.

"Give it to me," she says, extending her hand. "Give me the folder."

"Clare."

"Give me the folder."

"You asked me to come here, Clare. I wasn't expecting this. I want—"

"Give it to me!"

Malcolm returns to the bench to collect the folder. She snatches it from him without making eye contact. It's a coping mechanism, Clare's mother used to say to her. You're hard as a rock when you need to be. Malcolm waits for Clare to speak. But she doesn't. She takes a wide berth around him so that he cannot reach out to stop her from walking away.

"Clare," he says. "Please."

Through her sandals Clare can feel the dew forming on the grass of the campus green. Ginny's dorm room beckons her with its square of yellow light. Clare hugs the folder to her chest. She knows Malcolm is watching her. She can feel it. But she won't turn around, even if he calls after her again. She'll keep walking, holding whatever power is to be had by not looking back.

WEDNESDAY

The sleeping bag wraps Clare like a straitjacket. She pries hard against it, wriggling to sit up on the small bed.

"Ginny?"

No answer. The dorm room glows with hot morning sun. Nine o'clock. What time did she fall asleep? Clare stumbles to the bathroom and drinks three glasses of water in quick succession. She looks in the mirror. Her cheeks are flushed crimson. She is still wearing the clothes Ginny gave her yesterday.

"Ginny?" Clare opens the door to the hallway and peers left to right. Did Ginny come home? She searches the room for signs. Was her bed made last night? On the desk Clare finds the paper with Jordan and Ginny's cell phone numbers, scribbled in pink highlighter as a child would have done. She's fine, Clare thinks. She probably just went out for a coffee. Some food.

In the bathroom Clare locks the door and strips. Her body hums with energy as she steps under the cold shower stream. Her shoulder tingles. She allows herself two minutes under the stream before turning off the tap. She listens.

"Ginny?" she calls again.

Clare steps out of the shower and stands in front of the full-length mirror, assessing her naked body. She can picture Malcolm watching her from the bench last night. The warmth of his breath on her cheek as he leaned in. How unfamiliar her own reflection seems, her cheeks more concave. The red circle on her shoulder, a bull's-eye of scar tissue. When did she get so thin?

Her clothes hang on the radiator under the window. The bag of pills is still on Ginny's desk. Blue to relax you, pink to lift you. The white ones you can never be sure. *A surprise,* Jason would say, easing her mouth open by the chin to tuck one behind her lower lip. Clare grips the bag in her hand. Is it waning, she wonders, the urge to take one? It must be. There was once a Clare who would never have resisted this bounty. But now she needs to stay alert. To find Ginny. She digs her dead cell phone from the bottom of her duffel bag, which she realizes she'd forgotten to lock. Surely she'd have woken if Ginny had come home, had attempted to go through it. She finds the charger too and plugs it in. The file Malcolm gave her peeks out carelessly from under the laptop.

Clare sits at the desk and opens the file. The volume is overwhelming, three stacks paper-clipped together. The first are stories about Jordan and Philip Twining. In the top article they stand in a city alley facing the camera, Jordan with his hands in the pocket of his suit, tie loose. "Local Lawyers Take Up Legacy of Women's Causes." Lobbying, the article says, to have the city build a shelter on the abandoned lot next to their office. Working with local developers. A passion born from personal tragedy.

The second stack is articles about Raylene. "Prominent ER Doctor's Husband Not Guilty in Manslaughter Death of Twin Children." The most recent article shows an old family photograph, Raylene and her husband each with a smiling twin in their arms, an autumn scene of colorful leaves behind them. Clare studies the photograph closely. Raylene looks fifteen years younger, though Clare knows this shot is probably only five years old.

Under the desk Clare finds a plastic bag and puts the folder in it, securing it with an elastic band before depositing it in her bag. There is a strange fervor to each of her gestures. In three days she has gathered a lot of information. Made connections. Gone undercover by balancing her own truth with this false identity. But the largest pieces to this puzzle are still missing and it fills Clare with an energy unfamiliar to her. A spark. Something to harness. She lifts her phone and watches it come to life, then dials Ginny's number. The call is answered on the first ring.

"Hello?"

"Hi, Ginny. It's Clare."

"Why is your number blocked?"

"I don't like sharing it," Clare says. "You didn't come back last night."

"Aw," Ginny says. "That's so sweet. Were you worried?"

"Where are you?" Clare asks.

"Relax. I'm at Jordan's. I'd have texted you but you didn't give me your number. Your *blocked* number."

"Why didn't you just come back?"

Ginny sighs. "Very long story. Why don't you cab over here? I'll make brunch. I'll tell you all the sordid details."

"Is Jordan there?"

"Maybe. What do you care?"

"I don't," Clare says, surprised by the childish bite to her tone. "Give me the address."

"He lives above his office. On the fourth floor. Do you remember how to get here?"

"Yes. What suite?"

"The entire floor," Ginny says, drawling. "I get to buzz you up on his private elevator."

"Okay," Clare says. "I'll be there soon."

After hanging up Clare looks out the window at the empty campus green, at the distant statue and bench facing it where she'd met Malcolm last night. A lone figure appears from behind it and cuts across the lawn towards the dorm building. He looks up and waves, though surely he is too far away to see her. No. He wears a hat but curls of blond peek through around his ears. His gait lumbering but confident, as it has always been. The white T-shirt with the V at the neck, jeans despite the heat. Clare collects her duffel bag from the bed and throws in her phone and charger. She snatches the baggie of pills from the desk and drops it in the front pocket of her bag.

The figure out the window now jogs across the green. Clare watches him, her heart thudding against her chest. It surprises her when she starts to cry, the tears running freely down her cheeks, and soon she cannot catch her breath. She leans her forehead on the window. The man stands on the pathway right below her. He is waiting for someone. Then Clare sees her, a young woman in a sundress clutching her bag as she runs to him. He opens his arms to her and they embrace. The woman removes his hat and tousles his hair, not blond at all, not as curly as she'd thought from afar.

Of course it is not Jason. Clare wipes her tears and looks

down to the couple again. As she watches them kiss, Clare feels a painful shame, a loathing that clenches her fists until her nails pierce her palms. In the months since she left, some tiny part of Clare has imagined their reunion as a relief. The end of a long and lonely and terrifying escape. But, no. That tiny part of Clare is always overridden by the part that hopes she never lays eyes on Jason O'Callaghan again. So how could it be, Clare thinks, that in the fear and the rage she'd felt in mistaking this man for Jason, there had been a twinge of longing too?

The heavy dorm door swings open and Clare steps outside to get her bearings. Clare turns her face up to the bright sky. Already this day is too hot, the sun too glaring.

"Clare?"

A man leans against the building to Clare's left. She squints. Rourke.

"What are you doing here?" she asks.

"I was on my way out to High River. Thought I'd check in."

"How'd you know where I was?"

Rourke smiles. "We keep track of where all High River residents are staying while we execute the search."

"Right. Ginny's not here."

"I know she isn't," Rourke says. "Where are you headed?"

"To Jordan's place. To meet Ginny, actually. I was about to look for a cab."

"I could drive you."

"It's out of the way, isn't it?"

"Not by much," he says.

Rourke is flushed, the veins in his temples popped. He did not shave this morning, but his shirt is pressed. Clare can see the outline of a white tank top underneath its fabric. The half-smile he wears when answering her questions riles Clare in a way she can't understand.

"Come on," he says. "I'm broiling. Let's go."

"Okay," Clare says. "Thank you."

At the squad car Clare can feel the passing students watching her as she lowers into the passenger seat. Though the air conditioner blasts, the leather of the seat boils against her legs. A computer is mounted in the space between them, a CB radio fixed to the dash. They pull out of the parking lot and onto the main campus road. The radio screeches street names and intersections, call numbers Clare knows only from the cop shows. Behind her, scratched plexiglass separates the backseat from the front. When she peers over her shoulder Clare notices that the back doors have no handles. Rourke notes her curiosity with a grin.

"You ever been in the backseat of a cruiser?" When Clare doesn't answer, he drops the grin. "Sorry. That wasn't a very sensitive question."

"You know the way to Jordan's?"

"I was there last night, actually."

"Oh?"

"Ginny called me around midnight. Asked me to pick her up."

"Pick her up where?"

"She was at some rave in an abandoned warehouse. I guess some guy was following her around, creeping her out."

"So she called the police?"

"Not the police," Rourke says. "She called me. I gave her my cell phone number when we did the first round of interviews. I felt like she wanted to tell me something but couldn't. Or wouldn't. Thought I could befriend her a bit to squeeze it out of her. Encourage her, you know. Whatever she knows. She seemed to like the attention. Didn't figure she'd use me for a cab service."

Rourke places his arm on Clare's headrest and cranes to back out of the parking spot. He has the sort of face that would draw in a young woman like Ginny. Brooding, angular, older. Handsome. It takes a certain kind of man, Clare thinks, to take advantage of such a youthful crush.

"Why wouldn't she call Jordan to pick her up?" Clare asks.

"She said she couldn't reach him. He wasn't home when I dropped her off. Or he was sound asleep. I didn't see him."

"She invited you in?"

"I took her up the elevator. It opened, she stepped out." Rourke shoots Clare a jesting glance. "Don't worry. I'm aware that I'm a cop and she's just a kid."

"I don't know if she's aware," Clare says.

Out the cruiser window Clare watches the scattering of summer students, backpacks and earphones on, faces dipped to their phones. They reach the far side of the campus green. Clare rubs the back of her neck and looks to the statue where she'd stood so close to Malcolm yesterday. She pinches her backpack between her feet. What if Rourke asks her to open it? The file within it. The pills. The cell phone, the undeleted messages from Malcolm.

"You must be busy right now," Clare says. "I appreciate the lift."

"Autopsy's today." Rourke looks at his watch. "Right now, actually. Last night the coroner seemed . . . disturbed."

"A dead boy is disturbing."

"She's a coroner. She's seen it all. *Perplexed* is a better word. There were some anomalies."

If it were Somers driving her right now, Clare thinks, she would tell her what Raylene said about the boy's body and how he didn't drown. But she distrusts Rourke, a gut feeling that tells Clare to keep it to herself. They stop at a red light.

"Where's Somers?" Clare asks.

"At the precinct. She's on paperwork today. I'm on warrant duty." Rourke frowns and bites at his thumbnail. "When a body suddenly turns up in a place we combed over, the details are important. You never know what clue is going to lead you places. For one, the woman who found him shouldn't have moved him."

"You mean Raylene?"

"She should have left him there. There was no question about whether or not he was breathing."

Clare feels her skin prickle. "Would you have left a little boy underwater?"

A cyclist veers ahead of them and Rourke hits the brakes, swinging his arm to press Clare back into her seat, his hand landing on her breast. He retracts it at once.

"Sorry," he says. "Close call."

Clare nods without looking Rourke's way. He's too attentive, she thinks. It feels wrong. Forced. They turn out of the campus gates onto a four-lane road choked with morning traffic. Chilled, Clare fiddles with the vents to redirect the cold air away from her. Rourke wears his holster on his right hip, his gun within her reach. In a flash Clare sees Malcolm against the wall in the motel room, one hand raised. He is speaking to her. What is he saying? *Don't.*

"It must be awful for you," Rourke says, drawing Clare back to the present.

"What must be?"

"A friend gone missing. And then her boy found like that. Knowing that she reached out to you. That you didn't come soon enough. That's tough."

"It is tough," Clare says. "What else would it be?"

"I didn't mean it that way. What I meant is that I'm sorry you're going through this. I'm sorry you had to see that yesterday."

"So am I," Clare says. "Thank you."

For several minutes they edge along in traffic. Rourke flicks his sirens briefly to nudge the car in front of him forward so he can cut down an alley. They emerge a block later on a street devoid of traffic.

"Sometimes I think about packing it all in and taking off," Rourke says.

"Excuse me?"

He gestures to the traffic. "Leaving the city. Moving to some small town where it doesn't take twenty minutes to drive a block. You ever think about that? Jumping ship? Disappearing?"

Clare's ears buzz. She can't decode his tone. What bothers her about Rourke is not his attentiveness, his smiles or casual questions. The shared details, as though drawing her in. What disconcerts Clare is the prospect that he knows far more about her than he lets on. That he is toying with her. She takes a deep breath and shrugs instead of answering.

"I guess that was another insensitive question," Rourke says. "Given, you know. High River."

"Sally had every reason to jump ship," Clare says. "From her old life. Whether she jumped ship at High River, we don't know yet. Do we?"

"Her husband doesn't seem like a stand-up guy. He's got charges a mile long."

"Have you questioned him?"

"We got a local cop to do it. He was in jail the night Sally disappeared. Didn't post bail until two days later. There's a whole night's worth of footage of him wallowing in the holding cell. That's a pretty airtight alibi."

Clare thinks of Malcolm all those weeks ago in that roadside café, the weeks he'd spent closing in on her, the photos of her that Jason provided in the briefcase that rested at Malcolm's feet. Clare knew why he was there the moment she laid eyes on him. She'd felt certain in watching him across the café. He was there for *her*. Jason had sent him. The same could be true with Sally.

"Sally's husband could have hired someone else to do his dirty work," Clare says.

"Maybe," Rourke says. "The cop who interviewed him said he wasn't too bright. I'm not sure he'd be that sophisticated in his revenge. Plus his new fiancée was the one to bail him out of jail. Seems like he's moved on from Sally. But"—Rourke scratches at his stubble—"if nothing turns up in the next few days I might take a drive down and question him myself. Because you never know."

The cruiser slows on a street Clare recognizes. Up ahead she sees the construction site, the building. TWINING & HAINES BARRISTERS AND SOLICITORS. Clare looks up. The entire fourth floor, Ginny told her. They pull over in front of a construction site next door. JJ & SONS CONSTRUCTION LIMITED. Clare thinks of the article in the folder, Jordan and Philip Twining in the alley next to the abandoned lot.

"The builders," Clare says. "JJ & Sons? I noticed a sign for them out by High River too."

"Yep," Rourke says. "They've got a lock on pretty much every major construction project within twenty miles of the city."

"A shelter seems pretty small-time, then. For such a big operation."

"Maybe. Maybe it's a charity thing," Rourke says, tapping at the steering wheel. "He's an enigma, that Jordan Haines."

"How so?"

"Rich lawyer. Single guy, good-looking. Owns that whole building. Lives in this huge loft upstairs. And he's throwing all his coin into a shelter for abused women."

"His father shot his mother to death," Clare says. "That's a pretty valid driving force."

"Yeah," Rourke says. "My parents both died of cancer. For some reason I'm not donating every paycheck to find a cure."

"It's not the same thing."

"Maybe it isn't," Rourke says.

The radio squeals again. Rourke flips open the computer and frowns at it. The dash clock reads 10:00 a.m. Clare grips the handle and waits for Rourke to unlock the door.

"Thank you for the lift," Clare says. "I know you've got a long drive ahead of you."

"No trouble. Glad we could talk."

Clare collects her backpack and swings her legs to exit the cruiser.

"Hey," Rourke says, leaning over to touch her arm. "This case. It's a weird one. It's funny you arrived when you did."

"I should have come earlier," Clare says, careful not to shift her expression.

"Well. Who could have known?"

In the silence that follows Clare is certain there is more to his words. She searches his face for any glimmer, any notion of why he should fill her with the anxiety now whirring in her muscles. *He insisted on taking this case*, Somers said yesterday by the river.

"I should let you go," Clare says.

"You can call me," he says. "You have my card. I'm here to help. Say hi to Ginny for me."

"I will," Clare says.

Clare steps out and presses the cruiser door closed. The heat lands like a punch. Clare sways, light-headed, then gathers herself and walks to the door that leads to the upper floors of the building.

The elevator opens directly onto the sort of airy loft space Clare has seen only in magazines—huge windows and wide-plank wood floors. Ceilings two stories high. Ginny stands in front of Clare wearing a white T-shirt that must be Jordan's and, from what Clare can tell, nothing but underwear beneath.

"Ta-da!" Ginny says. "Hiya, stalker. Like my place?"

"It's beautiful. Is Jordan here?"

"You keep asking me that."

"Well," Clare says. "It's his place. And I'm in it."

"He's downstairs at work. Always working," she says. "I texted him to say you were coming. He'll be up in a minute."

Clare follows Ginny as she bounds to the oversized couch before taking a sharp turn to the kitchen. From the fourth floor the view out the window rises above the buildings across the street to a sweeping cityscape beyond them. South-facing. Clare sits on the couch and examines the space from her new vantage. The kitchen is industrial, metal and wood, a bar with

six stools. Along one wall, large sliding doors separate the bedrooms from the main space, along the other is an office with
an antique desk, a treadmill in the corner. The first floor of
Clare's old farmhouse would fit in this loft many times over.

"You hungry?" Ginny asks.

"I'd take a banana or something. Fruit."

"Catch," Ginny says, throwing an apple to Clare from such
a distance that she must brace for it, two-handed.

"Jordan's a stud, right?" Ginny sweeps her arm out to the
space, crossing the floor back to the couch.

Stud, Clare thinks. A strange way to reference your uncle.

"It's quite the place," Clare says. "Does he have a girlfriend?"

Ginny laughs. "Jordan? Um, no. Jordan likes dudes."

"Oh," Clare says, thinking of Jordan and Raylene embracing
early the other morning, Raylene's shoulders shaking as she
wept. How intimate it had seemed as Clare watched them
through the window. But maybe it was no more than one
friend comforting another. Or maybe it was something else, a
dynamic Clare cannot untangle in hindsight.

"I didn't know that . . . about him," Clare says.

"Of course you didn't. He comes off as straight so you assumed he was. That's what people do. They assume."

"Right," Clare says. "I guess I did. Does he have a boyfriend?"

"No. He's way too obsessed with work to bother with ro-
mance. He's obsessed with that stupid shelter. With making
sure Helen's okay. Too full of obsessions."

"Why wouldn't Helen be okay? I mean, aside from recent
events."

"She wants to sell the land to the developers. In her heart,
at least. Avoid the whole expropriation process. Jordan knows
she does. She needs to sell it and move on. But she's got so
much guilt. Guilt about women she doesn't even know. Guilt

about abandoning the land her mother loved so much and watching it get paved over by suburbia. So it's Jordan's job to convince her. And he's pretty fixated on convincing her."

"Why does he want to convince her?"

"He's been wining and dining with the developers for years. Calling in all kinds of favors because he's got this sweet land everyone wants."

"So the developers are building his shelter on the promise that they'll have dibs on the land?"

Ginny's eyes narrow. "Sounds kind of mafia when you put it that way."

"No," Clare says. "He could just be leveraging it to do good."

"Yeah." Ginny nods. "Exactly. Do you know how much that land is worth?"

"A lot, I'm sure."

"Forty million dollars. Half a million per acre. It's the only swath of untouched land left within twenty miles of downtown. It's basically made of gold."

"Forty million dollars," Clare repeats, picking at the peel of her apple. "Jesus."

"Jordan bought this building from Philip and Janice a few years ago when buildings were cheap. After the crash. It was a steal and they still gave it to him for less than it was worth. So it seems like Jordan's a high roller. But he's not. Not really. He and Helen bought Markus's share of the land a long time ago. When it was worth a tenth of what it is now, but it still strapped them to have to buy him out. Markus wanted to cash in his share and they had no choice. Jordan would have just sold the land outright then, but I was just a kid and Helen wanted to stay. I can remember Helen being so stressed about money for a while. Holding on to that land was hard for them. If they sell now, they both get super rich. Helen can find some other farmland somewhere or move to the city and get a real life. Jordan can build a shelter on every corner if his bleeding heart wants to."

"And Markus gets nothing," Clare says.

"Not a dime," Ginny says, mouthing the words again for effect. "And he gets turfed from his squatting grounds. But in the expropriation process he gets a stake because he lives on the land. He gets a settlement if they have to evict him. So it's way better for Markus if Helen refuses to sell and lets it go to the courts. Makes them take the land from her."

"That's really complicated," Clare says.

"You're telling me. Family. Right?"

Ginny flips over so she lies on the couch, her feet stretched up along the brick wall. Clare was never so comfortable in her own skin as Ginny seems to be. Even as a teenager she was acutely aware of showing her shape, of clothes that felt too tight. Hard as her mother would try to get Clare to wear skirts or dresses, sleeveless blouses, Clare always preferred loose and boyish. She feels her cheeks redden at the thought of the clothes she was wearing last night, whatever boldness had overtaken her in borrowing them. Braless in an oversized T-shirt, her legs bare against the wall, there is no shyness in how Ginny holds herself.

"I have these really early memories," Ginny says. "From when I was little. When we were all there. Helen, Jordan, Markus. Me. The four of us. It felt like we were a family. They'd come back to High River and were trying, you know. To live there. Jordan wasn't even eight and Helen was about to pop with me. It's crazy, because Markus and Helen were basically my age. But they had to be the adults. Running the show. Or Helen was, at least. Like I say, Markus was the resident weirdo."

"Helen had you," Clare says. "She had to be an adult."

"Markus used to babysit me. After he dropped out of college Helen started taking night classes. I don't think Markus ever really had a job. I remember us sitting in front of the TV watching these real estate shows, and he'd say he was going to make millions buying and selling property. Move to the big city and get rich. And famous." Ginny swings her legs back to the floor and edges closer to Clare on the couch. "This one time, he was babysitting me and I got really sick. I'd had an infection and I reacted to the medication. Instead of calling an ambulance he drove me to the hospital. Which makes sense." Ginny pauses. "It would have been faster to drive me himself. I remember that he let me sit in the front seat without my seat belt on. I remember the feeling of not being able to breathe."

"How old were you?" Clare asks.

"Seven."

"How scary."

"Yeah," Ginny says. "We pulled up to the emergency room and he carried me in, yelling for help. Shit, I was more scared by the way he was acting than by the fact that I couldn't breathe. The way he talked to the doctors. He waited so long to call Helen."

"Why would he wait to call her?"

"That's just Markus. When something crazy is going on, he wants to be right in the middle of it. I watched him from my stretcher. I had this oxygen mask on my face and he was standing by the nursing station, weeping his stupid face off. Going crazy. He wasn't trying to comfort me, though. It was all a show. I'm this little kid and I can't breathe and my fucking uncle is making a spectacle of himself for the doctors. He and Rebecca, you know? They're both so fake. Two-faced liars."

"What do you mean?" Clare asks. "Rebecca wouldn't have been there. You just said you were only seven."

To Clare's surprise Ginny slaps her hands to her face and begins to sob.

"I can't stop thinking about William. I can't. What the fuck is wrong with people?"

Clare collects a box of tissues from a side table and pulls out a wad. She pries one hand away from Ginny's face and dabs at the tears. How difficult would it be at Ginny's age, Clare thinks, to parse the details of your family's grievances, to make sense of why the adults around you behave as they do?

"Ginny," Clare says. "What does the story you just told me about Markus have to do with William?"

"Nothing," Ginny says, snatching her hand from Clare's grip. "Nothing."

"Do you think Markus could have hurt William?"

"No." Ginny sits up and sniffs, shaking her head briskly as if to cast off the tears. "Helen says he would never hurt a kid."

"Do you think Markus hurt you?"

"Who knows? Why don't you ask Helen?"

"Ask Helen what?" This is a man's voice.

Both Clare and Ginny turn to see Jordan standing by the open elevator. Ginny wipes her tears, then shoots Clare a look as if to silence her. She bounds to Jordan and rises to her tiptoes to kiss his cheek.

"You okay?" Jordan asks.

"Fine." Ginny turns her back to him. "Just hungover."

"I didn't hear you come in last night," he says.

"It was late. I forgot the key to my dorm room." Ginny points to Clare. "I didn't have her number to call and let me in. Thank God for your magic elevator and its secret codes."

"Your haven," he says, setting his satchel on the kitchen counter.

"I invited our friend over for brunch but all you have is fucking cereal and sour apples."

"I'm glad you're here," Jordan says to Clare. "I was hoping to talk to you today."

"Okay," Clare says.

"Maybe we can head down to the office after we're done with brunch?"

Clare nods. In the kitchen Jordan sits at one of the bar stools. Ginny circles behind the counter and fiddles with the coffee maker.

"Do I want to know where you went last night?" Jordan asks.

"I ended up at this random warehouse party on the outskirts," Ginny says. "You had to take these jagged rusty stairs to get in. The guy I was with abandoned me. I only knew one other guy there and he's got a bit of a serial killer vibe. So I escaped."

"Well." Jordan offers Clare a false smile. "I'm glad you made it here safely."

"It was remarkably easy to find a cab."

She is leaning into the fridge, so Clare cannot see the expression on Ginny's face. She cannot read the ease with which she just lied to Jordan. A cab. Of course Ginny wouldn't expect Clare to know that Rourke picked her up. Ginny sets out bowls and pours cereal for the three of them. Everything about her movements is so casual, so self-assured, no trace of the sadness choking her up only minutes ago, no trace of her deceptions. Ginny throws her head back in laughter at something Jordan is saying. *They're both so fake,* Ginny had said about Markus, about Rebecca. *Two-faced liars.* To bend the truth so boldly without flinching is a skill, Clare thinks. A skill that Ginny clearly has too. A skill that seems to run in the Haines family.

It feels like déjà vu to be sitting opposite Jordan's desk again, this time watching him sort through papers. He wears glasses Clare isn't certain he needs, the rims thick and black. After breakfast they'd left Ginny upstairs and taken the elevator down to the office at his request, leaving Ginny on the couch, absorbed by her phone.

"Ginny is lucky to have you," Clare says.

"I'm lucky to have her." He looks up over the rim of his glasses. "Give me a sec. I don't mean to hold you up. I just want to run something by you."

"I have nowhere I need to be," Clare says. "Not right now, anyway. At some point I'd like to go back to High River. At least to see Helen, if she's there. Until I can figure out next steps. But I'm not in a rush."

"I'm headed back there shortly," Jordan says. "You can come with Ginny and me. But next steps are actually what I want to talk to you about. Helen mentioned you might be considering other options. Ways to move on cleanly."

Cleanly, Clare thinks. An odd choice of word.

"I might be," Clare says.

"What if we started by giving you some new ID?" Jordan says. "Nothing too final."

"How is new identification not final?"

"You can choose whether you want to use it. Listen," Jordan says. "What if you retained me as your lawyer? No retainer or fees. No cost to you."

"Why do I need a lawyer?"

"That way anything we do, anything you tell me, is bound by privilege."

Clare rubs at her forehead. She thinks of the rudimentary identification Malcolm gave her before she left for Blackmore and again before coming to High River, the kit he used so basic that Clare couldn't believe the ID worked when it came time to flash it. Somehow she thinks Jordan Haines is capable of far more sophisticated work, that maybe she could benefit from having ID different from the one Malcolm provided. That maybe it would make her feel safer. Jordan slides a paper across the desk and sets a pen on top of it.

"This is a basic retainer," he says. "Just print and sign at the bottom."

What changes between them, Clare wonders, if she signs? Does it hold as a legal document if she isn't using her real name? Jordan watches her expectantly. She hovers the pen over the paper, thinking that she has yet to write *Clare O'Brien* on anything, that she never took the time to practice her signature. She holds the paper down and signs it with a flourish, the last name just an *O* with a squiggled line jutting from it.

"You hesitated," Jordan says.

"I like to read things first," Clare says. "Before I sign."

Next Jordan stands and pulls down a white screen on the

wall. He motions for Clare to step in front of it before collecting a camera from his desk drawer. Clare's own camera was left behind in the trailer in Blackmore, the one keepsake she'd taken with her when she left home, and the sight of this one fills her with an overwhelming dread. She stays in her chair.

I don't think I need ID just yet," Clare says.

"You might not. But it's good to have everything in place. A photograph. Authentic-looking ID can take some time to process."

"It seems too easy," Clare says. "To just create a new person."

"It's about knowing the right people," Jordan says. "About being willing to keep secrets. I'm good at it. Janice, Philip's wife, she was good at it too. Philip, not so much."

"Janice, Philip's wife. Where is she? I thought he said the other day that they were divorced."

"They are. Not by his choice. She got to the end of her rope."

"It was good of Janice and Philip to take you in after your parents died."

"That was all Janice. I get the impression Philip would have preferred the child-free way of life. He was good to us. But Janice was like a mother. The only one I knew, honestly."

"Are they still on good terms? Despite the divorce?"

"They aren't on any terms," Jordan says. "I get it. It doesn't come naturally to Philip to think about the people in his life. He's self-centered to a remarkable degree. I'm sure it was very hard being married to him. I think Janice kept her chin up for a lot of years, partly for our sakes. Once they adopted us, she probably felt like she couldn't leave. And then she stayed with him for decades even after Helen, Markus, and I moved out."

"Why did she finally leave?" Clare asks.

Jordan shrugs. "All I know is when she did, she ghosted him. Moved her things out, changed her cell phone number. Gone."

"But you know where she is?"

If he minds the question, there is no shift in his expression to show it.

"She's around. It's not like she ran away. She just cut him off. She was done. She wanted to live her own truth. But she keeps in touch with me. With Helen."

"Not Markus, though."

"I don't know who Markus keeps in touch with. We aren't close."

Clare gestures to the white screen.

"And Sally? Did you do this for her?"

"Helen said you might ask me that."

"Of course I'm asking you that," Clare says. "It's the whole reason I'm here. I want to know what happened to her."

Jordan leans back in his chair and smiles. He only seems to smile when he's displeased.

"I hope it doesn't bother you that Helen shared your story with me," he says. "The whole idea is that any story shared doesn't go beyond these walls. Whatever you tell me, or Philip, it stays here. I became a lawyer in part because I believe that keeping secrets is a virtue. Confidentiality. You could tell me anything about your life, confess to any crime, and I'm not going to tell the police. I'm your lawyer. My job is to help you, not turn you in."

"Isn't that breaking the law?" Clare asks.

The office door swings open, startling them both. It is Philip, his face red with anger, the underarms of his shirt tinted yellow.

"I wasn't expecting you in today," Jordan says. "You remember Clare?"

"You're something else," Philip says.

Jordan stands and circles his desk to shuttle Philip out of

the office. But Philip won't have it. He stops at the threshold and closes the door behind him.

"You're not supposed to make any promises to these people," Philip says sharply.

"Let's go to your office," Jordan says. "We can talk there. I'm headed out soon."

"I got a call from those lawyers today!" Philip raises his voice. "Do you know how angry they are? The dead boy could end this all."

What boy? Clare thinks. Surely he doesn't mean William. Jordan squeezes Philip's arm and yanks the office door open, guiding him down the hall. Clare can catch only a few barbed words of the muffled exchange through the wall. *Stop. Can't. Dead.* When her cell phone rings, Clare fumbles for it.

"Hello?" she answers.

"Clare. It's Somers. Where are you?"

"I'm at Jordan Haines's office."

"Is he there?"

"He's here. He's down the hall arguing with his partner."

"Listen," Somers says, "I was going to take a drive out to High River. I was wondering if you could join me." She pauses. "Just me. Not Rourke."

"Sure. Should I meet you at the precinct?"

"I'll come grab you. In twenty or so. Is that okay?"

"That's fine," Clare says. "I'll wait outside."

The conversation has moved to the office next door and dropped in volume now. Clare takes the pen from Jordan's desk and flips over the retainer to write a note on the back. *Somers called. Headed back to High River with her. See you there.* She sets the note on his desk and exits Jordan's office, cutting across the empty reception area and pressing the door open to the blinding heat of the street.

Clare. A voice.

Her heart lunges. Who is calling her name?

"Clare!"

This time it's perfectly clear. She follows the sound to the opening of an alleyway. Tucked into the shadow of the building is a figure. Malcolm. He wears the same shorts as yesterday, a golf shirt untucked, his briefcase in one hand. When she backs away he takes her by the arm and pulls her into the darkness.

"What is wrong with you?" she asks, tearing herself free from his grasp. "What are you doing here?"

"Listen," he says. "We need . . . You can't—"

"Somers will be here in a few minutes. The cop. You're going to blow our cover. *My* cover."

There is something desperate in Malcolm's body language, his eyes darting, weight shifting. He steps close enough that Clare can again feel his breath on her. It smells of mints.

"The police officer," Malcolm says, whispering. "The other one. You can't—"

"Can't what? Which police officer?"

"I went back to the campus this morning."

"Why didn't you text me?"

"Because I wasn't sure you'd answer me," Malcolm says. "After last night. I saw you in the parking lot. Getting into his squad car."

Malcolm's face is twisted in such a way that Clare wonders if he is holding back tears. A van turns down the alley. He presses himself back into the brick, pulling Clare closer. Her cheeks warm at the thought of Malcolm leaning into the statue last night, their faces inches apart. Now, in the light of day, she can see the thin lines around his eyes, the small dimple that forms in his cheek with the purse of his lips.

"The officer," Clare says. "His name is Colin Rourke. He's working the case. His partner is Somers."

The laugh that escapes Malcolm is short and shrill. He paces to the far side of the alley and back again. Clare is up against the brick, facing him.

"Colin Rourke." Malcolm shakes his head. "Working the case?"

"What? Why? Malcolm."

He doesn't answer. There is a puzzle in front of Clare, too many pieces still scattered, out of place. What has it been about Rourke since she first met him? His interest in her? What kind of questions has he been asking her? She presses her fingers to her temple.

"Do you know him?" she demands. "Detective Rourke? Do you know him, Malcolm?"

"Clare."

"You need to tell me."

"I don't expect you to come with me," he says.

"Come with you? Where? Malcolm—"

"That would be a bad idea."

"What are you talking about?"

"I'm not abandoning you. I know it's not over . . ." He trails off.

"Slow down for a second," Clare says, her voice rising. "Please tell me what you're talking about."

Malcolm steps even closer and boxes her in, his hands flat against the brick wall on either side of her. Clare can see the jagged path of the scar on his arm, the gnarled white of the tissue winding from elbow to wrist. The desperation in his eyes. She has seen it before, a man coming unhinged. Clare knows she must change her tack.

"Listen," Clare says. "You wanted to help me. You could have turned me in. But you didn't."

Malcolm offers a small shrug without looking up.

"And now you need to leave? But you won't tell me why."

"I can't tell you. I can't."

How formal he seemed in that first week in Blackmore, how robotic, devoid of emotion. Calm. A rendering of Malcolm so inverse to the man standing before her now, this tired and raw and scared soul who looks like a child in his efforts to stay composed. She tries again.

"What do you want from me?" she asks.

"Nothing."

"Do you want me to say thank you? Or sorry?"

"No," Malcolm says. "No. I want to say sorry to you."

"Then say it."

Malcolm edges closer, erasing the space between them.

"Say it," Clare says.

"I'm sorry." Malcolm looks right at her.

"For what?" Clare's voice is hoarse.

"I should have let you go. That first day. It feels so long ago. I thought I was giving you an option. A choice. There might have been another way."

Instinctively Clare presses her palm to his chest. His pulse is fast under her fingertips.

"I don't have a lot of time," she says. "Somers will be here any minute. Please tell me something. Anything. Am I in danger?"

"That officer," Malcolm says. "Rourke. He's not working this case. That's not why he's here."

"Do you know him? I don't understand what you're saying."

Malcolm looks to the ground.

"He has a partner," Clare says. "Somers. She's legit. I've been to the precinct. I saw his desk, his colleagues. And he's a real cop. He can't possibly be faking that part. He just transferred in from another precinct. So what is it? Malcolm. Please tell me. Please."

"I can't."

There is no way to discern it, the confused swirl of thoughts, where her loyalties should lie, where Malcolm's should lie, whether it makes sense to feel betrayed, angry. Scared. Clare sees Malcolm seated on the bed of the motel, concentrating. Close to her. She will try one more time.

"You asked me something," Clare says. "At the motel. You were changing my bandage. Do you remember that?"

"It doesn't matter," Malcolm says.

"Yes, it does. You asked if I felt hope. If I remembered what it felt like to feel hopeful. If I could imagine ever feeling that way again."

The words come back to Clare. She thinks of him reaching out to take hold of her arm, the way he'd loosened his grip on the bandage so that it fell to his lap. The way he lowered his head as he asked her about hope, unwilling to make eye contact. She thinks of her thumb edging along Malcolm's scar. Her palm on his chest. Touching him without shyness. She sees it fully now, how he'd leaned into her touch instead of pulling away. The hug between them. Malcolm's face as he pulled away, squeezing her hand. She sees the sorrow in the look he gave her then matching the one he gives her now.

"I said no," Clare continues. "I said I couldn't remember feeling hopeful. My answer was no. And you didn't say anything after that. Because I disappointed you. You thought I was going to say yes."

"He's dangerous," Malcolm says. "You need to stay away from him."

Clare feels her jaw clench. She reaches out and bunches the chest of Malcolm's shirt in her hand.

"If he's a threat to me," Clare says, "you need to tell me. You can't only protect yourself, Malcolm. You need to protect me too."

Malcolm snaps to attention, posture straight. He backs up to the far side of the alley and pulls his phone from his pocket. He reads a message, then looks up to Clare, his face flushed.

"I'm trying to protect you," he says. "I need you to trust me."

I don't, Clare is about to say, but a honking car drowns her out. Clare sees Somers's car parked at the opening of the alley, her window rolled down, her sunglasses perched on her nose. She is looking at Malcolm.

"Everything okay here?" she asks.

"Fine," Clare says.

"Do you know this guy?"

"No," Clare says. "I needed some shade. He was asking for directions."

"Directions," Somers says, deadpan. "You got what you need?"

Malcolm nods, eyes on Clare. She backs down the alley so Somers cannot see her face. Don't you dare leave, she mouths to Malcolm before jogging to Somers's car. Malcolm stands frozen in place. His lips part as if he is about to speak, but Clare ducks into the coolness of the car before he can.

S omers drives the first few
blocks in silence. At a red
light, she adjusts the rearview
mirror as if looking for Malcolm behind them.

"Directions, eh?" she says. "Because I'll be honest, it looked
to me like you knew that guy."

"I do know him," Clare says. "It's a long story. Not related
to Sally."

"Everything is related to Sally right now."

Clare cranes to look out the window as a means to end the
conversation.

"Warrant's turned up nothing so far," Somers says. "Not
much, anyway. We'll be doing another run tomorrow, I hope."

"That's too bad."

"Even the bunker. We found it. Nothing down there but
some food, powdered milk. Baby formula, like you said.
Oddball stuff."

"Guns," Clare says.

"Both licensed. Safely stored. Nothing illegal about that."

The trip out of the city to High River feels familiar to Clare now. Somers drives with one hand loose on the wheel. At the last light before the highway on-ramp, a young mother struggles to lift her stroller over the curb. The small child's face is red with the heat, the sunhat secured to his face with straps that bisect his fat cheeks. Clare watches them silently, noting from the corner of her eye that Somers is watching them too. They accelerate up the ramp and merge onto the highway in silence.

"Is he related to you?" Somers asks. "The guy, I mean. Just circling back for a second. You say he's not related to Sally."

"He's just someone I know."

The way Somers nods, her lips pursed, tells Clare her lie is not convincing.

"It looked pretty intense to me," Somers says. "You two huddled up against the wall like that." Somers pats the cruiser dashboard with feigned affection. "We know how to be stealthy, this car and me. We were watching you for a good minute before I honked. Like I said, it didn't look like two strangers talking directions."

It occurs to Clare to confess it all to Somers. To tell her about Jason, about Malcolm, about Blackmore. To peel back the layers to this story for this police officer, gauge her reaction, hope for some humanity in her response.

"Stealth or not," Clare says, "I'm surprised we didn't notice you."

"I'm not," Somers says. "Like I said, looked intense."

Clare opens her mouth to speak, then bites her lip to stop herself. Malcolm's words come back to her. *He's dangerous.* What if Malcolm is telling the truth? Clare thinks. What if Somers is dangerous too?

"Rourke thinks you're the key," Somers says as if reading Clare's thoughts.

"The key to what?"

"To this case. He thinks you know some things you're not telling us. He keeps bringing you up. Asking me what I think about you. He's been digging up info on you."

"He won't find anything," Clare says, her heart bouncing in her chest.

"Sometimes *not* finding anything perks us up even more than finding a whole lot, you know what I mean?"

"No," Clare says.

"I mean that a person with no verifiable past to speak of is probably hiding more than someone with a past a mile long."

"What about Rourke?" Clare asks. "You don't seem to know much about him."

"I know he's a cop," Somers says. "I talked to his previous captain. He doesn't exactly have a long list of commendations, but he's kept out of trouble. He's been on the job a while."

"Not all bad cops get caught."

"Believe me," Somers says. "I know that. But I think I'd spot it if my partner were corrupt."

The cruiser slows to turn off the highway onto a side road Clare doesn't recognize.

"Where are we going?" she asks.

"Just a shortcut," Somers says. "A back way. Not on the map."

The air-conditioning blasts. Clare feels disoriented. She rests her face in her hand.

"Listen," Somers says, reading the cues. "I'm not here to mess with anyone. You can trust me. If you know something, you can trust me with it."

Trust, Clare thinks, as if such a thing really exists.

"My guess is that you don't have many options," Somers continues. "Since you're here too. Since Sally e-mailed you to tell you this was a good place for you to be right before she disappeared. Maybe that guy in the alley, maybe he's part of it too, right? Maybe it's all about a lack of options. So if that guy has anything to do with Sally, I need to know."

How many ways might Clare respond? It makes sense for Somers to question why Clare ends up where she does, who that man might be. Clare should question it more too. High River. Blackmore. A dorm room on an unfamiliar campus. Malcolm. Her marriage. This police cruiser. Sometimes Clare imagines the ways her mother might press her if she were still alive, the harsh verdicts she would impose on so many of the choices Clare has made. Sometimes, she wonders how different her life would have unfolded if her mother were still alive to question her. Somers glances her way, awaiting a response. Clare wants to rage, to yell, to pound her fist into the bulletproof glass of her passenger window. Instead, she sighs.

"You run out of choices," Clare says. "When you run away, everything narrows. The options are few. I guess that's what High River is about. It becomes about survival."

Somers frowns, considering this. They pass the gas station. When they reach the driveway Somers rolls down her window and at once they hear it. Screaming. They clear the trees and see Rebecca and Markus next to the river, the little girl red-faced in Rebecca's arms. Helen stands nearby, and Clare can see Ginny and Jordan on the porch next to Raylene. They must have just arrived too. Markus takes hold of Rebecca's arm.

"Don't you touch me!" Rebecca says, snatching herself free.

"Jesus." Somers throws the car into park and steps out. Clare emerges from the car and watches Somers advance on them, her hand hovering above her gun.

"Rebecca," Markus says. "Please."

"You disgust me. You're disgusting!"

Helen approaches, arms open to the child. Clare cannot hear what she says over the din of the river. Rebecca turns and runs to the house, palm cupped to her daughter's head, a batch of papers clutched in her other hand. On the porch Jordan grips Ginny, holding her in place. The rest of them convene at the foot of the porch stairs, Somers and Helen, Raylene and Clare in a semicircle behind Rebecca and Markus.

"Ask your brother how much he loves his daughter," Rebecca says to Jordan, waving the papers. "How much his family means to him! Do you know what these are? I found a whole stash of them. Fucking little love notes. *Dear Markus, I can't stop thinking about yesterday. About the beautiful little child growing in me.*" Rebecca slams the papers to the ground and stomps on them, the child jostling in her arms. "Jesus Christ, Markus! Pregnant?"

Around her everyone is still, arms to their sides. Clare's gaze lands on Raylene biting her fingernails, across the circle, eyes darting from Rebecca to Markus. Clare edges closer to Somers.

"Well," Rebecca says, spitting the words. "You don't have anything to say for yourself? Nothing at all? To your family?"

Markus looks to his feet. Ginny rips herself from Jordan's grasp and descends the steps.

"You know what, Becks?" she says to Rebecca. "That's super shitty. What's worse than finding love letters between your husband and some other woman? Nothing."

"Shut up, Ginny," Rebecca says.

"Listen." Ginny shifts her weight, jutting her hip. "I know Markus is your knight in shining armor. I know you thought he was. But seriously? You've got to admit that your blinders are pretty thick. Because who else here didn't see this coming a mile away?"

"Stop it," Helen says, taking Ginny by the arm. "You stop it. Right now."

"You!" Markus points to Ginny. "You little bitch."

"Me?" Ginny sets a fanned hand on her chest in feigned innocence. "Don't pin this on me, Don Juan. You're the horrible husband. You're the pig."

"You think this place is yours?" Markus veers around Rebecca, his finger in Helen's face before turning to Jordan. "We all know you both want that highway paved right over us. We see the dollar signs in your eyes."

"This place means nothing to you," Jordan says, unflustered. "Your own family means nothing to you. To think you'd touch that poor woman. You're a piece of shit."

Somers raises her hand in a gesture of calm, then steps to the center of the group.

"Everyone here needs to take a step back and watch their mouths," she says. "No one wants to say something they'll regret."

"Pregnant," Rebecca says, spitting with rage, face-to-face with Markus. "All your little playdates while I was at work?"

The little girl on her hip wails now, her mouth round, head angled to the sky.

"Please," Helen says. "Please. All of you, let's stop."

"Here we go." Ginny rolls her eyes, then lands her gaze on Clare. "Just watch. Now she's going to defend him. Her piece-of-shit brother. 'He didn't mean it.' 'He can't help himself.' 'He had such a horrible childhood.' 'He's not very smart.' Blah blah blah. Right, Mom?"

But Helen doesn't speak. She looks almost vacant, staring ahead to the river, hugging herself as though warding off a chill. Even Rebecca watches her expectantly. Finally Somers sets her hand gently on Helen's shoulder.

"What I'm going to need is for everyone to go inside," Somers says. "Except for you two, Rebecca, Markus. You'll come across the river with me. We'll take the child with us."

From her vantage point Clare notices the cross now askew on the tree. The river, swollen from the rain, pushes up to the height of its bank, the roar is louder than it was yesterday. Clare ducks into the house with Helen, Jordan, and Ginny. Raylene is already in the kitchen. Even with the door closed, even as she can see them receding along the path, Somers between them, the little girl's wail still pierces the air.

The group sits scattered around the living room. Raylene, Clare, Jordan, Ginny. Helen in a chair in the far corner, gripping at the armrests, eyes to her knees.

"What do we do now?" Clare asks.

"Wait for Somers," Jordan says. "Nothing. Just wait."

"I knew she was pregnant," Ginny says. "I found the test."

At this a sob rises in Raylene's throat. "Oh my God."

"Did *you* know?" Ginny asks Jordan.

"Sally is my client. I can't talk about what I know. Knew."

"Right," Ginny says. "I forgot. That's your thing. Get these women to sign on the dotted line so you can keep all their dirty secrets. Maybe even use their secrets against them, or against the rest of us. Your master plan for dominance."

"Shut up, Ginny," Jordan says.

Tears spring to Ginny's eyes. She sits upright on the couch, hands folded on her lap, shimmying until she is pointed at Helen.

214

"Why do you let him talk to me that way?" Ginny asks.

"You're needling him," Helen says, her voice barely above a whisper. "You deserve it."

"I deserve it?" Ginny says. "You know what? I think you'd throw me in the river if one of your brothers asked you to."

"That's not true," Helen says.

"Your beloved brother Markus? He's disgusting. But you know what? I know why you defend him. Because *you* brought him back here. You let him move back. You didn't give a shit about how the rest of us felt."

"This is his home too," Helen says.

"He basically spat on the ground in good riddance when he left!" Ginny yells, rigid in her chair. "And when it all blew up for him, you just let him waltz back here and build that stupid house across the river and do whatever he pleases."

"That's your uncle," Jordan says. "Helen's brother. You don't have siblings, Ginny. You don't understand. What else was she to do?"

"He's your brother too, Jordan," Helen says, alert, shifting forward on her chair. "But when he showed up here destitute, all that family money burned up on oceanfront condos, he wasn't your problem either, right? He was mine."

"I was in law school," Jordan says. "You never even asked me what I thought."

"Law school," Helen says. "See? How wonderful for you. I was trying to do something with my life too. With this place. I was the one trying to build something here. But I've always been too busy taking care of others—of you!—to make anything of myself. To turn this into anything real. And now look at you on the front page of the newspaper, savior of women. You and Philip. Not a mention of me. Or of Janice! And look at her. She gave her whole life to Philip. Everything. Did all his dirty work, kept every secret, propped him up. Let the light shine on him. And what does Janice Twining get? St. Jude's. What do I get? Blamed."

Clare and Raylene exchange a wide-eyed glance, Clare working to process the details, the revelations, the undercurrents. What is St. Jude's?

"Come on, Helen," Jordan says. "Do you know how many times I've asked you what you want to do? Offered you counsel?"

"Counsel?" Helen says. "Ha. My baby brother and his wise counsel."

"We'll sell," Jordan says. "That's what you want, right? We'll sell for more money than you could dream of. You'll be free to do whatever you want. It's up to you. Sell. Or fight to keep this place. I swear. I just want you to tell me what you want."

"It's up to her?" Ginny says. "What about all your little meetings with the developers?"

"That's part of the process," Jordan says, exasperated. "You'd know nothing about it."

"You're right, Uncle," Ginny says, crossing and uncrossing her legs. "I know nothing about anything, right? But, hey. Did you know that Rourke asked me to spy on all of you? *Snooping* was the word he used, actually. He wanted me to *snoop*. And I remember thinking, why would he assume that I'd snoop on my own family and give him the goods like some third-rate snitch? But now I know why. It's because he sees the filth. Jordan? I love you, but you're stone cold. Offer Helen counsel? Get the fuck over yourself. And I swear, Helen, I swear you'd bury a dead body for Markus if he asked you to. I swear you'd put a gun to my head—to your own daughter's head—if Markus told you that would make him feel better. It's like the three of you are all tied together by your stupid little tragedy. But it's so over. It was over decades ago."

"Ginny," Helen says, her voice trembling.

"You see?" Ginny says to Clare, Raylene. "I'm the only sane one in this shitty family. That's what Rourke said. And he's right! That *I'm* the normal one. The only one who can actually help a frigging little boy and his mommy. A dead little boy, as it turns out. And a mom who's vapor. Vanished."

The room is quiet. For all her dramatic ways, Clare thinks, Ginny is wise, articulate. Smart. The front door swings open and Somers comes in, stopping short at the tension in the room. Jordan and Raylene stand but Helen stays fixed in her chair, eyes down again.

"I've got Rebecca in the squad car," Somers says. "She'll be coming back to the precinct with me."

"I'm sure you'll wring lots out of her now," Ginny says.

"Right," Somers replies, rubbing her forehead. "We've still got those hotel rooms. None of you are supposed to be here while the warrant is in effect."

"I'll take one," Raylene says.

"I will too," Clare says without looking at Ginny.

After a beat, Somers sits in the only empty chair around the room. She shifts her gaze on each of them in sequence, nodding, as if deciding whom to tackle first.

"Listen," she says finally. "I like to think we've been sensitive to each and every one of you. Taken all your concerns into consideration. But after what I just witnessed, I don't know if that was the right approach." Somers pulls a pad from her breast pocket and opens it. "Missing woman, pregnant? And some of you knew that and didn't tell me? Because this is the first I'm hearing of it. I'm also hearing that the boy's autopsy is yielding some surprising results. Arrows pointing in every god-damn direction." She pauses to inspect the room, her mouth in a tight line. "So I'm going back to square one. I'm going

217

to forgive you for not giving me the full truth the first time I asked. I'm going to give each one of you the chance to tell me anything and everything you know. About Sally. William. What they liked to eat for breakfast, what they were wearing the last time you saw them. Whatever you might have left out the first three or four or eight times I talked to you. Do you understand me?"

No one speaks or moves.

"The officers executing the warrant," Somers continues. "They were respectful. Dainty. No one ripped apart any furniture or broke any lamps or anything. Not a single hole was punched through the walls. I'm not sure I'll direct them to be so kind when they come back."

"Who says they're coming back?" Jordan asks.

"We have the right to access the property until we feel our search is complete."

"No you don't," Jordan says. "I know my sister's rights. The warrant was closed. I'm on the title for the property as well. So I'm going to ask you to leave, Detective. You can come back with another warrant. I'll have to assert our rights here."

"Oh," Somers says. "That's fine, Mr. Haines. I'm sure you know your own rights just perfectly. If you want to do things that way, that's fine with me. How about I work on getting a warrant for your office as well?"

Jordan smiles thinly. "Every single person in this room has retained me as their lawyer. Except for you, of course, Detective. Even her," he says, angling his head to Clare. "Signed me on about an hour ago, didn't you, Clare?"

Clare feels caught out, her voice retreating into her stomach.

"I'm quite sure you're not allowed to search a lawyer's office if your concern is with their client," Jordan continues. "But I can check on that if you'd like."

"Right," Somers says, standing. "Why don't I look into my options, and you can look into yours?"

"Will do," Jordan says.

Somers sets a card down on the coffee table.

"Your names are with the front desk at the hotel written on the back. You can take your chances, but I strongly suggest you vacate the property before my officers get back."

"I'll make sure everyone has a place to land," Jordan says.

Somers nods, her jaw still tight. She looks at Clare, disappointed, and Clare can only keep her eyes down until she is certain Somers is gone.

The city's light blares through the slit of the hotel room curtain. Clare wedges herself into the opening, the street below still bustling with cars, the odd pedestrian strolling though it is well past ten. A spider dangles from the ceiling on its invisible web, hovering along the window. When she closes her eyes she sees him. Clare sees Jason in their kitchen, squashing any insects under the toe of his work boots. In the first months of their marriage, Clare remembers watching in horror as he crushed the head of a dying mouse with the butt end of a broom. Putting him out of his misery, he'd claim, and while Clare knew the sentiment was right, it was the pleasure he seemed to take from it that disturbed her.

The knock on the door is so quiet that Clare doesn't hear it at first. She fumbles, reaching for the bedsheet and wrapping it around her, then dropping it in favor of the bathrobe that hangs in the closet.

"Hello?" she says, peering into the spy hole.

"Clare?"

Rourke. His face is bent into a strange angle as he leans into the door. A satchel is slung over his shoulder.

"Open the door," he says.

His tone startles her. She obeys before she can think better of it. When he enters the room she is aware of the mess, her clothes scattered on the floor, angry at herself for not holding him outside. He strides to the far end of the room and looks around. Rourke is in plain clothes. He wears a shirt unbuttoned, sneakers, and jeans, his gun holstered to his belt. Too casual.

"What are you doing here?" Clare flicks on every light switch, squinting. She tightens her bathrobe belt and sits on the far bed. "Where's Somers?"

"She's got a family. I take nighttime business."

"You have my number," Clare says. "Why didn't you just call me? Or text?"

"I did. You never responded."

Clare is certain she'd checked her phone too recently for this to be true. There had been no messages. She gestures for him to take the chair across from her. She thinks of Malcolm in the alleyway, the pained way he reacted to Rourke's name. *He's dangerous*, Malcolm said. Clare swallows. How does she choose which way to go next?

"You look nervous," Rourke says, half smiling.

"It's late. I wasn't expecting you."

"I'm not here to make you nervous. I'd like us to work together."

This surprises Clare. She must choose her words carefully.

"Can I ask you something?" she says.

"Anything."

"How long have you been working this case?"

"When did she disappear?" Rourke looks to his watch for effect. "Since then. Since the night she disappeared. Or the morning after, at least."

"Do you work more than one case at a time?"

"I have a few lingering ones. I've only been at the precinct for a month. I've had no time to settle in. I'm still living on my boat, looking for a more permanent place to land. Somers has a few cases from before I got here and I help her with those when I can. But obviously this is my focus right now. Our focus, I should say." Rourke pauses. "Why? You got something else for me?"

Clare shakes her head. She opens her mouth to speak, to ask the question: Do you know Malcolm Boon? But her heart races too quickly. She is too afraid of what his answer might be.

"Well." Rourke extracts a file from the satchel. "I have something for you. The autopsy report came back tonight."

His voice is raspy. He hugs the report to his chest for dramatic effect. Why would he come here with William's autopsy report? Clare wonders, noting the slight smile at the corners of his mouth. He's enjoying himself.

"What does it say?" Clare asks.

"The coroner believes the boy was dead before he went into the river."

"I know. That's what Raylene said."

"Well, she was right. His lungs weren't saturated. He hadn't aspirated any water. The only way you'd avoid aspirating any water is by not breathing. Not gasping for air. Which means he didn't drown."

Clare lets this sink in. She thinks of Raylene stumbling under the weight of the boy's body, the look of horror on Helen's and Ginny's faces as Raylene set him down on the grass.

"What does the coroner think killed him?"

Rourke opens the file to examine its contents, his forehead creased. "They found a meningococcal strain in his blood," he says. "Bacterial. Dangerous, but usually curable with antibiotics if caught early. The doctor said there were physical signs of high fever, that his blood counts were way off. No sign of antibiotics in his blood work. There were other things in his bloodstream, though. Not medical in nature. Lab's still working on those. Who knows what he'd been given. But there was evidence the infection had been allowed to progress."

"You're saying he died of an infection?" The implications wash over Clare. "Then someone put his dead body in the river?"

"It seems that way," Rourke says. "Yes."

Clare thinks of the way Raylene recounted the scene, Sally screaming. *Jordan told me to just tell it that way*, she'd said.

"Who would do that?" she asks.

Rourke shrugs. "That's the million-dollar question. I have my suspicions. You?"

He is leaning forward, his elbows resting on his knees. When the folder drops, Clare reaches to pick it up, their grips landing on it at the same time. Under her robe Clare can feel the pull of her shoulder, the new tissue resisting any movement in her arm. She winces.

"Are you okay?"

"I'm fine." Clare pulls the robe tighter. "What else did the autopsy say?"

"There was evidence of decomposition."

"Meaning?" Clare asks.

"That the body likely didn't go into the water immediately after death. That it spent time on land first. Or buried. Exposed to the elements. Which"—he pauses, scratching his head—"makes some sense given where it was found. Bodies underwater decompose differently. And we'd searched that area so thoroughly in the first day or two."

"So he died, and someone put his body in the water, then fished it out, then put it back in?"

"Or he never went in the first time," Rourke says.

Clare scrambles to recall her conversations with Raylene, Helen. With Ginny. Markus. Somers. The holistic measures. Rebecca's assertion at the eddy that Sally must have jumped. That she wasn't well. Where would you keep a body? A little lifeless child?

"So he had an infection and they didn't seek treatment," Clare says. "And he died. And they needed to cover it up."

Rourke is nodding.

"Then they killed Sally too? That's a stretch."

"Is it?"

"So what do you do now?"

A loud beep jolts Clare. Rourke fishes a phone from the back pocket of his jeans and reads the message. He stands, tucking the folder back into his satchel.

"I have to go," he says. "That's the coroner again. Pulling an all-nighter." Before she can move Rourke is in front of her, a hand on her tender shoulder. "Are you sure you're okay? I know she's your friend. I know this news it tough. You must be worried sick."

It takes all of Clare's might not to recoil from him, the disingenuous look on his face, closer to trickery than sympathy. He is not a good actor. And she worries now that neither is she.

"I could use some sleep," Clare says. "If you don't mind."

Don't touch me, she would like to say to him instead. To hiss at him. Instead she forces a smile and stays still as he gathers his things and heads for the door.

"You know where to reach me?" Rourke asks.

"I do. Thank you."

When he's gone Clare looks around at the room, the layout the same as so many she's known these past months. The fear coats her throat. She finds her phone on the bedside table and checks for messages. Nothing from Rourke, so that was a lie. But one from Somers.

Coffee tomorrow AM if u can? My treat. Just us.

Where? Clare types. Then she walks to the door and bolts it shut.

THURSDAY

Finally Clare spots it, the Hummingbird Cafe, its sign painted in lowercase across an old slat of barn board, its storefront set back from the curb. Clare takes a deep breath and opens the café door, scanning for Somers, then finding a table near the back when it's clear she's beaten her there.

At the next table a young girl slaps the salt and pepper shakers together like cymbals. The noise makes Clare's head scream. Clare closes her eyes and thinks of the grove behind the house where she grew up, the path to the river hardened by summer's drought. She pictures her nephew running that path, dodging craters of dried earth, a bucket and fishing net in hand. The quiet.

In the small hallway to the kitchen at the back of the café, Clare sees an old-style pay phone with a phone book dangling from a chain. She stands and opens the white pages. St. Jude's.

What does Janice Twining get? Helen said yesterday. *St. Jude's.*
There are three listings: a church, a school, and a hospice.
Clare rips the page out and folds it into her pocket before tak-
ing her seat again and ordering a coffee. A few minutes later,
Somers walks in and beelines to Clare. She sets her phone on
the table and plops into the chair.

"Sorry I'm late," Somers says.

"Five minutes. That's not really late."

The young waiter arrives with Clare's coffee and two glasses
of water. Clare watches Somers, the way she disarms the waiter
with a quick joke before turning serious eyes back to Clare.
Clare sips at her water in an effort to stay calm.

"Are you a cop?" Somers asks.

"No," Clare says, setting down her glass. "Are you?"

"Funny," Somers says. "You're funny. Listen. You've no doubt
noticed that I'm not terribly happy with how this investigation
is going. I'm picking up on some strange signals. Obviously
my job is a lot easier when people tell me the truth."

"I haven't lied to you," Clare says.

"You retained Jordan Haines as a lawyer."

"He asked me to," Clare says. "Maybe I haven't told you
everything, but I haven't lied."

"That distinction makes me antsy."

"Rourke showed up at my hotel room last night," Clare says.
"With the autopsy report."

"See? That makes me antsy too. I haven't read that damn
report yet. Why's he showing it to you before me? Why's he
showing it to you at all?"

The waiter arrives with Somers's latte and hovers as they
scan the menu. Clare orders oatmeal she knows she won't be
able to eat. After the waiter leaves they sip at their coffees and

observe each other. Clare calculates the pros and cons. The prospect of Somers as an ally perhaps outweighing the risks.

"Ask me anything," Clare says. "This time I promise to tell you the whole truth."

"Do you actually know Sally?"

"No."

Somers's eyebrows shoot up. "Okay. That's what I'd call a whopper of a lie."

"I lied about that," Clare says. "It was a cover. I needed a cover. To work the case."

Somers lets out a sharp laugh. "Work the case? You just said you're not a cop."

"I'm not."

"I'm confused. I really am. And I'm guessing you're not running from anyone either? That story you gave me the other day by the river? Just part of this con?"

"Actually, I am," Clare says. "Running from someone."

"You're losing me fast."

The con, as Somers called it, has gotten tiring. Clare takes a sugar packet and folds it until it breaks open.

"I was hired to investigate what happened to Sally Proulx and her son. I work for someone. The guy you saw me with in the alley yesterday. I work for him. We were hired anonymously. I'm like a PI, I guess. I don't know what you'd call me."

"Does anyone at High River know the truth about you?"

"No. I presume not." Clare pauses. "But since I don't know who hired us, it's possible that someone in High River did. And for the record, I did escape a bad marriage. Really bad. I left about eight months ago. I've been on the move ever since. So I guess my being at High River isn't a huge stretch for me in some ways. I wasn't lying about that part."

"I thought I was lost a minute ago," Somers says. "Now I'm truly at sea."

"That guy in the alley. His name is Malcolm Boon. In the winter, my husband hired him to search for me after I left him. I didn't pack a bag and leave a note. I ran away. Vanished. Malcolm caught up to me about six weeks ago. But instead of turning me in to my husband, he hired me as a kind of . . . apprentice. He looks for missing women. He's hired privately by whoever wants them found. And I guess he figured who better to look for a missing woman than someone who is one."

"You're shitting me."

"I'm not," Clare says.

"And why on God's green earth would you take the job? Did you even know this Malcolm guy?"

Good question, Clare thinks. One she's still unable to truly answer.

"I didn't know him. You remember yesterday on the drive to High River when you said you figured I didn't have many options?"

"Sure," Somers says.

"Well, I figure you don't know what that feels like—to have so few options that even bad ones start to make sense. You're not deciding between good options and bad options, you're picking the lesser of two evils. I know it made little sense to take the job. I knew that. But I took it anyway. Because if I had another choice at the time, I didn't know what it was."

Somers is nodding, arms crossed, sizing Clare up. "I get it," she says.

"Anyway." Clare tucks her loose hair behind her ears. "This is only my second job. I worked one other case before coming here. I really fumbled through the first case. It didn't end well. I mean, it did, in a way. I solved it. But I didn't go about it the right way. I got hurt. I thought this time I'd do better. Study up on Sally. Learn what I could. Go undercover. Come up with a backstory that would get me in. But I can't say I'm doing any better a job this time. And Sally is still missing, so—"

"Why didn't you just tell me this from day one?" Somers asks.

"Because you wouldn't have given me the time of day."

"I've worked with PIs before. I don't love it. Feels a bit like dabbling in amateur hour, to be honest. Like babysitting. But hey, I'm not above it if someone else wants to work the case. As long as they stay out of my way at the right times and work with me at the right times too."

The waiter arrives with their plates. Clare's oatmeal is beige and sodden. The smell turns her stomach. Somers collects a piece of toast from her plate and bites off the corner.

"So what now?" Somers says, chewing slowly. "We share what we know, properly this time?"

"You know everything I know," Clare says.

Somers makes a show of eating her eggs, eyes never dropping, a standoff. Clare hugs the warmth of her mug and fights a wave of nausea. From what Clare can glean, Somers has her life together. Marriage, children, a job she loves and does well. You need more friends like Grace, Clare's mother would say in the early days of Clare's troubles with drugs. More friends on the straight and narrow. But even then, Clare felt mostly jealousy towards Grace, as she does now towards Somers. Envy over a life on track. *Amateur hour*, Somers said. Clare takes a spoonful of her oatmeal and forces herself to eat it.

"This job is never boring," Somers says finally, setting down her fork. "It's always a jumble. You know, you start out clear. The details are clear and you just have to work every angle. Right off the bat, you get the forensics and the facts of it. The science is the easy part. But then you get in there and start dealing with people and everything gets jumbled. It's people who screw up police work. No one tells the whole truth. Every stone you turn over reveals a whole new layer of rot. Some of it is related to the case, and some of it isn't. But it's all rot. Markus and Rebecca and that whole shit show yesterday. Sally's pregnant, or so they say. And then there's Raylene."

"What about her?" Clare asks.

"Her husband's missing."

"Her *ex*-husband," Clare says.

"Right." Somers frowns. "Yeah. Of course. Anyway. Her story came through in our briefing last night. Her husband—*ex*-husband—disappeared a couple of hundred miles from here. He didn't show up for work. His parents called in. No one thought too much of it. Maybe he just went on a bender to Vegas or something. But a few days later they found his car on some lane a few hours away. No signs of anything else nearby. It seemed suspicious, so the local detachment sent out an APB. Our sergeant gave us all the case details, those two beautiful kids who died, the court case where he was charged and then acquitted, the whole background story even though we all remember it. We started talking about how he was let off and his ex-wife couldn't cope and took off, no one's seen her or heard from her in a few years. And my sergeant passed around the picture. And who is it but Raylene from High River. A character from this whole other story. Like I said, the layers of rot, right? The crazy thing is, I passed Rourke the picture and he glanced at it, but he didn't recognize Raylene. He's seen her, spoken to her. I'm pretty sure he even interviewed her, but it didn't click. Some cop, right? So, do I tell my superiors? Hey, want to hear something superfunny? We've actually got this Raylene woman booked at a hotel and we're paying for the damn room. Or do I stay quiet? Because do I really want five more cops on my case?"

The girl next to them bangs the shakers again, stopping wide-eyed when Somers glares at her.

"Are you going to arrest Raylene?" Clare asks.

"I was up all night asking myself that same question. Kids, you know? I love my husband, he wouldn't hurt a fly. But let's say he was a bad man and he laid a hand on my kids. I'd shoot him right between the eyes. So do I turn in this woman who ran away from the guy who probably killed her kids and got off? And there's another problem. She happens to be friends with Sally, the woman whose disappearance I'm actually supposed to be investigating. Or do I wait for some birdbrained officer to put two and two together and do the dirty work for me? You still with me? It's a shit show, like I said."

"Raylene's been at High River for months."

"Yeah. I know. Maybe she's got an alibi. Maybe her husband's guilt just got the best of him. Maybe he drove himself off a cliff." Somers scratches her head. "Or maybe not. I'm going to have to talk to her. But I'll give it a day. I've got a new warrant to get."

"My last case was hard," Clare says. "I faced a lot of questions. I turned up in this remote town and everyone had an eye on me. In High River, I fit in. I'm like these women. Weirdly, I fit in."

"Maybe you're learning how to do the job," Somers says.

"No. I still have no idea what I'm doing. I feel like I'm walking in circles."

"That's how it always feels," Somers says. "And I'm good at my job." Somers smiles. "My mom wanted me to be a nurse. I have four brothers who are either cops or firefighters. I'm the baby girl. I was her chance at something calmer. She put me in Girl Guides, ballet. She tried so hard to keep me soft around the edges. Imagine her disappointment when I joined the police academy."

A silence passes between them. The waiter comes to collect their plates but Somers waves him away.

"Sally's son was sick," Clare says. "That's how he died. His blood showed bacteria but no antibiotics. He didn't drown. That's what Rourke told me. He didn't drown."

"Rourke shouldn't be telling you anything."

"Neither should you," Clare says.

Somers shrugs. "Fair comment."

"Like you said," Clare says. "Rourke thinks I'm the key. But he's obviously off track. I think Rebecca is the key. Markus."

"Rebecca did say some pretty interesting things on our drive into town yesterday," Somers says. "I'm quite sure I can get her to talk."

"Talk about what? Did you let her go?"

Somers waves a finger at Clare. "Really? I'm not about to give up all my case secrets. I'm not under the same spell as Rourke."

What Clare wants to say is that Rourke's spell has nothing to do with Sally or her case. She thinks of Malcolm yesterday. *He's not working this case*, he said. *That's not why he's here.* Somers stabs a home fry with her fork and pops it into her mouth. Clare should know better than to trust her. Then again, Clare thinks, she should know better than to trust Malcolm.

"You're staring," Somers says. "You have something you want to say to me?"

"Ginny told me this story yesterday," Clare says. "This story about Markus taking her to the hospital when he was looking after her. She had a reaction to something."

"So? She's nineteen."

"No. This was when she was a kid. What if something—or someone—was making her sick?"

Somers frowns and sets down her fork. "Sick like William's blood work?"

"Right," Clare says. "I saw a documentary about that once. I Googled it this morning at the hotel. People who make their kids sick on purpose. It's a disorder. Think of the ways you'd benefit if people thought your kid was sick."

"I guess," Somers says.

"What if someone was making Ginny sick? And what if that same person was making William sick too? Or even Willow? Rebecca and Markus's daughter?"

"Who would do that?"

"I don't know," Clare says. "There's more than one adult who had access to both William and Willow. Who would have had access to Ginny. To all of them. The whole family seems to be fighting, but they're covering for each other too. I don't understand it. How could they cover for someone when there's a dead boy on their hands?"

"You'd be surprised," Somers says. "If fifteen years of police work has taught me anything, it's that people will go to extreme lengths to absolve their children or their parents or their partners or sisters or brothers or frigging second cousins of wrongdoing. No matter how horrific the crime. I've listened to mothers of sons who've confessed to murder argue their child's innocence. I've seen fathers hide damning evidence to avoid seeing their son charged with rape. Wives giving husbands false alibis when their guilt is clear as day. You'd be amazed."

Clare thinks of her own father. The year she was twenty, Clare was arrested at a party with a purse full of unlabeled prescription bottles. Her father had claimed the bottles as his own, called in a favor with the sergeant, a high school buddy of his, to have the charges dropped and a stern warning issued instead. And Clare remembers walking out of the detachment into the stark morning light, her father's grip on her arm as they descended the stairs to the car. We won't tell your mother, he said, opening the passenger door. Clare was supposed to feel gratitude, thankful that he'd sprung her, saved her from a trial and a sentence that would certainly have landed her in jail. But instead she felt helpless, angry even. The four hours she'd spent in the cell was the first time she'd considered the prospect of cleaning up, something she might have been able to do had she been left to pay the consequences of her crime, left to languish in jail.

"You'd have to be really evil to poison a kid," Clare says.

"I worked a case once where the mom was doing it. She'd had all kinds of troubles in her life and this was a way to be perceived as a hero. Caring for her own sick kid. That's another thing you learn in police work. Sure, some people are evil. You know, the serial killers who chop up children and leave them in their freezers or pluck women from the side of the road, then bury them naked in a swamp?"

"I try not to think about people like that," Clare says.

"Those are the crimes we hear about the most," Somers says. "The obvious psychopaths. But the vast majority of the time, lawbreakers are sane people, people who might even possess a reasonable moral compass. Like I said, your nice neighbor. But somewhere along the line, something's gone askew, and they're now motivated by a handful of things. Money, power, guilt, revenge. Love, even. The desire to protect something or someone they love. Sometimes purely one, sometimes all of the above. People will do profoundly stupid things, will commit the worst kinds of crimes or hurt innocent people, if one of those motivations is blinding enough. And if you throw in some hypnotic emotion like jealousy or anger, then all bets are off."

Jason, Clare thinks. Revenge mixed with anger and, should she feel generous, should she look deep, maybe even a tinge of love. Somers rubs her forehead and gestures for the bill. When her phone beeps she lifts it and squints to read a message. She gives Clare a curious look before typing her response.

"That was from Rourke," she says. "Asked if I was with you. He says he needs to see you. Says he has some things to clear up."

The room spins behind Somers. Clare grips the table to steady herself.

"Interesting, though," Somers says, laced with sarcasm. "He never mentioned the autopsy report or visiting you last night. You okay?"

"I'm fine," Clare says.

"Let's walk. The station's only a few blocks from here."

Once the bill is paid they both stand.

"Somers," Clare says. "I don't want—"

"I'm not going to give you away," Somers says. "Can you trust me?"

No, Clare thinks. The churn in her chest makes it hard to breathe.

"Listen." Somers takes Clare's arm, reading her fear. "I promise I'm not going to make anything worse for you. Maybe I can even help you. Can we keep this little breakfast meeting between us?"

"Sure," Clare says.

Outside Clare follows half a step behind Somers, the heat like a fog she must pass through. They pass a large convention center. Clare ducks under the awning to escape the blare of direct sun. Somers walks with her eyes on her phone, somehow still navigating the stream of men in suits, women in blouses and skirts. When they reach a revolving door Clare pauses to catch a blast of air-conditioning, watching the crowd. Then she sees the poster. Her. She sees *her*. Life-sized Grace, her white lab coat on, arms crossed with authority.

Today's Keynote Speaker:
Dr. Grace Fawcett
Support Patients' Addiction Recovery in
Your Family Medicine Practice
2–3 p.m.

Does Grace look older? The photo stares back at Clare. Has she aged in the months since Clare last saw her? Clare's breathing picks up. *Grace has been the worst,* Jason wrote in the letter he sent her in Blackmore, the letter still at the bottom of her bag. *Telling the cops to come after me and question me.*

"You okay?" Somers says. "You seem off."

Clare points to the poster. "I know her."

"That doctor in the ad?"

"I know her from home. She's a friend." Clare squeezes her eyes closed. "She *was* a friend."

"Did you know she was here?" Somers asks.

"No," Clare says.

"That's a coincidence," Somers says.

Bile rises to Clare's throat, nothing a coincidence anymore, everything converging, blurring. Without answering Clare starts walking again, fast enough that Somers must jog to catch up.

The interrogation room is a sweaty box. Clare rolls the water bottle in her hand, slamming it to the table and collecting it again, looking up to the one-way glass with as piercing a look as she can muster. The door opens and Rourke steps through, a thick folder tucked under his arm.

"Sorry about this. The AC is broken but there's not really anywhere else to go. It's just the easiest way to talk."

"Where's Somers?"

"I asked her to give us a minute."

Why would Somers have allowed this, have agreed to leave Clare alone with him? This small betrayal feels like a punch to the stomach.

"Listen." Rourke takes his seat. "I'm sorry I showed up at your hotel last night. That was inappropriate."

"Yeah."

"Believe me, Somers has made it clear that I was way out of line. I didn't mean to scare you. I just wanted to fill you in on the boy."

"Because I'm Sally's friend," Clare says, surprised by her own biting tone.

"See? That's where we need to talk."

The change in Rourke's expression is immediate, a frown that borders on distress. Did Somers tell him the truth about Clare just now? How far will her betrayal go?

"I've told you everything I know," Clare says. "I've told Somers everything I know."

"Right. But I haven't told *you* everything I know."

Rourke rests both hands flat over the folder on the table.

"It isn't the Proulx file," he says.

The smell of Rourke's coffee is too strong. He opens the file and hands her a large black-and-white photograph. She holds it facedown on the table, her hand shaking.

"Look at it," Rourke says.

"Who are you?" Clare asks.

"I want to be honest with you. I think I can help you. I think you can help me."

Clare turns the photograph over. It takes her a moment to process it, the tall man standing behind a woman, his arms wrapped around her. Clare feels it, the tectonic shift beneath her, this photograph changing everything. The woman bears a strong resemblance to Clare, smaller and slighter, her hair curly and long, her hands raised to grip the man's arms where they cross over her chest. Though he is younger, though he wears a smile brighter than Clare could imagine him wearing, though his arm does not yet bear the jagged scar, she knows this man as if he were here in the flesh. Malcolm.

"Where did you get this?" Clare asks.

"I've been tracking him for a long time. Trying to track him, at least."

"Malcolm Boon?"

"Yes," Rourke says. "That's not his real name, but yes. The man you know as Malcolm Boon."

Something in the photograph fills Clare with sadness, the way Malcolm's chin rests gently on his wife's head, their matching wedding bands. Rourke sizes up Clare so that she must carefully fix her expression.

"Who is he?" Clare asks.

"His name is Malcolm Hayes. The woman in the picture is his wife, Zoe. They were married for seven years, until she disappeared a little more than a year ago. Presumed dead."

Under the table Clare's legs shake. Rourke offers her a strange smile.

"Disappeared how?" Clare asks.

"You tell me," Rourke answers.

"Malcolm's never told me anything about his past. Except that he had a wife and that she disappeared."

"So he's told you a lot."

Clare's neck goes cold. She pries open the water bottle but can barely sip it.

"You didn't think to dig?" Rourke asks.

Clare shrugs.

"How long have you known him?" Rourke asks.

"A month or so," Clare says.

"And you work for him?"

"Yes."

Rourke taps his fingers against the file. A file that likely satisfies every question she's ever had about Malcolm, every detail filled out by her imagination, his tastes and his flaws, his family, his wife. Zoe. A month ago she might have dreamed of a file like this, its contents leveling the playing field between them, shifting the power to her. But now she feels an acute need to shield Malcolm. Why would she want to protect him from this man in front of her?

"I need your help," Rourke says.

"I thought you were looking for Sally," Clare says.

"I am. I asked to be put on the case. I needed a missing persons case. A woman."

"Why?"

"I needed to lure Malcolm here. I wasn't expecting him to bring you too."

Clare buries her face in her hands. Every conversation with Rourke swirls now, not her ruse but *his*, that he'd known all along why she was here. She thinks of Malcolm yesterday, coming unhinged, this reaction to her mention of Rourke's name. Had he felt a vise closing around him?

"He knows you're after him," Clare says. "And clearly you are. Maybe you'll tell me why."

"Shall I start at the beginning?"

Clare crosses her arms warily. Then he begins.

"Malcolm Hayes used to work as a forensic psychologist," Rourke says. "His father owned a tech company that made millions, but both his parents and a younger sister died in a plane crash when he was fifteen. He was taken in by an aunt on his mother's side. He inherited a massive trust the day he turned twenty-five. He spent five years floating. Then he met Zoe Westman and they were married within three months. They lived a nomadic life. New York City, Europe, even Rio for a while. You name it. They had very few friends. They were a strange couple by any measure. They finally settled in some old rambling house in Northern California. One neighbor said she could hear them fighting at all hours. Another said they were quiet as mice. Malcolm was finishing his PhD and was working on a book about—"

"What happened to his wife?" Clare asks, interrupting him.

Rourke lifts the photograph himself, scrutinizing it as Clare can guess he's done a thousand times, then opens the file to set it back in place.

"Zoe has a sister whom she confided in. She told her sister that Malcolm could be violent, would threaten suicide if she left him, would accuse her of marrying him for his money. But the sister said she suspected Zoe had something else going on too."

"You spoke to Zoe's sister?"

"I've been tracking him, like I said. Working the case. Anyway, there was more than one side. There were many sides. Zoe's sister said she didn't know which might be true. Then Zoe disappeared a year ago this past May. Went for a drive along the coast and never came home. They found the car a week later. Never found a body."

"And you think Malcolm killed his wife?" Clare asks, working to keep her voice steady. "He must have been questioned."

Rourke shrugs. "He didn't hang around long enough for us to get him. He was gone the day we found the car."

We, Clare thinks. We found the car. The door opens and Somers peers in. Clare feels a surge of rage at the look Somers gives her, sad and sorry. She drags over the corner chair and sits with them at the table.

"Everything okay?" Somers asks.

"I'm just filling her in."

"You knew about this?" Clare asks.

"Not until I got here today. I swear to God." Somers yanks the file away from Rourke. "He just told me. And I'm not happy about it."

"Listen," Rourke says. "I'm trying to straighten things out. Put it all on the table."

"Please tell me there's nothing else to put on this table," Somers says.

"Our fathers were friends," Rourke says.

"What?" Clare says.

"Malcolm and I. We grew up together, sort of. My dad worked for his dad. We didn't exactly run in the same circles. After his parents died his aunt sold off the company and it was shuttered. Parceled off. Tech was crashing. Long story, but my dad lost his livelihood. A lot of people did. Malcolm got rich." Rourke pauses. "This isn't coming out right."

"It most certainly isn't," Somers says.

"We both lost a lot. We kept in touch. We even went to the same college at the same time. I was lucky to get a full ride on a baseball scholarship. We didn't hang out, but I'd see him now and then. We'd exchange e-mails here and there. Keeping track of each other. I've known Zoe since we were kids. I was actually at the college reunion where he met Zoe. After they hooked up he was harder to pin down. Fast-forward to just over a year ago and she goes missing. It made sense for me to work the case because of all the background I had on him."

"Let me correct you there," Somers says, angling herself to Rourke, finger jabbing up. "It makes no sense at all for you to have taken the case. Didn't you learn about conflict of interest in your training, Rourke? Pretty basic stuff. You don't know when to stay out of things? Forget discipline committees. That's a firing offense."

"I know."

"Clearly you never told anyone at your last precinct that you knew him. Or that you knew *her*."

Rourke exhales. "I didn't tell anyone. That's true."

"Then you couldn't find him and the case went cold and you came here for a change of scene, right?" Somers's voice is low, angry. "Every cop has a case that eats them, and this is yours."

"This is mine," Rourke says.

"The crazy thing is," Somers says, her fist tight on the table, "even if you had caught him, even if you do catch him, you don't think he's going to tell the world he knows you? That you have a complaint with him? That his family screwed yours? That you grew up with his missing wife? Jesus Christ. You don't think that even if you could build a case without a body, any sane judge or jury would let him off?"

Rourke throws his hands up.

"That is without a doubt the sloppiest cop shit I've ever heard in my life," Somers says.

"I got to a point with it." Rourke sighs. "It became hard to turn back."

"Malcolm saw you yesterday," Clare says. "On campus. When you picked me up."

"That must have been a shock to him."

"How did you find him?" Clare asks.

"A few weeks ago the mine case in Blackmore was in the news. The missing woman gave a long interview on TV."

Yes, Clare remembers now, but it's all blurry, seen through the haze of the pain meds in that motel room. The missing woman from Blackmore, Shayna Fowles, selling her story to the highest bidder and sitting down for a one-hour exclusive.

"She talked about you in the interview," Rourke continues. "About a Clare O'Dey. The mystery woman who appeared in the mine, then vanished from the hospital the next day. She said you'd told her you were working for someone named Malcolm Boon, that you'd been hired to find her. I heard the name and I knew. I just knew. Boon was the name of the street he grew up on. Malcolm, the forensics guy. I saw the photograph of you and you looked like Zoe. It wasn't actually a stretch to piece it all together."

"You knew he'd be looking for missing women, for women beyond his own missing wife?" Somers says dryly.

"I know Malcolm. The way he fixates on things. They never fig-ured out why the plane carrying his family went down. Whether it was a mechanical issue or something more sinister. He became obsessed with unsolved mysteries. He doesn't let things go."

"Like you," Clare says.

"I actually wanted to be a baseball player," Rourke replies. "I was a good pitcher. But I blew out my elbow in college. Lost my scholarship."

"Jesus, Rourke," Somers says, eyes down on the open file. "Cry me a river."

"I took some vacation days a few weeks ago and flew to Blackmore," Rourke says. "Or flew to the nearest actual town, then drove to Blackmore. Did some police work. Found the doctor who treated you. Who hired Malcolm. He referred me to Malcolm's website, which is basically a single banner page with an e-mail address. He ID'd Malcolm from the picture, said he'd met him in the hospital after you were shot. I had my confirmation. When Sally Proulx went missing, I had my chance. It was perfect, actually. I got lucky."

"Lucky," Somers scoffs.

"So you lured him here?" Clare asks. "By hiring us?"

"I hired him. Not you. Set up an anonymous e-mail account. Said I was a citizen concerned about the goings-on at High River. That I didn't trust the cops to do it right."

"Is that ever rich," Somers says.

Rourke ignores her. "I had no idea how you fit into all this. I was surprised to see you in High River, needless to say. I recognized you right away. It kind of shook me, to be honest. You threw a wrench in my plan."

"Why?"

"Because who are you, really? I couldn't be sure how much you know."

Rourke drags the folder back over and uses a flag to open it midway. He runs his finger down the page in search of something.

"O'Callaghan," he says. "Clare O'Callaghan. One arrest for possession of illegals when you were twenty, a few domestic calls, spouse Jason O'Callaghan never charged. Disappeared December of last year—"

All sounds around them have ceased. Clare's ears ring with panic. She eyes the coffee still on the table, still steaming, still hot enough to scald.

"Don't say that name again," she whispers.

"We've had enough here," Somers says. "This is a lot to process. And I need to decide whether I'm going to get your ass fired."

"I'm not here to threaten anyone," Rourke says. "I think we all want the same thing. The three of us."

"You have no idea what I want," Clare says.

"Yes I do. You want absolution. Answers. You want this to end."

Rourke reaches to rest his hand on Clare's forearm.

"Don't touch me," Clare says, ripping her arm from him.

"I want to help you," Rourke says. "You can help me too."

"I don't work for you. You know nothing about me."

"I know a lot, actually. I've dug up whatever I can."

"Stop it!" Somers's chair slides back with a squeal. She stands and slams the folder closed. "Out," she says to Rourke. "Get out of here."

And then Clare feels it, watching Rourke as he backs to the door. The instant numbing, the icing over. Rourke is saying something to her, but Clare looks at him with such venom, such fury, that he quiets. Somers tucks the folder under her arm and follows him out, closing the door behind her. Clare stands and moves to the glass of the one-way window, pressing her forehead against it. She sees only black, but somehow she knows Rourke is on the other side. She can sense him there. Of course he is watching her. He has been all along.

C lare watches the spin of the convention center's revolving doors. She watches so intently that it dizzies her. She knows Grace's routine. A walk after each speaking engagement to quiet the nerves. A three o'clock finish, a short mingle with her audience, then her escape. After twenty minutes the doors spit out a familiar figure, Grace in a tailored pantsuit. Clare feels a deep pang as she spies her friend fiddling with her phone, looking north and south to pick a route. Always a planner. At once Clare remembers Grace in the yard of their high school, collecting signatures for a petition while Clare huddled with other girls, sharing a cigarette under the bleachers. At school their friendship went under the radar, their lives on different planes, Grace the star student and Clare the quiet brooder at the back of the room. But as they passed in the hallways they'd reach out to brush hands, some unwavering bond holding them together. A childhood friendship rooted deep.

The light turns. If Grace heads left after crossing the street, she will walk right by her. Clare emerges from the bus shelter, uncertain how to avoid startling her friend, shuffling her feet as Grace closes in. When Grace's eyes land on Clare, her expression remains blank. Then her head shakes vigorously.

"Grace," Clare calls.

Her friend takes a step back and shades her eyes with her hand.

"No," she says. "No."

"Grace. Please."

"No," Grace repeats, her voice cracked but firm. "No!"

By now there is only a few feet between them and Clare can see the look on her friend's face perfectly. Fear.

"Grace, I'm so sorry," Clare says. "I have so much to explain."

"You let me think you were dead."

"I know," Clare says. "Please. Let me explain—"

"How can you explain why we all thought you were dead?"

"Can I buy you a coffee? Can we just talk? A few minutes."

Clare reaches for Grace's hand. When she grasps it the tears come, to Grace first and then to Clare, and then they are hugging, and the familiar scent of her friend fills Clare with an anguish she must hold her breath to contain. When they finally break apart, Clare motions to the coffee shop on the corner. Inside, they order and take their hot drinks to a table at the back, silent. In the calm light of the coffeehouse Clare can see it clearly, how thin her friend has become, her hair flat, her face lean.

"I don't . . ." Clare begins. "I don't even know where to start. I'm so sorry."

"I thought you were dead," Grace repeats. "For months that's what I thought. Months."

"I know."

"Your father wanted to plan your funeral. Christopher wouldn't let him. He said we had to be sure." Grace fiddles with the string of her teabag. "We looked for you everywhere. Search parties for weeks. I left my newborn baby at home to trudge through fields of snow looking for your dead body."

"I'm sorry," Clare says. "I don't know what to say. After the baby died, this plan formed. You know? I had to leave. There was no other way. He wasn't going to just let me leave him. I had to disappear. There really was no other way."

Grace is unmoving, her lips a tight line. "If that was the case," she says, "you could have told me. Maybe I could have helped."

Clare feels her fists clench. *If that was the case.*

"You were done helping me, though. Weren't you? Both you and Christopher were done with me."

"I was done being lied to, Clare. You never told me the truth. You were stealing from me. Money, drugs. You took painkillers from my medicine cabinet. You pointed a gun at your own brother. We were all done with you. Can you blame us?"

"I was desperate," Clare says.

Grace takes a sip of her tea, eyeing Clare over the rim of the white mug. Her friend looks like she's aged ten years in the months since she last saw her.

"He tells a very different story," Grace says.

"Who does?"

"Jason."

At once the remorse, the love and pain and regret stirred within Clare since first spotting Grace are replaced by a flaring wrath.

"He was going to kill me," Clare says, her voice low and steady.

"You were going to kill yourself. You were one bad fix away from the morgue."

"Do you know what my life has been like since I left?" Clare asks.

"Do you know what *our* lives have been like since you left?" Grace's eyes well up again. "That's the thing about you, Clare. It was always about what your life was like. Ever since we were kids. Everything was always awful for you. You always had it worse than anyone else. Like you laid sole claim to misery. I know you had it bad. I know you lost your mom when you were way too young. But so did your brother, and Christopher's not a mess. I know Jason isn't a very nice guy. But none of it even matters. Because I swear you've been selfish since the day you were born. You only see your side. You hatched this escape plan because it suited you. It suited you to disappear into thin air. You didn't think about us."

"I thought about you all the time," Clare says. "You're all I think about."

"Did you know that my marriage ended?"

"No," Clare says, hand to her mouth.

"He left. Three months after Elliot was born. Or three months after you disappeared, however you want to count it. He dropped me for a nurse at the hospital. They moved to a condo in the city. He sees our baby every second weekend, give or take."

"God. I'm so sorry . . ."

"No you're not," Grace says, spitting venom. "Your whole issue from the beginning was that you thought my life was perfect. We were good until your mom got sick. After that, you hated that my life was going well. Never mind how hard I'd worked to make it that way. I remember in the weeks right after Brian left me, I missed you so much. I'd drink myself into a stupor in the kitchen and wish so, so badly that you were there with me. But then it occurred to me that maybe you'd have been happy that he left. That you'd have taken pleasure in seeing me knocked down a few rungs."

"No," Clare says.

But the tears that come tell another story. Even today when Clare saw the poster, that same jealousy mustered in her. The lab coat, the speaking engagements. And perhaps it does bring Clare some terrible satisfaction to know that Grace's husband has left, to see her friend experiencing the kind of loss and pain Clare could never seem to properly convey to her.

"I'm sorry," Clare says, wiping her eyes. "I honestly didn't mean to make things worse for you."

"Sure you didn't. You just let it be. Let us suffer. So here's what you don't know. We found out you were alive when we saw you in the news tangled up in someone else's mess thousands of miles away. You made this decision to vanish and you didn't think about what it might do to Christopher, or to your dad, or to me. Even to Jason. You—"

"Don't say his name," Clare says.

Grace crosses her arms. "He said I might run into you here."

"Who said that?"

The expression on Grace's face is unrecognizable to Clare. "Jason did. He said you'd left that mountain town. Blackmore, or whatever. That I might run into you here."

A fog descends over Clare, too many voices, the espresso machine earsplitting as it bursts forth steam. Clare feels woozy, untethered. She closes her eyes and thinks of the moment when she tumbled down the cellar stairs, her hand clasped to her pregnant belly, thinks of running through the back field, the ground cold and hard, of Malcolm the first time she saw him. Clare thinks all the way back to her mother's cancer diagnosis a few weeks before her high school graduation, of Jason locking eyes with her across the bonfire circle the night they first met. All these memories closing in on her at once, a flash sequence of her life as though she were dying. *You only see your side*, Grace said. Clare opens her eyes.

"Where is he?"

"Jason?" Grace says. "He's at home. Trying to move on."

"Trying to move on," Clare repeats, enunciating as though the words were in another language. "You said he was here."

"I said he figured *you* were here. He tells a very different story from the one you told."

Clare can no longer focus on Grace's face.

"I was horrible to Jason at the beginning," Grace continues. "I was sure you were telling the truth. Of course you were. I'd seen him at parties. He was an asshole. We all knew that. I told the cops not to bother looking at anyone else, that Jason had to be responsible for your disappearance. They needed to circle right in on him. I'd like to think they did. But after Brian left me, I didn't have the energy to keep on them. Do you know what Brian said to me when he left? That he needed to live his truth. I'm holding his baby in my arms as he says it. And then a month ago Jason shows up on my front lawn with this picture of you in this goddamn town in the middle of nowhere." Grace's voice cracks. "I'm pushing my kid on a swing and he shows up. And there you are, partying it up with these hillbillies. Smiling in some dive bar with your arm around some random coal miner. Jason was devastated. He wept when he handed it to me. I was confused, and I was devastated too. I told him I didn't believe it was you. But of course it was. There you were. Smiling at the camera as though everything was fine, as though you didn't have a care in the world, as though you hadn't left anyone behind. After that, everything changed."

"What do you mean, everything changed?"

"Jason. Me. We talked more. Our lives were both in shambles. I listened to him, Clare. Because Christopher wouldn't talk to me. He couldn't handle it, and Jason was the only person who'd talk about it. I needed to understand what would have possessed you to leave without telling me. And you know what? I got his side. He told me his side. His truth. And I understood."

Clare's head spins. She crosses her arms on the table and rests her head atop them. *Truth.* That word. The word connecting everything. Jason's word against Clare's. Which is true? Everyone in High River speaks of truth too, Ginny's stories, Jordan's, Helen's. Markus and Rebecca's. Malcolm insisting he's never lied to her, omitting instead, refusing to fill in the blanks.

"Clare," Grace says. "Look at me."

When Clare stands, a paper falls from her back pocket. She and Grace both bend to collect it. It is the ripped page from the phone book.

"Sit down," Grace says.

"No," Clare says.

"We need to talk about this. And you need help. I'm just sick of half-truths. I want to talk. I do."

But Clare is already backing up, knocking against a rack of mugs so that everyone in the coffee shop looks up to her.

"Clare!"

Grace's voice sounds like an echo. Before Grace can stand too Clare is out the doors, the street swirling beneath her. She flags a cab and is grateful when it stops. She jumps in and signals the driver to take her back to the hotel, catching only a small glimpse of the frown on Grace's face as the cab pulls away.

There is a memory of a motel room twenty miles from home. The first wedding they'd attended after getting married themselves. A coworker from Jason's factory and his bride. Clare remembers the dinginess of the motel room, the small window that wouldn't open, the smell of the beer cans tossed to the garbage unfinished. She remembers the needle on the bed, Jason splayed beside it, eyes closed, that half-smile of euphoria.

The curtains in this room are floor-to-ceiling sheer. Out the window Clare studies the people lined up to catch the bus. Their lives, their joys and sorrows, Clare imagines, all tolerable enough. After she left home, there were times when she allowed herself to feel safe, to feel free. As though no one were following, as though her past could be truly left behind. Times when she'd eat chips on the motel bed and watch TV, the gun she'd had then out of reach on the bedside table, falling into the laugh-track trance of whatever sitcom she was watching. Brief stretches of forgetting. Of normalcy. But the feeling was always fleeting. By the next morning, the anxiety was back. The fear.

He tells a very different story from the one you told, Grace said. *I got his side.* It feels too easy to imagine them, commiserating over their losses. Jason worming his way in.

It is a relief, Clare thinks. Grace. Malcolm. Jason. Sally. Rourke. This case. To be numb. To let go. The numbness a balm against the fear. It always amazed Clare that the farther along her mother's cancer got, the less fearful she became. When she'd jumped in the cab an hour ago and ridden back to this hotel, Grace in her wake, it had dawned on Clare. There was no need to continue. She owed her work to no one. A numbness set in.

Do you want me to be afraid? Clare's mother had asked, looking up from her deathbed. Because I'm not anymore. I'm relieved.

Clare takes the baggie of Ginny's pills from her duffel bag and selects the two she knows will wash her in dull light. Blue and white. She sets them on the glass desk. These motions are so rote, the tip of the hotel-logo pen to mash the pill, a straw to stir it around. She thinks of the look on Grace's face as she bolted from the coffee shop, on Rourke's face as he listed the dirt he'd dug up on her. Clare leans forward and presses a finger into one nostril, the straw in the other.

Don't. She hears a voice. His voice. If she stares at the wall long enough, she can almost see him. *Don't.*

Shut up. Clare can't be sure if she says these words aloud. I owe you nothing.

Clare leans back and hugs her legs to her chest. The scars on her arm still feel fresh. She remembers watching the young nurse fumble with her mother's morphine line, inserting and removing the needle, her comatose mother barely flinching at the indignity. How she'd wanted to offer to do it herself, well practiced as she was at finding a vein. Clare lifts the straw and leans in again.

Don't.

The scene comes back to Clare in perfect order. The motel room by the ocean. Not her room. Malcolm's. She'd knocked and he'd answered without a word. He retreated to sit on the corner of the bed, his shirt unbuttoned, his hair wet from an ocean swim. Clare stayed in the doorway. She'd only just started spending longer stretches on her feet, the pain of the bullet wound receding a little.

Still, she said. *I need more.*

You've had enough, Malcolm answered.

You're not my keeper.

It's making you foggy.

You're not my keeper. She was yelling.

Clare, he said, ever calm, *you've had enough.*

Something else had emerged in Clare then, a rage burning hot. Malcolm stood. She lunged for the desk drawer, expecting Malcolm to do the same, but instead he just watched her as she yanked it open. The pills weren't there, but his handgun was askew on the motel Bible. Clare lifted the gun and aimed it square at Malcolm's chest. He backed up reflexively, a look of shock on his face. Clare advanced until Malcolm was pinned to the wall, pressing his gun into the exposed skin at the V of his shirt.

Don't, he said.

I'll kill you.

She remembers everything. She's remembered all along.

Is that really what you want to do, Clare?

His voice was so gruff. The memory of it seems almost ridiculous to Clare now, how easily he might have overtaken her, swiping the gun to his right so that even if she'd managed to flick the safety and pull the trigger fast enough to pierce him, it would not hit his heart. Instead he kept his arms loose at his sides. Clare remembers the staccato of her own breathing.

I don't belong to you, she said.

No, Malcolm replied. *You don't.*

Next would have come the falling back onto the bed, thoughts erased. She can only guess, because the last thing she remembers for certain is setting Malcolm's gun back in the drawer, this time next to the Bible. She remembers standing up straight to meet his gaze, the anger she'd expected to see in him. But instead his face was cast in something closer to sadness, to disappointment, a look she'd failed to decode in the desperation of the moment. A look of longing.

Now, outside this hotel room, Clare hears voices, the fumble of luggage and keys. The squealing of children and a mother's gentle commands. I'll deal with the cart, Clare hears a man say. Then the family is in the room next door, their TV instantly on, a rhythmic thumping that must be children jumping on the beds. Clare drops the straw, her cheeks running with tears. Then she takes a deep breath and blows the powder from atop the table in a dusty poof. She props open the door to her room, crossing the hallway to toss the baggie into the garbage chute by the elevator. When she turns around, a boy of seven or eight stands in the doorway beside hers, his baby brother perched unsteadily on his hip.

"Hi," the boy says as Clare approaches.

"Hi," Clare says.

The baby flaps his chubby arm and utters a sound to mimic theirs, a rudimentary hello. Clare thinks of the way Christopher used to cradle his newborn son, cupping his soft head in his palm as though it were made of glass. It was never in Clare to be so gentle.

"Our house burned down," the boy says.

"Oh no," Clare says. "That's terrible."

"My mom says it's not so bad. We all got out."

"She's right," Clare says. "That might even make you kind of lucky."

The baby holds his brother's shirt with gripped fists and looks back and forth between them as they speak. This baby, fleshy and beautiful, the first wisps of hair curling around his pink ears, about the age Clare's son would be now had he lived.

"We have to stay here for a while," the boy says. "Until insurance comes. My school starts in two weeks and it's not too far."

"You must miss your home," Clare says.

"I don't know," the boy says, shrugging. "There's a pool here."

"That's a good thing."

"And I'm not dead," the boy adds matter-of-factly. "I didn't die."

Clare nods. She wipes at her still-damp cheeks. When the father calls to him, Clare offers the boy a wave, then ducks back into her own room, sliding the deadbolt over and throwing herself on the bed. She imagines the scene, the smoke detectors bleeping and the parents waking, then scrambling in terrified autopilot to scoop their children from their beds, nothing else important. Through the hotel room wall Clare hears the father's lilting voice, then the mother's laugh. She digs for her phone.

You owe me the truth, she writes.

The phone makes a swoosh sound as the message sends.

Malcolm, she writes. **You owe me.**

261

Clare grips her phone and waits. No answer. The folder Malcolm gave her is on the bed beside her. When this case turned up, when Malcolm arrived in her room with the file, Clare had taken it because she believed she could solve it. She'd learned the details of the case as she figured a professional would do; this the closest to a calling Clare'd ever experienced. This work absorbed her. Helen. Raylene. Markus. Rebecca. The Twinings. The pieces of the puzzle. Clare fishes into her pocket and pulls out the torn phone book page from the café this morning. St. Jude's. Another piece.

Her phone buzzes. Clare snatches it to read the message from Malcolm. One word.

Okay.

Clare sends him the address to the hotel and her room number.

Two hours, he responds.

The hotel business center is empty. Clare logs in to the computer and opens the search engine. She types in Janice Twining's name and finds photographs of her with Philip at various city events, articles on social issues, the dearth of women's shelters in the city. Clare tries social media sites but finds nothing. She opens the local newspaper's archive site and searches for the oldest entries. There is a short piece from forty-eight years ago. "Young Socialite Janice Godfrey Marries Up-and-Coming Lawyer Philip Twining in Lavish Ceremony."

In the photograph Philip feeds Janice cake, her dress modest but beautiful, their smiles young. Clare returns to one of the social media sites and tries again. This time, she types in *Janice Godfrey*. She finds one profile with its privacy locked down, but the profile photo is of a woman on a café patio. The woman could be Janice in a hat and sunglasses, the menu propped to cover the lower half of her face. Clare prints the photo and the article then clears the search and starts again, typing *Zoe*

Malcolm Hayes. But as soon as the results land, Clare flicks off the monitor. It is too much. She will ask Malcolm herself. He will be here in an hour.

In her room Clare takes a long shower, holding her head back under the hot water. How familiar it feels to be in an unfamiliar place, to squeeze shampoo from a bottle the size of her thumb. The cycle of rooms with their double beds, cheap patterned quilts versus the soft down bed of this city hotel. She steps out and wipes the fog from the mirror, studying her shoulder. The scar looks like a flower, the flaring red circle at its center surrounded by a wash of pink skin. She rubs body lotion into it, pressing into the dead tissue at the center, the pain duller. The case no longer needs to be Clare's to solve. But something compels her.

Maybe you're learning how to do the job, Somers said this morning in the café.

There is a knock. Clare goes to the spy hole with the towel wrapped around her. Why is he so early? But instead of Malcolm she sees Raylene standing there, arms crossed, nervous.

"One second," Clare says, toweling her hair. She dresses as quickly as she can and opens the door. "Raylene."

"I'm leaving," Raylene says, a rolling carry-on bag at her feet. "Taking a red-eye bus. I wanted to say good-bye."

"Where are you going?"

"I don't know yet. I'm going to book the longest bus ride I can."

Clare steps aside and allows Raylene into the room. Raylene leaves her bag at the door and walks to the window. Clare watches her as she peers down to the street below. Raylene wears clean clothes; a pink tailored T-shirt and dark capris. Her hair is combed into a neat ponytail.

"Your ex-husband was reported missing," Clare says finally.

"They found his car. An APB went out. It names you. Somers is on to you."

"I figured. So I'm leaving. Onwards."

"Raylene, do you know where Sally is?"

"No," Raylene says. "Do you?"

"I have a theory," Clare says.

"Everyone has a theory."

"Listen," Clare says, "I know you need to go. And you don't have to tell me what's going on if you don't want to. Will you be okay?"

"I've got ID," Raylene says. "Some money. I figure I don't have to worry about Sally taking heat anymore."

"Sally taking heat? For what?"

Raylene's eyes fill with tears. For a long time she stares at Clare, as if deciding. Gauging.

"He's dead," Raylene says.

"Who's dead?"

"Him. My husband."

"What happened?"

Raylene walks to the bed and sits, her hands folded in her lap.

"You know when you finally reach that point where it has to end?" she says. "One way or another?"

"Yes," Clare says. "I do."

"Three weeks ago he came to High River. I don't even know how he found me. Honestly, it occurred to me that Markus called him. Markus knew I was on to his affair with Sally. What better way to get rid of me than to tip off my husband? Anyway, it was a Sunday morning, and Sally and I were the only ones home at the big house. And William. He was there too. My husband arrived at the front door. Sally was the one who answered but I was right there in the kitchen eating a bowl of Cheerios. Right in front of him. He was wearing this stupid old baseball cap he's had forever. He took it off and held it to his chest. He had a picture of the kids. He sat at the table with us. Sally, William, me, him. He passed the picture to Sally, tousled William's hair. I remember Sally looking at me, the rage in her eyes, and she'd be nodding at me so slightly, like she was trying to send me a message, but then she'd turn to him and nod full out and frown like she was listening and wanted to hear his side. She amazed me, how quickly she could flip that switch just looking from me to him and back. I knew she'd do whatever I needed her to do."

When Raylene pauses, Clare touches her arm to coax her.

"He said he wanted me back," Raylene continues. "He asked me to drive with him to the grave. To their grave. I'd buried them in the same cemetery where my parents were laid to rest. A few hours from High River. Three hours. But, honestly? I never visited them. Not once. I couldn't bear it. And here he was, as if everything was normal. As if he were a normal husband just trying to make amends. I just couldn't bear it."

"Of course you couldn't."

"Sally took charge. She was being nice to my husband, but of course I knew. I knew her. She told him to get in the car and wait for us at the end of the driveway. We'd both go with him to the cemetery. Six hours round-trip. She took William upstairs for a nap even though it was morning. Then she came back down with this bag. She called Markus to come over and look after William. You know. She and Markus. Fucking Markus. He came over like this little puppy dog and she told him we need to take a run into the city and won't be back until after dinner. She told him she'd called us a cab to take us to the commuter bus station five miles away. She was all business. The way she just aligned the lies. It was remarkable."

When Raylene pauses again, Clare stands and collects two glasses of water from the bathroom. She hands one to Raylene and sits back down without a word.

"As we were walking to my husband's car, I'm freaking out, thinking he's going to kill us. No, Sally said to me, *we're* going to deal with this. Fuck this shit, she said. I got in the front seat and my husband smiled at me and squeezed my arm and I wanted to vomit. To punch his teeth in. We drove to the cemetery and Sally made small talk with him from the backseat. She talked about politics, the weather. Isn't the heat crazy? she was saying to him. I wanted to punch her too. I felt like I was going to faint. I wanted to die. To jump out of the car on the highway. Because I was listening to him talk to Sally and I could hear him talking to our kids at the dinner table or on the stand at his godforsaken trial. That same voice. Eventually we got to the cemetery and we were standing at the grave, the three of us. Sally excused herself. Said she wanted to give us some privacy. And I wanted to kill her but I was frozen there. Numb. Reading their names. Two years between birth and death. My husband was kneeling at the grave. He was crying. He was actually crying. Forgive me, he said. He said that. But then Sally came up. She was beside me and I could see that she was holding a tire iron. Where did she get a tire iron? She nodded at me. I nodded back. Then she took one swing, whoosh, just like that, and it cracked his skull. You could hear it. Crack. He crumpled."

"Jesus," Clare says.

"The worst thing was, he wasn't dead. He was unconscious, he was in bad shape. His skull was fractured, he probably had bleeding on the brain. But he was breathing. We dragged him to the car. What do you want to do? Sally asked me. She had this look on her face. Not fear. It was like exhilaration. I told her to drive. I'm giving her directions. It took us about half an hour to get to this place where my father used to take me. Deep in the woods. There's this abandoned cabin with an old well. My dad and I would go there so he could hunt."

Clare studies the details of Raylene's face, her stare fixed absently as she sips the water Clare gave her, the slight quiver in her lip the only sign of distress.

"Just tell me, please," Raylene says. "What would you have done if you were in the same situation? If it was him or you. Would you kill your husband? If it came to that?"

What a revealing question, Clare thinks. But Raylene's expression is so pained, pleading, that Clare answers.

"I would have shot him," Clare says. "I'm a good shot. I would have killed him in your shoes. But with a gun. To be certain."

"Guns aren't certain." Raylene points to Clare's shoulder. "Look at you. I learned that many times over in the ER. It's too easy to miss."

"I wouldn't miss," Clare says.

Raylene breathes fast to scuttle the tears.

"In her bag Sally had a sheet and some rope she'd seen in a closet at High River. Like some kind of well-trained mafioso. She asked me what I wanted her to do. And you know, I wanted a witness. I wanted someone to watch him die."

"I get it," Clare says, swallowing.

"He was lying there, and I was fumbling. Panicking. But then his eyes opened. He was groggy and weak, but he knew what was happening. He tried to stand up but couldn't get up past his knees. He touched the back of his head and felt the blood. 'Bitch,' he said. 'You dumb bitch.' His words were slurred. I pushed him back to the ground. Sally handed me the rope. At first I didn't know what I was supposed to do with it.

But I swear, I saw my kids. Something happened. Some kind of instinct took over. I wrapped the rope around his neck and pulled as hard as I could. Sally stood over me and watched. After he was dead we wrapped him up and threw his body down the well. Like a pair of psychopaths."

Raylene peels back the collar of her T-shirt to reveal faded scratch marks.

"I'm not a killer," she says. "Neither is Sally."

But you *are*, Clare thinks.

"You killed someone who you believed deserved to die," Clare says.

A silence falls between them. Clare knows Raylene is watching her. She imagines Jason in the woods, enfeebled by a blow to the head, lunging at Clare, calling her a bitch. In that scene Clare would have done it. She would have lifted her gun at him. The only uncertainty would be where to aim. His head or his heart.

"What did you do after you'd put him . . ." Clare can't think of the words.

Raylene sighs and looks to the ceiling. "We wiped down the car. His car. We drove it fifty miles in the wrong direction, away from the graves, from anywhere anyone would expect him to be. Parked it on an old road and walked to the nearest town. Bought tickets for a milk-run bus back to the city. At the bus station I remember feeling this weird energy, like I was high. But Sally couldn't stop crying. She was making a scene. That was the thing about Sally. It's like she was two different people. The one who could spur me to kill him, and the one weeping in the bus station. Over what? Maybe it's because she was pregnant. I wish she'd told me that. I wish I'd caught on."

"What happened when you got back to the city?" Clare asks.

"We bought new clothes, put our old stuff in a bag, and

found a Dumpster. Like a pair of criminals. Sally called Jordan and he picked us up and drove us back to High River." Raylene chokes on her sobs. "We were home in time for Sally to read William bedtime stories."

And then Raylene falls back on the bed, curling to a fetal position, fists in balls, weeping. Clare doesn't move. She doesn't have it in her to comfort this woman. Clare feels a strange mix of disgust, pity, relief. Even jealousy.

"You could turn yourself in," Clare says finally. "I could talk to Somers for you. With you. She'll help you."

Raylene rocks back to sitting and uses her shirt to wipe her tears. "No," she says. "No."

"You tell me all this and now you're just going to disappear? What about Sally?"

"Sally's gone. She's days ahead of me."

"You don't know that. Her son is dead. She could be alive. You're abandoning her. Somers is a pro cop. She'll figure this all out." Clare goes to the door and grips the knob. Malcolm will be here soon. She needs Raylene to leave. "Tell Somers. I'm telling you. She'll do her best to help you if you confess."

"I don't want her help." Raylene hoists herself up and kneels to open her suitcase. She unzips the inside flap and lifts a handgun from the bag. "I want to give you this."

"Jesus," Clare says. "Where did you get that?"

"It was Sally's. I've kept it. I was hiding it. I don't even know how to work it. But you do, right?"

"Yes," Clare says.

"I think she would want you to have it."

Clare takes the gun and breaks it open. It is loaded. She opens the top drawer to the dresser and sets it at the back. Raylene's movements are hurried now. She zips her suitcase and edges past Clare to the door. In the hotel hallway she stops and turns back. They stand in silence, Raylene's arms dropped at her sides, a zombie. Clare feels it, how she distances herself from this woman and her pain. She cannot take it on. It is not Clare's job to take it on.

"Just so you know," Raylene says, her voice dull, "I was Sally's friend too."

Too, Clare thinks. Raylene will never know of the lies Clare told to reel her in, to gain her trust. Before Clare can respond Raylene spins on her heel and turns the corner to the elevator bank. *It suited you to disappear into thin air,* Grace had said in the café. *You didn't think about us.* And perhaps she'd been right, Clare thinks as she hears the ding of the elevator carrying Raylene. Sally might still be alive, but Raylene is leaving anyway, abandoning the friend who'd stood with her as she did the unthinkable.

Malcolm Boon sits on one bed, Clare facing him on the other. At exactly eight o'clock he'd knocked and this time, she'd let him in. When the door closed behind him, they did a small dance, before settling in front of each other, knees nearly touching in the space between the beds.

"Where do I begin?" Clare says. "Colin Rourke? The cop you were telling me to stay away from? The dangerous one? He told me about you. About your trust fund. Your family and the plane crash. Your wife who vanished. The case that has you as the prime suspect. You're Malcolm Hayes. Your wife is Zoe."

Clare pauses but Malcolm only returns her stare, unblinking. How familiar he's become to her in the last month, his features, his hair grown out, his skin a hint darker from the summer sun. The scar.

"He lured you here," Clare says. "Did you know that? Lured us here."

A wave of understanding passes over Malcolm's face. He

presses his hand to his forehead, a gesture Clare now understands as his way of shielding whatever rage or fear or sadness is passing through him.

"You've been lying to me this whole time," Clare says.

Malcolm shakes his head. *No.*

"About your wife. About why you do this work. About your childhood friend the cop?" Clare feels her voice rise, tremble. "He has a file on me too, you know. He knows my real name. He knows all about Jason."

Still Malcolm can only shake his head, his lips parting then closing as if the words won't come. Through the hotel room wall Clare hears the din of cartoons. The boy and his family.

"But," Clare continues, tapping her forehead with a finger. "But! He says he's trying to help. And you know what? I've been thinking about it. What if he actually is trying to help? I know it's a big what-if. So there's the question. Who am I supposed to believe? You? The man who basically entrapped me and has been lying to me ever since? The man who might have killed his wife? Or Rourke? A bona fide police officer who seems like he wants to solve cases?"

"Clare," Malcolm says, his voice a whisper.

"It's not a question of trust, really. It's a question of which of you do I distrust the least."

"You know nothing about him," Malcolm says.

"I know nothing about *you*! By your design, I know nothing about you."

"You know more than you think. Maybe you don't remember—"

"You keep saying that. See? But I do. I remember the gun in the motel room. I remember pointing it at you, okay? Like some junkie needing her fix. But Malcolm, I'm past that. I think I am. And I'm tired of people telling me what I do and don't remember. You were trying to control me. I'm done being controlled."

"No. I was trying to help you. Because I—"

"Right. Men say that all the time. But you don't know what it actually means to help."

"I had the best of intentions."

"You changed my bandages and gave me food," Clare says. "Like a guard might for his prisoner."

"I was trying to help," Malcolm repeats.

"And maybe Rourke's trying to help you. If you're not guilty of killing your wife, what are you worried about? He's your friend, isn't he?"

"You of all people should know how little that means."

The words are meant to pierce, and they do. A knot forms instantly in her throat.

"Maybe you did kill her and this is your way of dealing with the remorse."

Finally it alights in Malcolm, the temper she always suspected was there. He stands and paces before slamming a fist into the wall, the drywall buckling. He retracts his hand and rubs at his knuckles, pacing again. His eyes lock with Clare's. Through the wall, the TV sounds are gone.

"I would never, ever hurt her."

"You don't get to be angry with me," Clare says. "Is she dead?"

"No."

"How do you know?"

"Because she's sending me messages."

"What kind of messages?"

"Letters. Not letters. E-mails."

"Can't you trace them?"

"I've tried. She's very smart. Smarter than me."

"Why is she sending you e-mails?"

"Because. You don't know her. She's . . ." Malcolm breathes deeply and sits on the corner of the bed. "Her family. There's this whole side to her I knew nothing about when we got married. Five years ago her father was shot to death while eating dinner at a local bistro. There were these ties. These dealings. She was always good at keeping terrible secrets. Good at behaving as if my money was irrelevant to her. She and Colin knew each other before I even met her. They dated all through high school. He was in love with her. Did you know that? Did he tell you that? They have a long history."

As he speaks Malcolm runs his finger up and down the length of his scar. It might seem implausible, Clare knows, the notion that deep secrets could be held in the confines of a marriage, that you could marry one person, then watch them turn into another before your eyes.

"If she's reaching out to you, why don't you just show Rourke the e-mails?"

"Because I think he's part of it. I think they . . ."

"You think they *what*?"

"Clare," Malcolm says, looking up at her. "Do you really not trust me?"

"You don't get to ask for my trust when you've never offered me yours."

Malcolm stands and takes a step towards Clare.

"You don't know him," Malcolm says, his tone pleading. "You don't know Colin. What he's capable of. He's got a vendetta against me. Always has. Blames me for things I had no control over. My family's business was sold when we were young. I know it wasn't good for his family, but it wasn't my fault. He turned to ice. Eventually he came back into my life. He got a dozen scholarship offers but ended up at the same college as me? He was like a shadow. Especially after Zoe and I got married. I'm telling you, he covers it well, but Colin Rourke is made of something different. You have no idea. You have no idea what he might have done to lure us both here."

"What are you talking about?"

"Sally Proulx."

"What about her?"

"Why would she disappear? Have you found any good reason?"

"She has enemies. She has a husband she left behind. She has a dead son. She had a lot of reasons to run away. More than you can possibly know. Malcolm, you're being paranoid."

"Don't say that," Malcolm says. "Have I ever said that to you? Have I ever called you paranoid?"

"Yes," Clare says. "You have."

There is a knock at the door that startles them both. They stand frozen. A voice drifts through. *Is everything okay in there?* Clare points at Malcolm to stay back before she fiddles with the chain to unlock it. A man stands at a safe distance from the door, angled so that only Clare can see him, his hands raised defensively. By his looks Clare can tell at once that he is the father from the room next door.

"Sorry," he says. "We just heard a bang. Some . . . loud voices."

"Yes," Clare says. "Sorry about that. I knocked over a lamp. We're just, we got a little hotheaded . . . it's fine."

The man stares directly at Clare, eyes narrowing.

Are you okay? He mouths the words.

In a flash Clare sees Christopher in her kitchen at home, hand on her back. *Are you okay? I don't think you're okay.* The way she'd snatched herself out from under his touch, the exasperation she'd felt at his concern. Clare feigns her gentlest smile and gives the man a thumbs-up. He doesn't retreat. She looks him square in the eyes.

Thank you, she mouths back.

When she closes the door and turns back, Malcolm hovers close.

"Colin paid me up front," he says. "Wired me the money. For this case. Obviously I didn't know it was from him. He was clearly trying to guarantee I'd come." Malcolm points to an envelope on the bed. "It's all there. I have to go."

"Go where?" Clare says.

"I can't stay here any longer," he says.

"At some point don't you think it's better to stop running?"

"You confused everything," Malcolm says. "We confused everything. I did. That was never my intention."

"And now you're leaving," Clare says.

"I don't have a choice. I shouldn't have come here."

When Malcolm bends to rest his cheek on Clare's shoulder, she freezes. On her inhale she can smell him, a musk. His face buries into her neck and he shakes. She can feel his beard, the wet of his tears on her skin. Clare lifts her hand and combs her fingers into his hair. Malcolm raises his head and puts a palm to her cheek, his thumb tracing her lips. He hovers, about to kiss her. But when he leans to close the final space between them, Clare presses her hand to his chest.

"Don't," she says.

"Clare."

But now she can't look at him.

"Am I in danger?" Clare asks.

"He's not after you. He's after me."

"Then you need to go. You should go."

Clare moves to the door and holds it open, eyes averted, steadfast.

"I want to say . . . I don't know—"

"Malcolm," Clare says. "You need to go."

Without a word he sweeps past her into the hall. Clare hears the ping of the elevator and the doors open and close, swallowing him. Just like that, Malcolm Boon is gone.

FRIDAY

The hospice looks like a home, the branches of a large maple tree on the lawn sweeping against the windows of its second floor. Clare presses the buzzer and waits, the exhaustion deep in her bones. She had stayed awake in the hotel room all night, recounting everything, the contents of the folder spread across the bed, Clare searching for missing clues. She understood that it wasn't just Sally she was searching for anymore. She understood that this somehow connected back to Malcolm. But how? By dawn Clare had charted a path, made a plan. She'd wrapped the gun Raylene gave her in a hand towel and set it at the bottom of her backpack.

First stop: St. Jude's. A hospice, Clare discovered in her research. PALLIATIVE CARE CENTER, a plaque on the door reads. Janice Twining is dying.

The woman who answers the door wears scrubs with a badge pinned on her breast. SUZANNE. CLIENT CARE COORDINATOR.

"I'm here to see Janice Twining," Clare says.

The woman leads Clare into a large foyer that feels as warm as it is outside.

"Can I tell her who's here?"

"Her niece," Clare says. "Clare."

"Wait here."

Suzanne ascends a long set of mahogany stairs. Despite the homey touches, this place still feels medical, emergency plans lining the walls, a box of latex gloves on the table at the foyer's center. The smell is too sterile. Clare wants to gag. Suzanne reappears at the top of the stairs and waves Clare up.

"She'll see you now in her room."

Clare follows her up the stairs and down the hallway to the very end. Suzanne guides her into the last room. Clare gathers herself before crossing the threshold. She finds Janice on a bed angled up to sitting, her legs covered by a homemade quilt. In her profile her jawbone is pronounced, her skin tinged yellow, a plain blue scarf tied over her head. She barely resembles the woman from the pictures Clare found online. Janice's gaze is fixed out the window.

"I don't have any nieces," she says.

"I took my chances," Clare replies.

"You knew me by name. You must have a reason to be here."

Clare hovers, uncertain. "Do you mind if I sit?"

"I can't stop you."

Clare sets her backpack down in the corner, heavy with the weight of her gun. She pulls up a chair so it faces Janice. She thinks of her mother's hospital room, the snow-coated parking lot out the window, the highway beyond it. Her mother had wanted nothing from home, no attempt to warm her room with photographs or trinkets, just as there are none here in Janice's room beyond the quilt. I can't bring any of it with me when I go, her mother mused from her wheelchair as they surveyed it together. If she understood that room would be the last place she'd ever see, she showed no regret over it.

"You're one of Helen's lost girls," Janice says.

Clare bristles. *Lost girls.* "No. Well, not exactly. I'm here about Sally Proulx."

"Ah," Janice says. "Clare. Yes. Jordan mentioned you when he was here last night. He said you're an investigator."

So, Clare thinks, Jordan knows she is working the case. Someone must have told him. Somers, or Rourke? At this point Clare knows it no longer matters. The act is over. It ended yesterday when Rourke revealed himself to Clare, when Clare told Raylene the truth too.

"Yes," Clare says. "I've been undercover at High River. And I know that you've been part of helping women escape their pasts for a long time. Helping your husband with his work."

"Helping my husband?" Janice says. "No. This has been *my* life's work. Philip was just along for the ride."

Now it makes sense, Clare thinks, why there is no sign of Philip in this room. Not a single reminder.

"I don't mean to pry," Clare says. "But I've met Philip. At his office. He said he hasn't seen you. He doesn't know you're . . . here?"

Janice smiles. "He does not."

Clare isn't sure what to say. Even in divorce, terminal illness seems like quite the secret to keep. Janice studies Clare, reading her thoughts.

"Philip took forty-eight years of my life," she says. "I figured I'd take back my own death. Go it alone. He'd just make it all about him anyway."

A nurse appears in the doorway. Janice lifts a limp hand to wave her off.

"I'm not hiding from him," Janice continues. "I just haven't told him where I am. Unsurprisingly, he's not putting much work into finding me."

"Does he even know you're . . ."

"Dying?" Janice says. "No. He doesn't."

The tray is out of reach, so Janice must lean forward to collect the Styrofoam cup of ice cubes. She lifts one and runs it over her flaked lips before sucking on it. Janice looks just as Clare's mother did in her final weeks, gaunt and wispy bald under her scarf.

"I'm sure he'd want to see you, especially if he knew."

"It doesn't matter what he wants," Janice says.

"What about what Helen wants? Or Jordan? Markus?"

Janice smiles, wistful. "Jordan looks so much like his father," she says. "It's striking. I find I have a hard time looking him in the eye these days. All I see is Gerald. His father. He's the spitting image."

Clare says nothing, allowing Janice room to continue.

"Gerald was a star. There's no other word for it. He was just gorgeous."

"You're speaking about a man who murdered his own wife," Clare says.

"Believe me, I know," Janice says. "By the time it happened, he and Philip had been law partners for ten years. Margaret was my best friend. I adored those children. They were all so beautiful, just like their parents. Philip and I weren't blessed with any children of our own, so I thought of those kids as my family. We were all like family. Philip said Gerald had a temper. But don't we all have tempers? I never realized . . ."

Janice's expression turns mournful, her hands folded across

her chest. Clare thinks of the way Jason's friends would glance at her when Jason flared over a football game or a lost poker hand, as if they understood how that temper might translate behind closed doors.

"I just missed the signs," Janice says. "They were there, and I missed them. And my dear friend Margaret didn't feel she could confide in me, and then she was dead. She paid the price. After that it became my life's work, to make amends to my friend for not helping her in time. Raising her kids, working to help as many women as we could to escape men like Gerald."

"That must have been difficult for you," Clare says. "And the Haines children, they must have—"

"They were traumatized. The older two, at least. Helen was nearly fifteen. Almost a grown-up. Markus . . . he struggled. He was angry. And Jordan was just a sweet little baby with no inkling of the injustice the world had already dealt him. They lived with us for five years, until Helen inherited the house and the trust fund and took on her brothers' care herself."

"And she wanted to move back to the High River house?"

"She was insistent," Janice says. "We tried to support her, Philip and me. She wanted to make it a refuge. To do the same work we were doing. But that house. It's so awful. So . . . haunted. Full of ghosts. Her mother's blood is in the soil. And Helen? She was damaged. Iced over." The shift in Janice's expression is immediate. "And pregnant, of all things."

"Pregnant with Ginny?" Clare asks.

Janice clenches at the quilt, her fingers too bony.

"Did you ever meet Ginny's father?" Clare prods.

"Oh, I've met him. I know him very well. He couldn't help himself."

"Oh," Clare says.

"He just couldn't."

Clare feels her stomach twist. It clicks. Another piece. Philip in the office the other day, swooping Ginny into his arms, offering her money, coddling her as a guilty father might do.

"How old was Helen when . . . ?" Clare begins.

"Eighteen when he got her pregnant," Janice says. "Nineteen by the time Ginny was born."

"Does Ginny know Philip is her father?"

"I'm quite sure no one knows. Except Philip, Helen, and me. And now you." Janice straightens up, her collarbones angling out sharply.

"Why the cover-up?" Clare asks.

"I ask myself that question now more than ever. The truth is, I don't know. To save face, maybe?" Janice lets out an anguished laugh. "At first Helen and Philip tried to hide it from me. I'm astounded that I couldn't see it. Couldn't see the way they were carrying on. Or maybe I just didn't want to see it. Philip whistling while he shaved, hitting the gym to pump iron. Helen quiet, never looking me in the eye. Wearing baggy clothes. She was six months pregnant before I even realized. I think she was in denial too. She'd yet to see a doctor. How stupid can you possibly be? By then there were no viable options but to have the baby."

Janice looks to the ceiling, her eyes glassy with tears. Clare is silent and still in the chair.

"What was I to do?" Janice continues. "I offered to keep the baby myself. But it was clear Helen wasn't going to give it up. She wanted that child. It became clear to Helen too that Philip wasn't her knight in shining armor. That he was a weak fool. He behaved the worst of anyone. Offering her money to give the baby up. But she refused. She swore to me she wouldn't tell anyone if I didn't, provided she could keep the baby. She had enough of her own money and said she wanted nothing from us but our silence. She came to me one night, her belly all the way out to here, and told me she was sorry. Said it was her fault. That she'd let it happen. She didn't stop him when he tried to seduce her. Can you believe that? A child, apologizing for the transgressions of a grown man."

"So Helen just left?" Clare asks. "Went back to High River?"

"We made a pact, Helen and I. Promised we'd keep the secret. We confronted Philip together and gave him an ultimatum. He would keep the secret too, and he would never touch Helen again or go near her or the child. And Philip, the great savior of women, never seemed terribly troubled by our pact, by abdicating responsibility for his only child. As long as no one openly besmirched his virtue."

There are many questions that might come next. About why Janice chose to stay with Philip, to keep his dirty secret. About why Helen would want to return to a house filled with such harrowing memories. Janice lifts a wand cabled to her morphine drip and presses the button.

"Why are you telling me all of this?" Clare asks.

"Because you asked. Because I've made mistakes. Because who else is there to tell? Not Jordan. It would break his heart. So, lucky you! Happening upon my final confession."

Clare cannot look at Janice. She fixates instead on the contents of the bedside table. Hand cream, a half-eaten packet of saltine crackers, a pad and pen, a box of tissues, a rosary.

"The strange thing is," Janice says, "I didn't hate him. After the kids were gone, things went back to normal, in a way. Philip and I just continued on with our lives. I buried it. Women are capable of that. Of burying things. I've had a full life. He was good to me in a lot of ways, probably making amends too. But recently, it all bubbled back up. Maybe it was the cancer growing in me. Forcing things out."

Imagine, Clare thinks, considering yourself lucky to be married to a man who fathered a child with a teenager you'd promised to protect. The act of dying leaves you bitter or wistful, Clare's mother used to say on their visits to the hospital for her treatments, and the luck of your actual life doesn't predict which way you'll swing.

"This can't have anything to do with Sally Proulx," Clare says.

"Don't be so sure," Janice answers.

Clare feels a swell of impatience that shames her. "Janice," she says. "Please. If you know anything about Sally, can you tell me? I'm afraid for her."

"I have an apartment," Janice says. "A hideaway. One of those little buildings I've always loved. You know, with a courtyard pool? I rented it for over a year before I left Philip. It sat empty, waiting for me. That's how long it took me to build up the courage to leave him."

Clare opens her mouth to speak, but Janice lifts a hand to stop her.

"I lived there for five days before I got the final diagnosis. Five days free of him. That's all I got. The liver, you know. No one lasts long when it hits the liver. I'd been having symptoms for months. Deep down, I knew. Maybe that's why I finally left." She lets out a long sigh. "Life is cruel, isn't it?"

The warbled slur in Janice's voice is familiar to Clare. Morphine.

"Janice—"

"Helen called me," Janice says. "A week ago. Less. She was desperate. There was a woman who'd made some terrible mistakes, she told me. A dead child. Helen needed to get her out of High River fast. She needed a place to go."

"Is Sally Proulx at your apartment?" Clare asks, her voice rising.

Janice nods almost imperceptibly. With great effort she draws herself forward and collects the pad and pen from the bedside table. The address she scribbles is barely legible, but Clare can just make it out.

"You're making me anxious now," Janice says, falling back to her pillow. "I need you to leave."

Janice presses the button again, this time with urgency. Clare collects her backpack and rests her hand on Janice's leg, so brittle through the blanket that Clare worries it will crack under her touch.

"Thank you," Clare says.

Janice nods, eyes closed. Clare exits the room and winds down the hallway. She takes the stairs two at a time, pressing onto the street before anyone from the hospice can intercept her.

Clare jogs down the leafy street until she matches the address on the building to the one scribbled on the paper. Number 4316. An old brick low-rise apartment with a gated yard. In the courtyard an older man swimming laps in the pool climbs out and towels himself off. Clare approaches the door. It's locked. On the call list she finds the listing J GODFREY under apartment 2A. She makes a show of searching through her bag until the old man meanders over and uses his own key to let her in.

Clare takes the stairs to the second floor and walks the long hall. She knocks on 2A and listens. Shuffling. She knocks again.

"Sally?" she calls, ear to the door. "Sally?"

The door opens. Helen Haines, her shoulders slumped. Exhausted. She steps aside wordlessly and allows Clare to enter the apartment. The living room is sunny and lined with boxes and packages of unassembled furniture. *Five days*, Janice had said. Clare looks left to right, peering through the doorways to the kitchen, to the bedroom, for any sign of someone else.

"Where is she, Helen?" Clare asks. "Where's Sally?"

Helen sinks into the couch. "She's gone. I came here last night and she was gone."

Clare sits at the far edge of the couch, allowing Helen a wide berth.

"Do you know where she went?"

The look Helen gives Clare is pure anger, ice. "Somers told me the truth about you," she says. "A hired PI. And here you are. Investigating."

"I'm sorry I wasn't honest with you," Clare says. "But you never would have let me stay if—"

"No," Helen says. "I wouldn't have."

"Helen," Clare says, reaching for her hand. "Let's start at the beginning. Tell me what happened. I can help you."

"Ha." Helen laughs bitterly. "You can help me? You were never even her friend."

"No," Clare says. "But what I told you by the river about my own life? That was true. I left my husband and I've been on the run ever since. I really do care. I want Sally to be safe. I want you to be safe. Raylene. Ginny too. Where is Ginny?"

"She's on her way," Helen says.

"Good," Clare says. "We can get to the bottom of this. Truly. I want to help. Let's just start at the beginning."

Helen sighs and presses her fingers to her temples.

"He was already dead," Helen says. "By the time I got to Markus and Rebecca's, he was dead."

"William?"

Helen nods.

"Okay," Clare says.

"The boy had been sick for a week, maybe more. We all knew he was sick, fevered. Rebecca had been treating him. She has these . . . potions. These tinctures she was giving him to break the fever. Tinctures! Sally seemed okay with letting them take care of him. I told Markus they needed to take William to the hospital. But Rebecca . . . she kept interfering. And Sally trusted them. She trusted Markus, especially. I talked to Markus that very afternoon and he said the boy was getting better. He promised me they'd take him to the hospital the next morning if the fever hadn't broken. Rebecca really wanted to see what she could do on her own. But later that night Sally came to find me. She was beside herself. By the time we got back to Markus's house, William had stopped breathing. There he was, this tiny little body, pale as a ghost on their couch. And Rebecca said nothing when I came in. Nothing. It was like she was made of stone. Sally hugged William to her. He died in her arms."

"Jesus," Clare says. "Why didn't you call the police then? Or an ambulance?"

"Because everyone panicked." Helen wipes a tear. "I went to call 911, but Markus stopped me. 'You can't! They'll arrest us,' he said. 'They'll call it neglect. They'll blame Rebecca. We'll go to jail for years. They'll take Willow.' And Rebecca, I turned to her then, and I don't even know that she was flustered. Maybe she was in shock. All she said was that she didn't understand why the tincture didn't work. Like some kind of fool! And Sally was hysterical, saying over and over that she wanted to die. And if that wasn't enough, Markus started going on about Jordan. How hard he'd been working on my behalf with the developers. How a dead boy might mean the property couldn't be sold. A scandal. An end to the safe house. To Jordan's reputation. And when I mentioned the police again it was Sally who started screaming, 'No police! They'll arrest us!' I couldn't think straight. I didn't know what to do."

Clare sees it, the stillness of the boy's body, the chaos, Sally's terror. She must have known that if the police came they might also trace her to the scene of Raylene's husband's death, that her crimes extended beyond the agony of her dead son.

"So what did you do?" Clare asks.

"I phoned Janice," Helen says. "I couldn't think of anyone else. Anyone I could really trust. She's the only person I know who could hide something of this magnitude. There she was, dying of cancer in a hospice bed, and she took control. She told me to get Sally to the bridge right away. Walk her a mile beyond it. She would find someone to come for her. Someone she could pay off to keep quiet. Janice had people. People to call. She'd seen it all before. That operation Jordan and Philip say they run? The work they do? It was always Janice. She is the brains behind everything."

Helen is curled over, head lowered, her hands wringing furiously between her knees. Her composure finally unraveled.

"What did Janice tell you to do with William?" Clare asks.

"She told me to hide his body." The words come out in a wracking sob. "She told me to get Markus to bury him somewhere deep on the property. Told me the story we'd tell was that Sally and her boy just left. That they left High River on their own and we didn't know why. No one would question that. Women leave High River all the time. Come and go, sometimes under the cloak of night. Janice promised me that she would help Sally. We both would. Help her like we've helped so many women before. Help her escape and start a new life. Once she was here in this apartment, we'd figure out where she could go next. Except her son wouldn't be with her."

"You must have known Raylene would wonder what happened to her friend. Sally's things were still at the house. They were close and—"

"I had a plan for that. We had a plan. But when Sally and

I were headed for the bridge, she collapsed by the river. She was clawing at the ground. She was trying to throw herself in. She screamed. It took all my might to keep her from jumping. I managed to calm her down and get her away from the edge. I promised her everything would be okay. I told her to think about the baby she was carrying."

"You knew she was pregnant?" Clare asks.

Helen only blinks. But it's all the answer Clare needs.

"Raylene heard Sally's scream," Clare says. "By the river. But she didn't see you."

"Yes," Helen says. "She heard her. And Raylene came to find me to tell me something was wrong, but obviously I wasn't in the house. She'd seen Sally earlier, before the boy was dead, and Sally had seemed so agitated. So Raylene phoned Jordan. She told him something was very wrong. That she thought she'd heard Sally screaming by the river. And now she couldn't find Sally, or me. After they hung up Raylene ran out to the river, but Sally was already gone. Jordan phoned the police from his loft. And imagine." A desperate laugh escapes Helen. "By the time I got back from leaving Sally at the drop-off point, the police were arriving. Then Jordan arrived too. The cops were searching the riverbank, and Jordan told Raylene to *lie* to the police, to say she saw Sally go into the river instead of just hearing a scream. Because Jordan—good-hearted, sweet Jordan—was afraid that if Raylene didn't say that, that if there was no eyewitness, the cops wouldn't dredge the river. Sally would be treated as just another troubled woman gone missing. Another woman who probably just ran away."

Another troubled woman gone missing. Those words jab at Clare.

"Sally was in a getaway car by then," Helen says. "One of Janice's trusted crew was driving Sally here. And Janice was in her bed at the hospice, orchestrating it all. William was dead and Markus was trying to hide the body. And I was on my porch at High River watching the police look for a woman I'd vowed to protect and her young son when I knew exactly where they both were."

Now Clare cannot recount the specifics of her conversations with Helen in the days since arriving at High River. She remembers only the composure, the stoicism masking both this terrible story and the deception required to cover it up.

"I still don't understand how the boy ended up in the river," Clare says.

"Markus was beside himself. His one job was to take care of the body. But he panicked. He told me that he found a spot and buried him. And the search parties came and went and then the boy turned up in the river days later. 'What did you do?' I said to Markus. He told me he panicked. He realized the body would be found when the developers razed the place. So he dug him up and put him in the river so it would seem like he'd drowned." Helen shakes her head. "Markus doesn't think. He's not a thinker. He doesn't think of the science, the logic. That the coroners would uncover what he'd done. He thought the water would wash away the truth."

It strains Clare to mask her disgust with Markus, with Helen. How could you do that? Clare wants to ask. How? She thinks of Somers in the café yesterday. *People will go to extreme lengths*, she said, *to absolve their loved ones of wrongdoing.*

"And Sally," Helen continues. "She was crazed. The grief was too much, especially on top of the pregnancy. We needed to figure out something for her, but she said she didn't want to stay here. We got her sleeping pills, had someone with her around the clock. But she wanted to see Markus. Markus!" Helen straightens up. "You know, if I were to do it all over again, I would not have lulled any of the women in my care into feeling safe. I would have given them all the same things. A roof over their heads, options for the future. But I would have told them there's no such thing as safety. Because sometimes even the people who mean well end up being a danger to you. You will always be a rabbit in a hole. You should never let go of the fear."

Helen's expression is impassive. Empty.

"It's not too late to tell the truth," Clare says. "You can still help Sally. We can find her."

"I watched my father kill my mother," Helen says.

"I know you did."

"Do you remember what it's like to be fifteen? Imagine seeing such a thing at that age. Your brother is screaming, hiding under the sink. And your other brother, a baby, is asleep upstairs. And your mother is dead on the lawn and your father is standing in front of you holding the gun that killed her."

"Markus did the right thing, killing your father," Clare says. "He had no choice."

"Ha!" Helen says. "See? You don't know. No one does. Markus? He stayed under that sink. Cowering and crying. I got the gun, not him. *I* went and got the gun. I stood by the sink to make sure my father wouldn't kill Markus too. I had no idea how to fire a gun beyond what I'd seen on TV. All I remember thinking is, Don't let him speak. My father, I mean. Because I knew he'd say something to stop me. He'd make an excuse. He'd blame my mother. She deserved it, he'd say. Or maybe he'd try to convince me it was an accident. I knew I couldn't let him say anything. So when he came through the kitchen door, I fired right away. Got him in the arm. And he stumbled back, then looked down in shock at the blood. Like he couldn't understand why he was bleeding. The second shot got him here."

She touches the soft spot at the base of her neck. "There was no look on his face after that. No expression. He fell over like a log."

The scene paints itself perfectly in Clare's mind, where Helen would have stood in the kitchen, the very place her father would have fallen dead to the floor.

"Why didn't you tell the truth when the police showed up?" Clare asks.

Helen's gaze is far away. "Markus climbed out from under the sink. I handed him the gun and went over to my dad's body to make sure. I turned him over so Markus wouldn't have to see his face. I told Markus to call the police then I went upstairs to get Jordan. He was so heavy for such a little boy. It was hard for me to carry him. By the time I got to the bottom of the staircase the cops were busting through the front door. A neighbor had called them when they heard the first shot. And Markus was standing where I'd left him. He was still holding the gun. It was chaotic. And the cops just assumed."

"They assumed Markus killed your father," Clare says. "Because it could never have been you. The girl."

"That's right," Helen says. " 'You're a hero,' one cop said to Markus as he stood over my dead father. 'You saved your sister's life.' The ambulance drivers, all the cops who showed up, the detectives. They all chimed in. And Markus basked in it. He needed the attention. It was a distraction for him, a distraction from losing his parents the way he did. I couldn't tell the truth after that. And Markus was quick to embellish the story, to add details every time he told it. He needed to be the hero. He was just a kid."

"You were brave," Clare says.

"No, I wasn't. I was vengeful. I hated everyone after that."

"Of course," Clare says. "What happened was traumatizing to you. To Markus."

"Once we moved in with the Twinings, that's when Markus started to get angry too. We were both angry, but he couldn't bury it in the same way. He'd come into my room at night and lean into my pillow. 'Why did you kill our father?' he'd ask me. I couldn't understand the question. In some ways, he was gentle, kind. Most of us are a mix of our parents, a bit or a lot of each. It's taken me a long time to understand that my father's weakness is in him too. Markus isn't a smart man. He doesn't think. I don't know if the trauma froze him in time, or something. Left him with the brain of a child. All I can do is love him anyway, right? Protect him. I can't—"

There's a knock on the door. Both Helen and Clare jump.

"Ginny," Helen whispers.

Clare stands and looks through the peephole. She sees Ginny's face in close-up, her chin raised in defiance. Clare opens the door. Ginny looks shocked to see her. Clare steps aside and allows her to pass.

"What is she doing here?" Ginny asks Helen. "Do you know she's a cop?"

"I'm not a cop," Clare says.

"Rourke said you were lying about being Sally's friend. Who lies about something like that?"

Rourke. At the mention of his name Clare feels the goose bumps crawl along her skin. Ginny looks around the apartment, backing against a far wall, as much distance from Helen as she can create.

"What is this place? You just text me a random address?"

"It's Janice's apartment," Helen says.

"I've been trying to call you," Ginny says to Helen, choking on tears. "Since yesterday! Where the hell have you been?"

"Ginny," Helen says. "There's a lot I can't—"

"I heard you!" Ginny yells. "I fucking heard you!"

"You heard what, Ginny?" Clare asks. "What are you talking about?"

Ginny jabs her finger at Helen, her voice piercing. "I was ready to just forget *all* this shit. Focus on school. Stay at the dorm and forget my crazy fucking family. But I was freaked out. Yesterday, after that whole stupid scene at the house. All of you—my whole family—you're all bat-shit crazy. And I was in my dorm room and I kept seeing William's body. Every time I closed my eyes. It's like I can't even remember what he looked like alive anymore. I even Googled him just to see if I could find an actual picture of him from the news to remember what a cute little guy he was in person. You know? The curly hair, the big eyes. To clear the image of his dead body from my head."

"I'm so sorry," Helen says quietly. "Ginny. I'm so sorry."

"I took a cab all the way back to High River so I wouldn't be alone," Ginny continues. "And I came in through the kitchen and you were in the living room. You were on the phone, all whispery. So I stood back against the wall like some kind of spy and I heard you. 'Sally!' you're saying. 'Sally! Calm down. No one knows where you are. No one knows where Janice even lives.'" Ginny mimics Helen on the phone, hunched and secretive. "And I'm like, *what*? My delinquent mother is talking to the missing woman? What the fuck?"

"I was trying to protect you," Helen says.

"That's what you always say!" Ginny is yelling now. "But what have you ever done to actually protect me?"

The air between them, mother and daughter, is heavy. But Clare feels something else wash over her. A certainty, the dots connecting. She sees the panic in Ginny's eyes.

"Ginny," Clare says. "What did you do after you heard Helen on the phone?"

"I called Rourke," Ginny says, sniffling. "I went outside and called him. He said he would take care of it."

Clare feels light-headed. "Did you tell him where Sally was?"

"Yes!" Ginny says, her voice rising again. "I was freaking out. So I told him! And you want to know what he said? He said I was basically responsible for solving the case. He told me not to tell anyone. Not yet. 'Can you get back to the dorm without anyone seeing you?' he asked me. Oh, sure. I walked to the end of the driveway and called another cab. Rourke told me to wait at the dorm. So I did. And I just sat in my room all night freaking out. I haven't slept, not at all. I was just waiting for someone to call me. You, Helen! But no one did! Rourke wouldn't answer my calls and neither would *you*, Mom. I was afraid to tell Jordan, like he'd freak on me too for trusting Rourke, or for whatever. For fucking up. And I thought about calling Somers, but what if she arrested me? And I kept going online to see if the news had broke that Sally has been found. That she was safe. But nothing ever came up, there *was* no news, and—"

"I don't understand," Helen says to Clare. "I don't understand. If Rourke came to get Sally, why wouldn't he—"

"Ginny," Clare says, cupping Ginny's face and adjusting her own gaze so they are eye to eye. "Listen to me very carefully. Is there anything else you can think of? Anything else Rourke said about where he was going? Anything?"

Ginny thinks for a moment. "He has a boat," she says.

"Yes," Clare says. "He mentioned that once. So?"

"He offered to take me out on it a few days ago. Told me this story about buying a new sail, blue and silver, his baseball team's colors, wanting to try it out on the water. And last night I was lying in bed, and I was thinking about you. And Sally.

Like if you're really an investigator, what sort of things would you be looking for? And a few times, Rourke had these coffee cups, when he'd show up at the house, these cups from some place called the Havana Café. I Googled it, and it's right across from the marina. The marina on the river."

"Yes," Clare says. "Good. How far is that marina from here?"

"Ten-minute walk," Helen says.

The three of them squeeze in, huddling close on the couch. Helen grasps Ginny's hand hard.

"Okay," Clare says. "Listen to me very closely. I'm going to the marina now. And you two will call Somers. And you'll tell her. You need to tell her everything you just told me."

Clare pinches her backpack between her feet, the shape of her gun against her toes. All along she's been searching for the connection, the missing piece tying Sally to Rourke to Malcolm. And now she finally sees it. She understands.

It's me, Clare thinks. I am the final piece of this puzzle.

Clare ran the entire distance to the marina. Now she stands on the dock, working to catch her breath, scanning the rows of boats, the gun hidden against the small of her back, tucked into the waist of her jeans, her backpack left behind with Helen and Ginny. In the farthest row she spots a sailboat with a blue-and-silver sail wrapped around its mast. She closes in. *Homer*, the boat is called. Not the poet, Clare thinks. Homer, as in home run. Baseball.

"Rourke!" Clare calls from the dock. "Rourke?"

Clare hears a latch and the door swings open. Rourke pops out and up the stairs to the deck. If he is surprised to see Clare, he masks it well. He wears a T-shirt and jeans, his gun holstered to his belt.

"You're here," he says. "I'm glad you're here."

"Where is she?" Clare demands.

Rourke scans the docks. "Come on board. We can talk," he says, extending a hand to Clare.

"There's no way I'm getting on that boat."

"You probably should," Rourke says, unholstering his gun and pointing it at the ground, arm straight. "I think you should do what I tell you to do."

There it is, the stillness Clare has felt so few times in her life. The steady calm. The docks are empty, the rows of boats bobbing, the tallest masts tilting in the breeze. No one else in sight. Clare arches. She concentrates on the feeling of her gun against her back, its metal cool. She will go.

"I know you don't want her to get hurt," Rourke says. "Come on."

The effort to pull herself onto the deck rips at Clare's shoulder. Her eyes lock with Rourke's, his face set in a smirk. He gestures for her to descend belowdecks. The boat's cabin is cramped, the walls a faded mahogany, its ceilings too low to fully stand. And seated on a built-in bench at the cabin's far end is Sally Proulx. Pale, thin, the smallest hint of a round belly poking out from under her shirt. Her hands are folded in her lap, her wrists bound together with zip ties. She looks at Clare, eyes vacant.

"Sally?" Clare says. "Are you okay?"

Sally nods too slowly, dazed.

"Sit," Rourke says, motioning to the bench next to Sally with his gun.

Clare obeys, crossing the cabin and resting a hand on Sally's. If he frisks her, Clare knows, this will not end well.

"It's okay," Clare says to Sally. "Everything will be okay." Then, in a hiss to Rourke, "What did you give her?"

Rourke blocks the door to the deck, his gun tight in his hand.

"It's been tough keeping her calm. She's got a lot on her mind. Don't worry. I've been feeding her. She's fine."

"Sally," she says. "My name is Clare. Has he hurt you?"

"I don't know any Clare," Sally says, barely a whisper.

"Everyone's been looking for you. I've been looking for you. Tell me. Has he hurt you?"

A whimper emerges from deep in Sally's throat. She slouches forward, her shoulders shaking. Clare hears the engine of a passing boat. Two seconds, Clare thinks. It would take her two seconds to snatch the gun from behind her back and aim it at Rourke. A second longer, she knows, than it would take him to aim and fire. Rourke reholsters his gun and crosses the cabin. He takes Clare sharply by the arm and grabs a tie from a shelf behind her to secure her wrists too. Clare does not resist, does not fight it, too afraid that her gun might come loose. Once Rourke is back across the cabin she feels it, the well of frustrated tears at a question she's asked herself too many times before. *Why didn't you fight?* Clare presses back into the seat to feel the gun against her back. What good is a gun if your hands are tied? Clare thinks. She must gather herself.

"Why did you bring her here, Rourke?" Clare asks. "What are you doing? What do you want?"

"I have the same questions for you, Clare. What are *you* doing?"

"My job," Clare says.

Rourke smiles. "That's cute. Your job. I like that."

"You found her," Clare says. "So why not just bring her to the station?"

"Because it's not Sally I'm after," he says.

"If you're after me, just let her go."

"Women. You always think you're one step ahead." Rourke removes his gun again and firms his hold on it, straightening his arm to point it right at Clare. "I'm sure you understand why I can't do that."

Sally eases closer to Clare and lists into her, whimpering. Clare scrambles for what to say.

"Just call Somers now and tell her you got a tip and you

found Sally. This"—Clare gestures to the boat, to the zip ties on their wrists—"Somers doesn't need to know. Sally is so far gone. She's not lucid. When she comes to, trust me. She won't even remember—"

"Somers reported me. I was put on leave yesterday afternoon. Unpaid fucking leave. She's officious, that woman. And she doesn't think I'm the sharpest tool in the shed. But I'm not as dumb as she thinks. I had this hunch. You know what I'm talking about, Sally?"

Sally blinks, moaning. Clare shushes her. Their hands intertwine on their laps, tied wrists pressing together.

"I charted it," Rourke says. "Let's say two women were out on a mission. Let's imagine these lovely ladies out there where Raylene's ex-husband's car was found, and they needed to get back to High River. Now, what route might they take?"

Clare breathes to steady herself. Rourke watches her as though he expects an answer. He taps the gun against his chest.

"No answers, ladies? None?"

"What does this—"

Rourke interrupts her. "What if they were in a car? But that seemed unlikely. What if they weren't? I called the bus depot and got this bored security guard on the line. At that point I figured I was just looking for Raylene. One woman on a mission. But the security guard e-mails me some footage of these *two* women buying one-way tickets to the city. Funny luck. He'd remembered them." Rourke points to Sally. "Because one of them couldn't stop crying. That stuck with him. And he goes deep into the tape and finds them for me, because what else does a lonely security guard have to do on an overnight shift? And lo and behold, it's not just Raylene, but our friend Sally here too. Sometimes in police work, you just get lucky. Somers, I know she thinks I didn't catch on at the briefing . . ."

"Rourke!" Clare says, her voice desperate. "Then just turn Sally in! Why are you doing this?"

Rourke ignores the question. "I'm doing good police work here. Solving murders, finding missing persons. And as I'm packing up my desk yesterday . . . Did you know they give you two minutes to pack up your desk when you're put on leave? With some junior beat cop breathing over you to make sure you don't take any case files or steal a stapler? Yeah, so I'm packing up and I'm thinking of Malcolm. And I'm thinking about how he takes every single thing. Takes every single thing away from me. First, my father's job. That destroyed my family. Then he takes Zoe too. Right out from under me. And even when that's not going his way anymore, he can't leave it alone. And here I am, trying to do good work, I'm trying to solve these cases *and* bring him to the justice he deserves, but no. He takes my job too. If that's not enough to send a guy over the—"

"Please," Clare says. "This isn't—"

"I know what Malcolm sees in you," Rourke says. "You're smart. Figuring out where I was, where Sally was. That took smarts. I was trying to figure out how to get you here, lure you, if you will, but you're one step ahead. So smart. You remind me of Zoe too."

Clare thinks of the photograph from Rourke's file, Malcolm and Zoe arm in arm. She'd seen it too, the resemblance between her and Malcolm's wife.

"Just tell me what you want," Clare whispers.

"I want you," Rourke says. "No. Sorry. That doesn't sound right. That sounds creepy. I want Malcolm."

"You had him," Clare says. "You could have had him. He was here."

"No," Rourke says. "I couldn't. Because he sent *you* instead. He stays underground. It's hard to smoke him out."

Clare feels Sally's fingers grip her arm. She is crying, eyes closed.

"He won't come," Clare says. "He's gone."

"Is he, though? Because I think he probably loves you. Or something like that. I know how he works. He doesn't easily let go of women he loves. He doesn't let go of anything. We have that in common."

"You said yesterday that Zoe was presumed dead."

"Presumed." Rourke smiles. "They never found a body."

She's sending me messages, Malcolm had said of Zoe yesterday. *She was always good at keeping terrible secrets.*

"Listen," Clare pleads. "Just let Sally off the boat. You have me now. You don't need her. She won't remember this. It's between us."

"Hey," he says, waving the gun to Sally. "Do you still want to die? Remember what you told me last night, Sally? Your son's dead. You killed a man. You said you wanted to die."

Sally's eyes are wide, panicked. There is a strange cadence to Rourke's voice. Clare has witnessed this many times before. An angry man losing his grip.

"No," Clare says, placing her tethered hands on Sally's pregnant belly. "Tell him. You don't want to die."

"Please," Sally says, her voice small, cracking. "No."

"Rourke," Clare says, meeting his gaze head-on. "You're a police officer. You're not a killer. Whatever is between you and Malcolm, I can help. I can work with you. We can search for him together. Bring him in. Bring him to justice. For whatever he's done to you—"

"Yeah," Rourke says. "I've read your file. I know all about you. I even talked to your husband. Jason's his name? He's got plenty to say about you."

Clare feels it, the quiet rage at his name. Jason. The rot in the pit of her stomach.

"Bottom line is, I can't trust you, Clare. No one can."

Clare stands, her legs surprisingly firm beneath her. Rourke takes hold of his gun and points it at her chest.

"Sit," he commands.

"Do you hear that?" Clare asks.

Sirens. Rourke frowns, ears piqued.

"Ginny Haines?" Clare says. "She's the smart one, Rourke. She figured out exactly where you were. You left a trail of crumbs and Ginny collected them. She and Helen called Somers. That siren? That's the squad car. And a dead body is bad news for you at this point. Two dead bodies, even more so. So put the gun down and let us off the boat."

Rourke cocks his head, as if Clare is playing a game and he's enjoying it. The siren drones in the background. He swings the gun side to side, aimed at her, then Sally, then her again.

"If you move," Rourke says, "I'll kill you. If you scream, I'll kill you both."

Then Rourke is out the door, climbing to the deck. An engine turns over. Through the small cabin window Clare can see him on the dock. He yanks at the ropes, untying them, tossing them onto the boat. Clare sits again. *Think.*

"He's going to kill us," Sally says over the noise of the engine.

Clare closes her eyes. *I'll kill you.* How many times did Jason utter those words to her? No, Clare thinks. No. She falls into Sally as the boat shifts position.

"Listen to me right now," Clare says. "We are going to get out of here."

Sally nods. Clare twists away, her back to Sally.

"See behind me?" she says. "Look at my back, Sally. Lift up my shirt. See the gun? Give it to me. Lift it out carefully and set it down beside you."

Sally does as she's told. Clare turns and lifts the gun, fumbling to get a proper grip with her hands tied.

"Hurry," Sally whispers.

"You stay in here," Clare says. "I need you to get up and open the door."

"Okay."

The calm. The calm of her movements. Clare adjusts the gun in the space between her tied hands so that one finger can rest on the trigger. She unlatches the safety with her thumb and aims the gun at the doorway. Sally unlocks the door and stands aside for Clare to pass. Don't think, Clare's father used to say when she'd hesitate after aiming at her target.

Never think. Just aim. Shoot.

As she climbs the stairs to the deck, Clare must squint against the bright sun shimmering off the water. One eye closed, she spies Rourke down the barrel of her gun. Her wrists scream, the ties cutting into her skin. His back is to her as he fumbles with the final rope. He cannot hear her. The boat's engine is too loud.

I'll kill you.

No, Clare thinks, bracing herself by wedging a knee against the boat's railing, gun aimed at his skull. No. You won't.

A squad car pulls up in the parking lot. Rourke jolts and turns. His hand swings down to its holster, but before he can raise the gun, Clare has already fired. The bullet strikes Rourke in the shoulder, the exact spot where Clare took her own bullet weeks ago. He falls to his knees then on his side, crouched in fetal position, clutching his arm. Clare rushes to him and kicks his gun from his reach. Then she takes several steps back, aiming at him again.

"Don't," he says, shielding himself. "Don't."

Somers has emerged from the squad car. She runs to them. Over the engine Clare hears Sally wailing in the cabin. Rourke looks up at her. What is his expression? Shock. Fear. Anger. Clare lets her finger hover over the trigger, surprised by the steadiness in her hands.

SATURDAY

Last night the rain came to lift the heat, the grass now wet with early morning dew. A pigeon hops along the water's edge, pecking at litter. Across the pond is the bench where Clare sat with Malcolm only days ago. She thinks of him then, the frown, the distracted way he fiddled with his phone, the effort it must have taken not to fill her in. Malcolm, a cracked dam trying not to breach. Clare sighs and pulls out her phone to check the time. Somers is late.

Only six days ago, she'd woken in the room in High River, Raylene asleep beside her, all the unknowns of that place and its people before her. And again, she's done it. She's solved the case. It might be, Clare thinks as she watches the joggers along the path, ever scanning their faces, that she is good at this job, that her senses are tuned for it. That she was meant to do this work.

I can't run forever, Clare thinks. I can't. She takes her cell phone from her pocket again and enters the code to block her number. Then she dials home. As it rings, she cannot compute the time difference, whether it's later or earlier for Jason, time and place strange muddles to her now. After three rings he answers with a blunt hello. Clare waits without a word, the phone held to her lips so that he might at least hear her breathing.

"Clare," he says, a whisper.

Though she opens her mouth, no sound comes out.

"Clare? I know it's you." His voice is pleading. "Come on. A blocked number? I know it's you."

"It's me."

"God," he cries. "My Clare. Clare! Please. Please don't hang up."

"I'm not coming back."

A pause. Clare's heart bangs against her ribs.

"Please," Jason says again. "I loved you. I love you still. I tried. Am I really that bad?"

His face comes to her in perfect clarity, the angles of his jawline, that slight and beautiful smile as he sat next to her at the kitchen table, taking her hand to make amends, tracing a finger along the ache of her jaw. *Am I really that bad?*

"We remember things differently," Clare says.

"I guess we do." He clears his throat. "I'm sorry we do."

His answers are so lucid. There is such ease in his voice.

"I'm not coming back," Clare says. "I just wanted you to know that."

"Come on. That's not why you called."

Suddenly Jason laughs, sharp and uproarious, and Clare can imagine his head thrown back as he stands in their kitchen, one hand on the counter to steady himself.

"Jason." His name sounds foreign on her tongue. "You won't ever see me again."

"Now you're just rubbing it in. You called to rub it in."

"I'm calling you because I want this to end. I saw Grace. She told me you're trying to move on. She said you knew I'd be here. I don't know how you knew that. But I'm tired. I'm done. I want you to move on. I need you to let it go."

And then, despite the vast distance between them, Clare feels it, the heat of his wrath through the phone.

"Now you know I can't do that, Clare. Because I promised you. You promised me. 'Til death, right?" He breathes hard into the receiver. "I know you've got yourself a little bevy of men out there to keep you company. I know you're not exactly lonely. That cop guy called me. Told me all about the fun you're having. You and that Malcolm. That you're getting around. But me? I'm lonely. Grace, she tries. She tries to be a friend. But I need you. I need you back."

Somers emerges over a rise across the pond and scans until she spots Clare. She lifts the two coffees she holds, a kind of wave. Clare is immobile, her phone hot to her cheek. Silent.

"Clare? Don't you hang up. Clare!"

There is something in Somers's gait, the ease of her stride. A strength, a poise. A lack of fear. Clare drops the phone to her side without hanging up. She can hear Jason's voice, distant, barking her name.

"Clare! I swear, if you—"

"Jason?" A pause. "Listen to me. I'm done. This is over. If you come after me, I'll kill you. Do you understand me? Come after me and you're dead."

"Don't you—"

Fuck you. Clare can't be certain whether she says the words aloud before ending the call with the press of her thumb. She looks down at the phone in her hand, its screen reflecting the rising sun. Then she tosses it into the pond.

"Jesus," Somers says, handing Clare one of the coffees. "Who was that?"

"No one."

"No one, huh? Tell that to your phone."

"It doesn't matter." Clare shifts to make room for Somers on the bench.

"I've got a lot to say to you," Somers says.

"I know."

"I could lose my job, cutting you loose like that. They'll want you for more questioning. They're going to wonder where you've gone."

"I know," Clare says. "Thank you."

"Rourke came out of surgery early this morning. Looks like he'll pull through. Jesus. I've heard of dirty cops, but he takes it to a whole new level. He hasn't been questioned yet. Today, hopefully. I don't expect they'll get any reasonable answers from him. He's clearly not driven by reason."

Clare takes a sip of her coffee. It burns her tongue.

"Sally confessed," Somers says. "She admitted what happened with her son. The whole thing."

But not what happened with Raylene's husband, Clare thinks. She could tell Somers now. The whole truth, return the favor, solve another case on Somers's behalf. But she thinks of Sally below that boat deck, the grief and terror mingling within her. She will keep it to herself.

"Can she go to jail for not taking him to the hospital?" Clare asks.

"Unlikely. Rebecca's taken full responsibility, believe it or not. She told us she was the one who convinced Sally not to take her son to see a doctor, that she believed her alternative therapies would work. She'll be charged. Criminal negligence. And Markus, what he did with the body, throwing it into the river like that. More than stupid. I'm sure he'll see the inside of a cell for that."

He doesn't think, Helen had said yesterday. *Markus isn't a smart man.* That is no excuse, Clare thinks.

"Anyway," Somers says. "Social services has been called in. They have the little girl. I'd like to see a family member take on guardianship for now. We'll see."

"What about Helen?"

"That's a tough one," Somers says, thoughtful. "Do you punish someone for trying to do good, even if they bend the law from time to time? I don't know. I don't know the answer to that. I'll leave it to my superiors to decide." Somers lifts the lid from her own coffee, swirling its contents. She shifts on the bench. "Where are you hiding?"

"I'm at a motel," Clare says. "Not far from here. I won't stay in town much longer. I need to leave."

Somers pulls a thumb drive from the inside pocket of her blazer and hands it to Clare.

"What's this?" Clare asks.

"Anything I could dig up on this Malcolm Boon guy. Malcolm Hayes, actually. To be honest, there wasn't much on him. Lots on his wife, though."

"Like what?"

"Her father was a business mogul of the very shady variety. About five years ago, her father was shot in the head while finishing his tiramisu at a restaurant. I remember that case because it was such a goddamn embarrassment for the cops. Couldn't get anyone to talk. Not even Zoe. And she and Rourke? Turns out they go way back. A couple all through high school. All kinds of mess. It's all on that drive."

"Thank you," Clare says.

"Also," Somers says. "Whatever he had on your husband. On you. It's all in there."

"I'm grateful. Really. Thank you."

"Tit for tat. I'm a little mortified by how much legwork you did on this Proulx case. You cracked it. You're a natural at this, you know."

"Maybe. Maybe it's an easier job to do from the inside."

"Could be." Somers draws a circle in the grass with her heel. "You going after this Malcolm guy?"

"I have to," Clare says. "I need to find him."

Somers nods.

"He helped me," Clare says. "Gave me this job. At first I thought . . . he was crazy. But now, it seems to fit. Like I was meant to be doing it. Then we were together for three weeks in between jobs. I'd been shot and he didn't abandon me there. I wanted to hate him, but I can't. It's hard to explain. And Rourke. I don't know what the full story is, but I need to find out."

"You've got the bug," Somers says. "You solve one case, and it infects you."

"I guess so," Clare says.

"Be careful. That's all I can say. This one seems messy. You don't know what you're going to find. You're peering down a dark well."

"I know."

"Well, not sure you want any help, but you know where to reach me." Somers casts Clare a sidelong glance. "I saw an old police report in the file Rourke had on you. Domestic. You filed charges against your husband and then you dropped them."

"I declined to testify," Clare says.

"Right. So what about him?"

"My ex? What about him?"

"Do you think he'll come after you?"

"He'd better not." It's all Clare can say. "I'm tired of it. Tired of running."

"I imagine it would get tiring after a while."

They sit in silence, Clare aware of Somers's gun on the bench between them. Somers fishes her cell phone from her jacket and lowers her gaze to read an incoming message. She jots a quick reply and stands.

"You have my card."

"I do," Clare says.

"If you get into any trouble . . . if you need any help. Any help at all. You know?"

"I know," Clare says. "Thank you."

The rising sun forms a halo behind Somers's head. Whatever this is, Clare thinks, this new footing between them, it feels something like friendship. Somers turns and walks briskly down the path, cell phone in hand. As Clare watches her disappear back over the rise, she slides her hand under her shirt and rests it on her shoulder. Though her skin is warm under her palm, it no longer aches when she presses her fingertips into the scar.

Somewhere along the line, Clare realizes, she stopped counting the days since she left Jason. She now counts the days since she met Malcolm. Since he came searching for her. The days since he arrived in that coffee shop, clean-cut and well dressed, briefcase in hand, his own secrets buried deep under that stoic and inscrutable guise.

Forty-seven. Forty-seven days.

Clare grips the thumb drive that Somers gave her tight in her fist. She will walk the few miles back to the motel and get started on her search for Malcolm. There is much work ahead. She needs a plan. She needs a place to begin.

ACKNOWLEDGMENTS

MUCH IS written on the wild and often difficult experience of writing a sophomore book. My own journey to finishing *Still Water* included suffering a concussion at the midway point. This muddled me and made me draw even more on help from my incredible group of family, friends, and colleagues. I am grateful to be here, this book in hand, my brain intact, knowing the path was paved by the support of so many of you.

I'd like to begin by saying thank you to my fellow educators. I have worked as a teacher and guidance counselor for over fifteen years, and I understand that for all its rewards, teaching is sometimes a lonely and difficult gig. In my life I have been lucky to have had many excellent teachers and I would like to name them here. In the early years: Eugene Di Sante, Barbara Terpstra, Glenda Romano, Janice Fricker, Jennifer Walcott, and Gerry Lazare. In university and beyond: Lesley Shore, Sioux Browning, Alistair MacLeod, Glen Huser, Michael Winter, and Lisa Moore. To all my fellow educators in Toronto and beyond, and especially to the Alt9 family, including Sally Sinclair, Lee Sheppard, Jeff Kozopas, Cassandra Kirchmeir Gitt, Tamara Nedd-Roderique, Geraldine Diamond, Michelle Hadida, Alcidia Cabral, Grant Fawthrop, Mike Gurgol, Andrea Parise, Anna Gemmiti, Jeff Caton, and to all my amazing students at WEA with love and thanks. To the hardworking teachers who encourage my sons every day on their own learning lives: I am grateful for everything you do. In particular I would like to acknowledge and thank my high school English teacher David Reed, a true great who inspired me not only to write from the bones but also to try to be an educator worthy of every student who enters my classroom.

To the incredible teams at Simon & Schuster Canada and Touchstone Books; watching *Still Mine* launch into the world really showed me the magic you are capable of. To Kevin Hanson, Patricia Ocampo, Sarah St. Pierre, Amy Prentice, Adria Iwasutiak, Felicia Quon, Brendan May, Catherine Whiteside, Siobhan Doody, Lauren Morocco, Jessica Scott, David Millar, and the wonderful sales, publicity, and marketing teams, with many thanks. A special thank-you to my American editor, Tara Parsons, for championing the books so fiercely, and to the singular and incredible Nita Pronovost, a truly gifted editor who knows how to push and encourage in equal measure.

To the team at the newly minted CookeMcDermid, especially my wonderful agent Chris Bucci, as well as Martha Webb, Monica Pacheco, and Anne McDermid. To booksellers across Canada and the U.S. for placing me on their shelves and for everything they do for writers once the books leave our hands. We owe every reader to you.

The greatest support has come from the people around me every day as I wrote. To my parents, Dick and Marilyn, my sisters, Katie Flynn and Bridget Flynn, and my sister-in-law, Beth Boyden, as well as to Mark McQuillan, Chris Van Dyke, Jamie Boyden, and Tim Stuart and Anne Wright, with all my thanks. To all the Flynns, Keefes, Boydens, Carraghers, Browns, Stuarts, Manuels, Wrights, Van Dykes, McQuillans, Bradleys, Wilsons, and beyond who shouted from the rooftops when *Still Mine* was released and have bugged me in the best ways to finish its sequel. To my nieces and nephews: Jack Boyden, Charlotte Boyden, Jed Van Dyke, Stuart Boyden, Peter McQuillan, Margot Van Dyke, Luke Boyden, Sean McQuillan, and Owen McQuillan with lots of love.

To the women in my life who keep me buoyed: Elisa Schwarz, Kendall Anderson, Deanna Wong, Allyson Payne, Mariska Gatha, Sarah Faber, Jenna King, Tara Samuel, Aviva Armour-Ostroff, Allison Devereaux, and Claire Tacon. To my friends-who-are-like-family who help us in the crazed logistics of everyday life, especially Hollis Hopkins, Doug Stewart, Darcy Killeen, Kirsten White, and all the Sharks and Titans parents and players who make being in a rink late on a Friday or early on a Sunday pretty fun. To my fellow coaches Ian Clapp, Carlo Caravaggio, Fausto Presta, and Caroline Godfrey for making my third job on the hockey bench my favorite gig of all. To my aunt Mary Flynn for being "My Mary" to our boys and caring for them with so much patience and love.

Above all, to Ian, for never wavering even when I did, and for living your life with remarkable kindness and good humor. To Flynn, Joey, and Leo, who became my mini-publicists when *Still Mine* was released and who fill my days with joy and craziness. Every day I think of how proud Sue would be of you. Of all of us, I hope.

ABOUT THE AUTHOR

©PAIGE LINDSAY

Amy Stuart's debut novel, *Still Mine*, was an instant national bestseller. She was nominated for the Arthur Ellis Best First Crime Novel award and was the winner of the 2011 Writers' Union of Canada Short Prose Competition. Her writing has previously appeared in newspapers and magazines across Canada. Amy lives in Toronto with her husband and her three sons. *Still Water* is her second novel. Visit her at **AmyStuart.ca** or **@AmyfStuart**.